DARK WEB SPIDERS

R JULIAN HAFNER

Publisher:
Australian Self Publishing Group, Pty. Ltd. / Inspiring Publishers
PO Box 159, Calwell, ACT 2905, Australia.
Phone: 61-(0) 2 6291-2904
http://australianselfpublishinggroup.com

A catalogue record for this book is available from the National Library of Australia

National Library of Australia Prepublication Data Service

Author: R Julian Hafner

Title: **DARK WEB SPIDERS**

ISBN: 978-1-923449-58-9 (print)
ISBN: 978-1-923449-59-6 (ePub2)

Dedication

This book is dedicated to the late Paul Eckert, who nurtured, challenged, stimulated and amused me throughout our long friendship.

CHAPTER ONE

George was startled by the roar of a car engine behind him. He swung round and threw himself sideways as the black 4WD hurtled at him. He felt a sharp pain in his left foot but was able to stumble to his feet and stagger towards an alley that he had just passed. He wedged himself behind a green dumpster and prayed that whoever had almost killed him would not try to finish the job.

Silence, except for some jazz coming from an apartment further down the alley. George was strangely gratified to recognise the music as a track from one of his favourite groups, the Oscar Peterson Trio. After about twenty minutes he limped towards the entrance to the alley and peered out. There was no sign of the black 4wd. His left foot was excruciatingly painful, but George managed to get back to his town house on

Crown Street in Surrey Hills, a Sydney suburb in which he'd lived for over ten years.

He poured himself a hefty gin and tonic and settled into an armchair. He gingerly examined his left foot and was relieved to find no evidence of broken bones, just some bruising. He had some oxycodone, prescribed years earlier, and thought the pain in his foot was severe enough to justify swallowing a dose. A measure of calm restored, George rang his friend and colleague Fred.

'Someone's just tried to kill me'.

'Christ! What happened?'

'Can you come over right now? I'll tell you while it's still fresh in my mind. Perhaps we can work out who might want me dead.'

'I've got a friend with me. She's been assaulted and needs my help. I'll contact you when we've sorted things out.'

Fred saw that his friend Sue's left cheek had turned red and was beginning to swell.

'I'll get an ice pack from the fridge and wrap it in a dish cloth. Lie down on the sofa and hold it against your cheek. It'll help the pain and reduce the swelling. Don't worry, you're still beautiful!'

Sue did as she was told.

'Tell me what happened,' Fred said as soon as he'd made Sue as comfortable as he could.

'I've been working in this café bar for about a month. After we closed today, my boss, Aldo, tried to kiss me. I pushed him away and he grabbed my arms and tried again. I freed myself but then he became violent. He hit me hard in the face and I fell backwards onto a table. This hurt my back so much that I screamed. Aldo backed off, and I was able to run out. I thought of the police, but my mobile was in my handbag which I'd left behind. Then I remembered that you lived only a few blocks away. Luckily you answered the door.'

'The bastard!' Fred exclaimed. 'What do you want me to do?'

'I always put my handbag under the bar, where it's out of sight. Aldo knows this. The bag has my car and house keys, credit cards, driver's licence and mobile phone. But it also has a jewelled necklace, a family heirloom, that I'd taken to a jeweller for valuation and some minor repairs. I'd picked it up at lunchtime and hadn't had time to put it back in the safe at home. It's worth about forty thousand dollars. If he finds it, he'll take it and deny it was ever there.'

'So, we need to go and get your handbag right now. Are you up to that?'

'Let's go. We can park behind the café.'

'Is Aldo a big man?'

'Not tall, but he's bulky and strong.'

'Then I'll take my revolver.'

'Isn't that a bit over the top?'

'It's just insurance. I don't want to get into a fist fight. Take the ice pack with you.'

Lights were on in the café. Fred and Sue went in through the rear entrance. Aldo was standing behind the bar, the contents of Sue's handbag spread before him.

'I'm surprised you've come back so soon. Who's your friend?'

'I'm Fred. We've come to get Sue's handbag.'

'What if I decide to keep it? If you make a fuss, I'll say it was never here.'

'Look at Sue's face,' Fred retorted sharply. 'If she goes to the police, you'll be charged with assault. Give us the handbag and we'll call it quits.'

'I don't believe you. If you want the bag, you'll have to take it. And I'm a bit bigger than you.'

Fred took out his revolver and pointed it at Aldo, who laughed.

'You won't use that. Just bugger off, the two of you. If you contact the police, I'll deny everything.'

Fred fired a shot into the ceiling. The gun's silencer muffled the sound into a sharp pop.

'I won't shoot you unless it's self-defence. But this baby can do a lot of damage. So can we. Go and sit over there.'

Fred fired another shot into the ceiling. Aldo did as he was told. Sue made sure that all the bag's contents were back inside it.

'I'll be sending someone round to make sure you don't assault any more of your staff. They'll do a much better job than the police.'

Sue and Fred went straight to George's town house, one of the very few that had a double garage. They parked next to George's car and went inside.

'Drinks?' asked George.

'That'd be a lifesaver,' said Sue, holding the ice pack against her cheek. ' Can you manage a whisky and dry?'

George pointed to a well-stocked bar on the wall opposite the French window.

'Easy.'

'I'll have one too,' said Fred. 'Make it a double.'

Between them, Fred and Sue explained what had happened.

'Will you go to the police?' George asked.

'No. Aldo would just deny everything. It'd be far too messy.'

'I told Aldo I'd send a frightener round,' said Fred.

'What's a frightener?' asked Sue.

'A tough guy who threatens to beat the shit out of someone if they don't cooperate. Or just beats them. They work in pairs. Shall I send a couple to the café?'

'That'd make me feel a whole lot better. But just a roughing up, with a threat to come back much harder if he ever did it again.'

Sue waved her empty glass. 'I'm feeling better already. Another of these and I'll be fine.'

George limped to the bar and refilled all their glasses.

'Now,' said Sue, 'it's time to hear from George.'

Fred looked at George. 'First, I should let you know that Sue and I are just good friends. Sue knows I'd like it to go further. But ...' He waved his hands in a mixture of hope and dismissal.

'Our work is difficult and dangerous,' said George. 'If we tell you about it, you must promise not to tell anyone else.'

'You can trust her,' said Fred. 'I've known her long enough to be sure. So let me begin the story. George was a very successful psychiatrist but was struck off the register for two years after having sex with Julia, a patient.'

'This was totally out of character', George interrupted. 'It was a set up. Julia literally threw herself on me. She used this one episode, backed up by forensic evidence, to blackmail me into helping her to bring her step-father to justice. He had brutally and repeatedly raped her as a child. He was a Cabinet Minister, and also a patient of mine. Some weeks later, he was murdered. Julia was cleared of any suspicion. Shortly after his death, I was given a flash drive, a duplicate of which he had sold to Iran. It contained enough data to allow the construction of a nuclear bomb.

The minister had arranged for me to get the drive in the event of his death. It was supposed to protect me, but instead, it put me in grave danger. After two attempts on my life, I was able to give the drive to MI6. I then went to the Swiss bank where the minister's payment had been deposited. Using the codes he had given me, I withdrew the money. After sharing it with those who had helped me, I was left with eight million dollars. With what I'd been through, I thought it was okay to keep it.'

Fred continued the story. 'I had helped George by using my hacking skills. When he told me he had no wish to go back to psychiatry, I offered him a job. He insisted on contributing most of the eight million to our work together. We decided to greatly expand my original mission aimed at eliminating illegal arms dealers. We now target a whole range of baddies.'

'Thank you for trusting me with all that. But your plans sound, if you'll forgive me for saying so, almost impossibly ambitious. How on earth will you be able to do all this?'

'The dark web,' replied Fred. 'What do you know about it?'

'Almost nothing.'

'Then let me explain. When I started my work, the dark web existed, but on a very small scale. I didn't need to grapple with it. But it has hugely expanded and become the engine that drives much of the evil in this world. It is a parallel internet that can be accessed by connecting to a Virtual Private Network server, downloading the Tor Browser, and installing a search engine that indexes the dark web. Duck and Go is a popular one that doesn't track your searches. You are guaranteed total, absolute privacy in your dark web dealings.'

'So, anyone can access it?'

'Just about. It can be put to good use as well as bad. Journalists, for example, can use it to circumvent censorship and publish information that the mainstream media would suppress. Julian Assange is the best-known example of someone who gleaned classified information from the dark web and then, to his great cost, published it on the open internet. And then there are those who wish to guarantee their privacy for legitimate reasons. We plan to use it to track down the baddies and then expose them.'

'You mentioned that the use of the dark web has greatly increased,' remarked Sue. 'How come?'

'Bitcoin,' replied Fred. 'Before it was invented, anonymous payments on the dark web were almost impossible. Paying for an illegal service risked exposure. Bitcoin can be used with total anonymity. It is this currency that's allowed such a massive expansion of the dark web, which in turn explains why Bitcoin's value has increased so vastly.'

'A thought has just come to me,' George exclaimed. 'Sue, you're currently out of a job. Maybe we can offer you some work. But first, tell me a bit about yourself.'

'My father's a Lutheran pastor here in Sydney. My mother has devoted her life to supporting him. I see them fairly often. I've never asked them for financial help. Their money's always been tight and so has mine. The café job paid just enough to cover the rent on a tiny flat that I share with a friend.

I studied Art at uni for three years and then went to NIDA – Sydney's National Institute of dramatic Art – and completed their Bachelor of Fine Arts. It covers all aspects of live performance. But I haven't been able to land an acting gig. Most unis run courses similar to NIDA's. They churn out far too many graduates for far too little work.'

'Before we talk about a possible job offer,' said George, 'we need to explain more about our work. Fred can do this best.'

'Thanks George – I think! We can't reliably hack into the dark web. We've tried, but if a user gets the slightest whiff of our presence, they close the site and move to another. And a couple of times, a user was able to identify us and threaten a response, not just on the internet, but in real life. So, hacking into the dark web can be difficult and dangerous. The best way to access it is to become part of it. That's what we're planning to do. We need help. Especially from a trained actor. But the work could be dangerous.'

'Before I decide, I need to know more about your whole set-up.'

'We used George's money,' Fred responded, 'to set up a totally secure location and install the most sophisticated equipment on the market. Our income comes mainly from activities on the deep web, of which the dark web is actually a fairly small part.'

'My brain's beginning to hurt' frowned Sue. 'What, for Heaven's sake, is the deep web?'

'The deep web is over 90% of the entire internet. It can't be accessed using standard search engines like Google. It includes emails, paywalled sites such as Netflix, chat messages, bank statements, health records, and all other electronic data that can be accessed only by permission. We've gained a reputation among major financial institutions for exposing and eliminating money laundering. Payment for this is our main source of income. We think we can rely on it well into the future. So now we use some of the money to fund what we really want to do - confront those evils embraced by the dark web.'

'Exposing money laundering must invite a response from the perpetrators. Could this be behind the attempt on George's life?'

'Almost certainly. Although this work involves the deep web, not the dark web, it can't be dealt with entirely online. George recently gained access to a law firm which the police suspected was a front for a money laundering and drug dealing outfit. He posed as a cleaner but was caught download-ing data from a computer. They held him in the building until, after some physical persuasion, he admitted to being a private investigator. Obviously, they feared that George had enough information to expose them. They were desperate enough to try and kill him or at least scare him off. With a hit and run, his death could never be traced back to them.'

'So, if I came to work for you, I'd presumably be doing the same thing as George. It's obviously dangerous at times. But not nearly as dangerous as entering the dark web. Would I need to be involved in that? George implied earlier that this would be a priority.'

'Absolutely not', said George. 'But we needed to explain from the start that the dark web will become a major focus of our work. If you joined us, we'd do our utmost to protect you from danger. Unless of course you agreed to accept a measure of risk as part of doing what you believed in.'

'I don't share your passion – perhaps obsession is a better word – for confronting evildoers. But I have a highly developed social conscience. I've often thought of using my acting skills to somehow make the world a better place. My father never preaches at me, but he's instilled in me the idea that we are here to embrace, in his own words, "Prudence, Temperance, Justice and Fortitude." I'm okay with prudence, but not so good with temperance. I'm passionate about the need for justice. And

I believe I've shown much fortitude in what has, at times, been a difficult life. So, start talking about the terms and conditions of my employment.'

'We're in a position to offer job security,' said Fred. 'We've earned good money, and on top of that we've been very lucky on the stock market - no insider trading, I swear! It adds up to over ten million dollars. We can pay you a salary or you can have a one third share of the profits from any successful projects that you're involved in. It's your choice.'

'In for a penny … I'll take the profits.'

CHAPTER TWO

Two days later, Sue, Fred and George met in the secure location that housed their equipment. It was in Paddington and comprised a large basement floor which Fred and George had restructured to create a central room holding their equipment. They had kept two bedrooms and a bathroom to allow for overnight stays. Great care had been taken to protect against break-ins. The intruder alarm was linked to their smart phones. The ground floor had been converted into a storage area and garage.

George opened the meeting.

'First we need to decide whether or not to continue the investigation into the law firm.'

'I think we have to let it go,' responded Fred. 'Our cover is blown. They'll boost security, maybe even relocate. All we can do is update the police and withdraw our services.'

'I agree, 'said George. 'Disappointing, but it's the only sensible thing.'

'So, what now?' asked Sue.

'The dark web stuff hasn't really got going,' Fred replied. 'We can put it aside for now and focus on the deep web. We have two remaining projects. One also involves money laundering, based in a casino. The other is personal, not business. An aunt of mine – one of my mother's two sisters – was scammed out of $30,000, money she could ill afford to lose. I'm very fond of her, so I agreed to try and get the money back. I told her that the chances were pretty slim. Obviously, we have to focus on the casino job. Pursuing the scammers will have to wait.'

'Tell me about the casino job,' said Sue.

'High stake gamblers, also known as high-risk gamblers, can hide their true identity. As money launderers, they buy large amounts of casino chips and use them in high stake card games or on the main floor of the casino. They play cautiously to minimise their losses. Then they cash in their chips for legitimate money. Electronic transfer of the funds is their preference, since bank accounts in tax havens such as the Cayman Islands are virtually untraceable. The money is then ploughed back into drug trafficking or other criminal activities.'

'The authorities must know about this. Why don't they crack down?'

'AUSTRAC has repeatedly demanded that casino operators check the identity of high-risk gamblers more rigorously, but money launderers always find new ways of avoiding detection. Crown Resorts, which owns the Sydney casino, has asked us to help them deal with the problem. Their casinos can be hugely profitable, and Crown is desperate to keep its licences.'

'Made much progress?' asked Sue.

'We've managed to identify one launderer, a man in his forties. Through him we hoped to identify the organisations that he works for. We know where he lives, but his apartment is totally secure. We just can't get in. And without knowing his true identity, we can't hack into his computer. He's secured his smartphone with Express VPN and Total AV, so we can't get into that either. In short, we're stuck.'

'I have an idea,' said Sue. 'What if I sit beside him while he's gambling on the main floor. Start a conversation, act a bit seductive, get him to invite me back to his place? Then get as much data as possible from his computer or any paper documents I can find.'

'That's far too risky,' said George. It's out of the question.'

'There's something I haven't told you,' said Sue. 'My older sister got addicted to heroin and died of an overdose. Just over five years ago. I'd been using coke and cannabis, but I've been clean since my sister died. Now, of course, Fentanyl is the drug of choice, and its wreaking havoc. So, I've got my own reasons for hating drug runners, and the money launderers who keep them in business. Since there's no other way to get these vermin, I'm willing to take the risk.'

'We'd need to train you up in accessing computers,' said Fred, 'and in the use of a miniature camera.'

'Let's do that. Then I'll go to the casino. You've got his photo of course.'

Sue went to the casino twice without seeing the money launderer. On the third occasion she saw him at the roulette wheel. He was clearly trying to gamble in a way that fitted his assumed identity as a high-risk punter. For each spin of the wheel, he placed chips worth a thousand dollars, but he nearly always picked the safest bets, choosing red or black, or odds/evens, which gave him an almost fifty percent chance of winning. Sue's bets were a little riskier, but she placed only one ten-dollar chip at a time. Occasionally the money launderer placed a five-hundred-dollar chip on a single number. When he chose thirty-three, she placed a bet on the same number. The wheel stopped at thirty-one.

By this time, she was standing next to him.

'God, that was close,' she said, looking directly at him. 'I hoped you might bring me some luck. You seem to be doing pretty well.'

He smiled. 'But the house always wins.' Then he introduced himself as Paul. Sue saw a good-looking man whose physique suggested hard work in the gym. She found him very attractive. A conversation began which continued at one of the bars. When Paul invited her back to his place, she feigned reluctance, making it clear that she wasn't one of the prostitutes who chose the casino as a potentially lucrative beat. This increased Paul's attentiveness, and she found herself charmed.

Finally, she agreed to his suggestion, adding: 'but just for a drink and a snack.'

Paul's apartment occupied the third floor of a small block of flats. The door had two locks. After turning the two keys, Paul pressed an app on his phone and Sue heard a muffled grating sound. Opening the door, Paul said:

'I'm a bit paranoid since my last place was burgled, so I installed a steel bar across the door that only I can retract. The door itself is made of steel.'

'Easier to get into Fort Knox,' Sue quipped, bringing a smile to Paul's lips.

'Show me around?'

Paul looked surprised but took her on a brief tour. There were two bedrooms with ensuites, and a third toilet. The kitchen was at one end of a large sitting room, and there was a study, the door to which Paul did not open. The furniture was contemporary and tasteful. Three abstract paintings hung on the walls. Sue sat down on a lounge and Paul, armed with their drinks, sat beside her at a respectable distance. As an after-thought, he got up and rummaged in the kitchen, coming back with a bowl of mixed nuts and some cheese crackers. When, after more drinks, Paul gently kissed her, Sue became strongly aroused. She let herself be ushered into Paul's bedroom, thinking, 'all in the line of duty.'

Paul was a surprisingly gentle and thoughtful lover, and Sue found herself responding to his caresses with something close to passion. When both were sated, Paul fell asleep on his back, snoring quietly. Sue slipped gently out of bed and went into the ensuite, carefully closing the sliding door before leaving through a second exit. The study door was unlocked. A desk held a screen and a keyboard as well as a laptop. As she had hoped, the desktop was not password protected.

'He must be very confident about his security,' Sue thought while opening the computer. She quickly transferred all accessible files to a flash drive, and then opened the desk drawers, taking photos of documents that might yield useful data. Taking care to leave no trace of her espionage, she re-entered the ensuite and slipped back into bed. Paul was still snoring gently.

In the morning, they sat on kitchen stools and ate muesli, washed down with superb coffee from an expensive looking machine. Paul asked Sue for her phone number, but she politely declined, saying she would be much more comfortable contacting him. He hesitated and then gave her a number.

Sue went straight back to HQ. Both Fred and George were there. Eagerly they downloaded the contents of the flash drive.

'Bullseye!' shouted Fred. 'There's enough here to identify the organisation that employs Paul. We don't need to do any more. If we give the data to Crown Resorts, they can decide how to use it. Case closed! Sue, you're a hero! Without you, we'd still be stuck at square one. Once Crown has paid us, you'll get your share. One third of two million less overheads.'

'I'm a bit dazed,' said Sue. 'I can't believe I did it. So many things could have gone wrong. And so much money!'

'A baptism of fire,' said George.

'My father,' said Sue 'once described that as the Holy Spirit descending in tongues of fire to cleanse and purify. That's exactly what we're trying to do.'

'Enough of the theology,' smiled Fred. 'We've got to decide whether to help my favourite aunt get her money back or organise another paying project.'

'Twenty minutes ago,' said George, 'I got a call from Julia. She was desperate. Someone has created a deep fake porn video of her and published it on the web. I took the liberty of inviting her round. She should be here shortly.'

'Not THE Julia?' exclaimed Sue. 'The woman who got you struck off the register?'

'I haven't told you the whole story. Julia was a lawyer in a small firm. The arms dealers discovered that she was a patient of mine and threatened to harm her unless she delivered a copy of the flash drive. ASIO got involved. Working with the Australian Federal Police, they subpoenaed Julia's case file which led them to accuse her of killing her stepfather. Luckily, she had an unshakeable alibi.

Dealing with all this, including threats on my life and an attempt to kidnap Julia, drew us together. We became lovers. We stopped the arms dealers getting the flash drive and, thanks to ASIO, the threat to our lives was removed. She came with me to Switzerland to help get her stepfather's ill-gotten gains from the bank.'

At this point the doorbell rang, and Fred let Julia in. Although obviously distressed, her thick auburn hair unkempt, she was still beautiful. Once Julia and Sue had been introduced, and Sue's role explained, George told Julia where he had got to in explaining their relationship.

'Let me finish the story,' said Julia, 'It'll help me settle down a bit. Once we'd returned to Sydney and rewarded all those who had helped us, often at danger to themselves, my share of the money enabled me to train as a barrister, a long-cherished ambition. It totally consumed me, and I rather neglected George. We ended our sexual relationship but have stayed good friends. I've successfully prosecuted some very nasty crims. I'm pretty sure that one or more of them is behind the fake porn. The video was sent to me with a request for a million dollars to stop it being published on the web. Foolishly I thought my legal expertise and contacts would somehow protect me, and I refused to pay. They became impatient and gave me one last chance. I was close to yielding but still delayed any payments. They then flooded the web. All my colleagues either saw it or heard about it. My career was destroyed.'

The tears came. George and Sue instinctively moved to comfort her, then helped her settle into an armchair.

'It's not just the obliteration of my career,' said Julia when her tears had eased. 'I feel violated. As if I've been gang raped by all the men I've helped send to jail.'

'Are you sure your career has been destroyed?' asked Sue.

'Absolutely. If you saw the video, you'd under-stand why. It's graphic. Shots of me having sex with both men and women. Close-ups. Anal, oral, vaginal. Ugh!'

'You know I'd do anything to help you,' said George, 'But it seems that the damage is done. Is there anything I can do apart from being there for you?'

'This may sound crazy' Julia replied. 'What if I joined your team? My legal skills might be a useful addition. And you won't have to pay me. I'm still a very wealthy woman.'

There was a stunned silence, broken by Fred.

'We've worked closely together to stop the flash drive getting to Iran. I think you'd fit in really well.'

'It's a no-brainer,' said George. 'But we need a consensus. Sue?'

'The three of you have worked together before. Julia, you will be invaluable. Welcome aboard!'

CHAPTER THREE

A few days later, George, Fred, Sue and Julia met in the secure location which they now called HQ. Julia had resigned from her job. Fred had removed the fake video from the internet but could not locate its source. He suspected the dark web.

Julia looked her normal mid-thirties self apart from dark rings under her eyes. Asked how she felt, she responded at some length.

'I was beginning to pick up a bit until I realised that only one of my friends and acquaintances had contacted me. She was more interested in who might have posted the video than in my wellbeing. Then I had the most horrifying thought: what if I was seen by viewers of the video as a willing participant rather than a victim? I dismissed the thought because the video seemed staged and was so over-the-top. And because the utterly obscene, demeaning voice-over must surely be directed at a victim. But could it be seen differently? Yes, if the viewer, disgusted, shut it down before the end.'

'People have short memories for what they see on the internet,' said Fred. 'In time, all this will be forgotten.'

'Whether or not that's true, I realise I must try and put it all behind me. Focus on the future. At least I have a job!'

'Which we don't!' exclaimed George. 'I can't remember the last time this happened. Usually there are at least two projects waiting for us. We usually choose the most interesting, not always the best paid.'

'I have an idea,' said Fred. 'Let me make a phone call. Meanwhile, why don't you familiarise Julia with the set up here?'

'I'm ready for that' responded Julia. 'Something else to help me take my mind off the video and look to the future.'

An hour or so later, Fred returned to the central room and invited everyone to sit down.

'Good news' he said cheerfully. The Federal Government is increasingly worried about the impact of scammers, who recently created a fake MyGov website that scammed many thousands of dollars from those who could least afford it. I told my government contact that we'd be interested in trying to track the scammers down. I got a message to phone the Department of Foreign Affairs on a secure line. The Minister herself answered. She knew of our work and, such was her concern about the situation, she offered to send me a contract at once. While we're waiting for it, let's decide if we want to take the project on, and how we might begin to grapple with it.'

'What sort of fee can we ask for? asked Julia.

'Always the lawyer,' quipped Sue. This raised a laugh, even from Julia.

'Surely that's the bottom line.'

'Not necessarily,' responded Fred. 'As I've mentioned before, we are very well funded and have the luxury of accepting projects of the greatest interest rather than the best paid. In this case, I suggest we charge a million up front, and another million if we deliver a positive outcome.'

'Will they wear it? 'asked Sue.

'I think so,' Fred replied. 'In the scheme of things, it's actually a very reasonable fee.'

'But can we actually do it?'

'That's the big question' replied Fred. 'I hadn't kept up with the latest in scams and scammers, so when my favourite aunt asked for help, I contacted some fellow hackers to get up to date. Now that

I've learned more, I'm convinced that scams are a huge and increasing threat, not only to individuals but to society at large. Once scammers have mastered the use of AI, they'll be able to create deep fakes of increasing sophistication. They've already scammed huge sums by creating the images and voices of celebrities and politicians to endorse investment opportunities which seem very attractive, but which are designed to steal the most money from the most people as quickly as possible. In truth, no-one is safe.'

'You must have some idea about how to stop them' said Julia, 'Otherwise you wouldn't even think about taking the project on.'

'At first,' replied Fred, 'I thought that the only way to stop them was through greater security on the social media platforms that the scammer infiltrate. I know that the operators of platforms such as Tik Tok, WeChat, Instagram, Facebook, and many others, struggle hard to contain scams, but they are constantly outsmarted by the scammers, who pay the best hackers huge sums. Then I realised that there is another way. Scammers rely on hackers. Hackers rely on their relationships with other hackers to keep their edge. These networks are highly exclusive. I'm already part of a network, but it's focussed on legitimate goals, not scams or scammers. I think I can use it to springboard into the scammers' networks. That would be a start.'

'How confident are you?' asked Julia.

'Pretty confident, but I'm less confident about how to take things further. I need to think a lot more about that.'

'So', said Sue, 'You are asking us to take part in a project that requires you to think a lot more before we know how to proceed, or even if we can proceed.'

'Look at our track record. George and I have often succeeded against seemingly impossible odds. Now that our team includes new talent, I'm sure we'll be even better at doing what seems impossible. Have faith in our ability to be clever, resourceful, creative and persistent, until we achieve our goals.'

'That's impressive rhetoric,' said Julia, 'But if you will forgive me for saying so, it is just rhetoric. You've taken me a little closer to a decision, but I'm not there yet. I need more facts. Something more. Joke all you like about my legal background, but my training insists on a more rigorous argument.'

'I think I can give you that something more,' said George. 'As part of my own research I have discovered what most Governments and their security services have become deeply afraid of. The CIA,

MOSSAD, MI5, MI6, the FSB – Russia's new name for the KGB – see deep fakes as the greatest threat since nuclear annihilation at the peak of the cold war.'

'Please tell us why,' said Julia. 'It seems a bit far-fetched.'

'It's all about the ability to create the images and voices of famous or influential people. Scammers have got very, very good at this. The emails, messages, videos or podcasts that they put on the net are totally convincing. Even experts struggle to identify them as fakes. And the scammers will only get better. The introduction of ChatGPT has made it even easier for them to get the background information they need. That's one of the reasons why Elon Musk and some other tech titans are against any further development of ChatGPT.

If we succeed in shutting down scammers in a way that makes it more difficult for them to do their evil work, this in itself is a big win. But imagine what success will bring to our business! We'll have more work than we could have ever imagined.'

'I'm in,' said Julia.

'Me too,' said Sue. 'We know that George is keen, so let's get started.'

CHAPTER FOUR

'Good news,' announced Fred at a team meeting two days later. 'I let it be known in my hacker's network that I was desperate for money and would be open to any offer. There's no way anyone can discover my true financial status. I got three responses. Two were dead ends. The third came from the dark web. I replied, and a woman named Zelda got back to me at once. I've recorded our correspondence, and I'll read it out verbatim. I want you to capture its flavour.'

'I've confirmed your identity, Fred, and I've established that you are seen by your fellow hackers as one of the very best. I think I can help with your financial problems.'

'That sounds like good news. Tell me more.'

'Before I do so you need to understand that what I tell you is in the strictest confidence. You must agree to abide by that condition. If you fail to do so, bad things will happen.'

'I understand. You have my word.'

'How much do you know about deep fakes?'

'I keep in touch with developments, but to be honest, I've never created one myself or collaborated with others to do so.'

'That's okay. It's your top-rated hacking skills that are important here.'

'So, what's the deal?'

'I'm part of a business that creates deep fakes and publishes them on the internet, mainly the deep web. We have no problem hacking into all the social media platforms, as well as YouTube.'

'What sort of deep fakes?'

'You name it, we make it. The most difficult, but by far the most lucrative, involve creating communications from celebrities, well known businesspeople, politicians, the more successful influencers, and anyone who happens to have captured the headlines. We use these fakes to scam money, disrupt elections, incite public unrest, even rebellions. Even wars. But we must constantly fight attempts by the owners of the social media platforms to stop us. Sometimes Governments join forces with them. This is where you come in.

With the very best hackers and programmers, we stay ahead of the game.'

Fred stopped reading from his laptop.

'There's more, but I'd like your impressions up to now.'

'Are deep fakes,' asked Sue, 'really as powerful and destructive as Zelda claims?'

'I'm afraid so. And they'll get more so. The programmers will make full use of developments in AI. And the scammers already rely on ChatGPT to glean background information on their targets. Now here's the rest of my conversation with Zelda.'

'Tell me about your setup. You must have a physical location.'

'Of course. Please remember the importance of total confidentiality. What I tell you could, in the wrong hands, be harmful to us. You probably think we are just one of many groups doing the same thing, but that isn't the case. The supply of genius-level hackers and programmers is limited. We have to compete for them against not only the social media platforms, but many other individuals and organisations, both private and Government. Especially the security agencies. You'll know that programmers and hackers have their own code of ethics. Most would refuse to work with us, or with similar organisations. I'm confident we've identified those organisations that have potency comparable to our own. There are only two. One is based in Russia, the other in China. I don't know the physical location of either group, although I could find it if necessary. I'm based in New York, together with four colleagues. We find that physical interaction greatly enhances our creativity and efficiency. We know the physical locations of most of our hackers and programmers, but that is of little importance since we work with them almost exclusively online. Is there anything more you need to know before I make you an offer?'

'An offer I can't refuse?'

'Ha ha. We're not the Mafia, although I confess to working with them at times. I won't offer you a written contract. Everything will be based on trust. Your starting salary will be four million Australian dollars a year, paid monthly in bitcoin. No income tax!'

'That really is an offer I can't refuse. When do I start?'

'There are a few things I need to put in place. What about next Monday morning?'

'That's fine with me. Should I contact you, or will you get in touch?'

'The time difference between Sydney and New York is currently sixteen hours. Eight a.m. in Sydney will be four p.m. the next day in New York, so let's say nine a.m. your time.'

'I look forward to hearing from you.'

'That's the end of our correspondence,' said Fred. 'What do you think?'

'I think you should have discussed it with us before accepting,' said Julia.

'Of course, I thought of that, but to me the situation demanded immediate acceptance. I was supposed to be in a desperate financial situation. A delay would have undermined that notion.'

'I'll accept that,' responded Julia, 'But you are taking on a huge risk. At the moment it's just you. What about the three of us?'

'I can't see that I've put any of you in danger. Our defence systems make it impossible for Zelda to discover the location of HQ, so it really is just me. But I'll need your help and support. We'll still be a team working closely together. Any time away from the project can be used to get you and Sue more skilled in using the computer network. Is that okay with you George?'

'Of course. I think I've learned enough to turn them into budding hackers and programmers!'

The team gathered at HQ fifteen minutes before nine the following Monday morning.

'Remember, Fred cautioned, 'that I have sworn an oath of confidentiality. There can be no hint of your presence.'

'We'll be quiet as mice,' Sue quipped.

At exactly nine o'clock, Zelda sent a message suggesting they should switch to voice mode. Fred pressed a few keys.

'Can you hear me, Zelda?'

'Loud and clear.'

Zelda's voice betrayed the trace of a mid-west accent. She got straight down to business.

'Our current project targets Robert F. Kennedy, who Trump has appointed Secretary of the Department of Health and Human Services. We plan to create a video of Kennedy pledging to ban all vaccination of children from the first of January next year. He is a well-known anti-vaxxer, so people might actually believe what he says. Of course, the video will cause total panic and outrage.'

'You'll have to be at the very top of your game for this one,' said Fred. 'His speech impediment will be incredibly difficult to get exactly right.'

'With you on board it's a no-brainer,' quipped Zelda in a surprising display of levity.

'I'm surprised you want to undermine Trump,' Fred continued, 'I thought you'd be a fan.'

'Not relevant. We're a business. Certain enemies of the US are paying us mega-bucks to do this.'

'What exactly do you want me ...'

Fred was interrupted by a loud sneeze.

'You are not alone! Zelda exclaimed. 'You've broken the most important rule before we've even started!'

'It's just one of my team. I really need her to work with me.'

'I told you that bad things would happen if you broke your word. You will never be safe again.'

Zelda broke the connection.

'Oh God, I'm so sorry,' said Sue, almost in tears. 'It just exploded without warning. This has happened before when I'm anxious or excited. I shouldn't have been here.'

'It's my fault,' said Fred. 'I should have insisted on being alone. Perhaps unconsciously I wanted a way out.'

'You were having second thoughts?' George asked.

'Yes. I'd come to realise that my duplicity would be discovered by Zelda as soon as I started probing. So, to be honest, I'm relieved.'

'Zelda promised bad things for you,' said Julia. 'Is she serious, do you think?

'I don't see how she can harm me physically. She can create problems online, but I'll sort them out. Let's take a break. Meet again this afternoon.'

The late afternoon meeting was understandably subdued. George volunteered to tell the Government contact of their failure. Fred was about to thank him when his phone rang. 'It's the intruder alarm at home. It's been triggered. I've got to go.'

Fred lived in a duplex in Redfern, which he had bought before the suburb became fashionable. It took half-an-hour before he drove into to the built-in garage facing the road. Opening the car door, he smelled gas. Instinctively he backed out, colliding with another car. The sound of the crash coincided with the deafening noise of an explosion that showered both cars with debris. When the smoke and dust cleared, Fred saw that his duplex was almost completely destroyed.

At HQ the next day, Fred explained that he had finished with the police and insurance company. Before he found another dwelling, he would live at HQ, where he had often stayed at busy times. He had stored all work-related material, important personal documents, and his few valuables in a robust safe. They had survived intact. He took them to the safety of HQ.

'Well,' said Sue, 'we're out of a job. What next?'

'This will sound crazy,' Fred responded, 'but I still want to destroy Zelda's outfit.'

There was stunned silence.

'Why on earth?' demanded Julia.

'There's something I've never told any of you, not even George. Both my parents were shot dead just as they were leaving our home in Melbourne. I had lagged behind and so escaped injury, but I saw everything. The police explained that it was a case of mistaken identity at a time of intense gang warfare. I've never doubted that. I went to live with the aunt who I've already told you about. Her love helped me seal over the emotional scars, but even now, talking about it is unbearably painful.'

Fred started to sob, his shoulders shaking. He let the tears flow.

'I can't remember the last time I cried,' he said, when finally, his tears stopped. 'It must be a delayed response to losing my home. Anyway, ever since the murder, I've had this rage inside me, a rage relieved only when I'm trying to destroy bad people. But the main reason for destroying Zelda is to stop her killing me.'

'You're sure Zelda was behind the explosion?'

'Absolutely. I made no attempt to hide my home address. She could have found it easily and clearly did so early on. She must have paid someone to make the explosion look like a gas leak. Someone was waiting for me to drive into the garage. He or she triggered the explosion a few moments later, giving me time to enter the house. But I was incredibly lucky. My backing out of the garage must have been obscured from view by a truck. It's a busy road for transport vehicles, including those enormous road trains. I'll stop swearing at them from now on!'

'I still don't understand why Zelda wants to kill you,' said George.

'I think it's personal. She feels betrayed. But more important, I know enough about her set-up to endanger it. I even managed to find out her physical location in New York. Zelda might think that I'm desperate enough to go over there and try to eliminate her. She'd have learned from the hackers' network that I'm capable of killing if there's no other option.'

'Oh!' exclaimed Sue, 'I didn't know that!'

'So, I've decided to go to New York. Alone. There's no way I'll expose any of you to more danger.'

There was a brief silence, broken by George.

'I'm going with you. My work as a psychiatrist was part of a strong need to right wrong. I still have that need though it's not as fierce as yours, Fred. Even more important, I have an unshakeable sense of loyalty towards you. You helped save me from the assassin's bullets. And I'm as determined to destroy Zelda as you are.'

Both Sue and Julia insisted that as part of the team, they were coming too. Under protest, Fred yielded.

'Okay,' he said. 'Let's start planning. I'll let the Government representative know what's happening.'

CHAPTER FIVE

It took three days to make the arrangements for the stay in New York. The excess luggage bill was eye-watering. Fred needed to be sure that he had enough equipment to meet all possible challenges. They arrived at JFK airport on Friday morning and took a cab to the three-bedroom apartment they booked on West End Avenue, a location chosen because it was walking distance from Zelda's HQ. It was booked for two weeks at almost twenty thousand dollars. Fred assured them that money wasn't an issue.

After settling in, they walked over to Zelda's HQ. It was a four-storey brownstone set in a terrace on a relatively quiet street. To their astonishment, a large, unmarked truck was parked outside. A heavy box was being loaded. Then the doors were closed, and the truck's engine started.

'We're going to lose them,' George exclaimed.

Without a word, Sue ran towards the truck and sprang onto its rear board just as it started to move.

Julia couldn't stop herself shouting, 'Sue, you're crazy!'

'That's the only way we'll ever find them again,' said George. 'They've hired the truck privately, not from a removalist. The number plate has been deliberately obscured. Zelda wants to foil any attempt to find her new HQ. How extraordinary that we arrived when we did. A good omen, perhaps.'

Twenty minutes later, they got a call from Sue.

'You won't believe it, but they've moved to another brownstone only a kilometre or so from the old one. I'll get a cab back to the apartment. See you there.'

'Without your crazy heroics,' said Julia, 'we'd be totally fucked. You are truly a hero.'

The others loudly voiced their agreement.

'It's my NIDA training,' quipped Sue. 'I suddenly felt I was in a movie, one of those where the hero does the same trick.'

'I'd love to celebrate,' said Fred, 'but we've no time to lose. Let's get a cab and check out Zelda's new HQ.'

Taking care to keep out of sight, they saw that the brownstone was the last in a terrace that ended in a cul-de-sac.

'Clever,' said Julia. 'No through traffic and mainly local pedestrians.'

'let's make a detour to the other side of the cul-de-sac,' said George who knew the city well. 'Often these cul-de-sacs have an alley for pedestrian access.'

George was right. The side of Zelda's brownstone faced a narrow alley that linked the cul-de-sac with an adjacent street. The windows on the side wall were high up and barred.

'This type of brownstone,' continued George, 'is called a classic. You can see the steps leading up from the sidewalk to what is actually the third floor. This normally contains the living and dining rooms. The floor below is called the garden level, which usually includes the kitchen and laundry. You can't see them from here, but there are steps down to the front basement, a small area for storage of garbage bins. The windows to the basement floor itself are always barred, of course. That floor usually has a spare bedroom or two, and storage.'

'They may well have knocked down a wall or two before moving,' said Julia. 'Is there any way we can see inside?'

'Theoretically we could access the basement of a facing brownstone and use thermal binoculars with a laser rangefinder, but it's not worth the risk. Zelda's installed closed-circuit cameras that will record any nearby movement.'

'Even if we know the layout, I don't see how we could get in,' said Sue.

'We can't,' said Fred firmly, 'so let's get back to the apartment and discuss alternatives.'

Although sex-role stereotypes were anathema to her, Julia had none-the-less taken on the role of house mother. Aided by Sue, who had similar views about gender roles, Julia kept the apartment well stocked with food. Once they'd eaten and settled into their chairs, Fred began the discussion.

'We have only one option, he said. 'Blow the place to smithereens!'

'You can't be serious,' exclaimed Julia and Sue simultaneously.

'Zelda blew my house up. We're going to pay her back in spades.'

'But what about collateral damage?' asked Sue, 'and how can we be sure that only Zelda and her team of four will be there?' Even more important, do you really want to kill Zelda?'

'I have to kill her. If I don't, she will kill me.'

'What about the other four?' Sue continued.

'They're probably as bad as Zelda. I don't want to kill them, but I will if I have to. I understand your concerns about collateral damage, so I'll take the risk of placing a mini spy camera that will send images of all who come and go. George says there's a back door, but it's just for access to the garden, which is fully enclosed.'

'If we get the go-ahead,' said George, 'we have two huge problems: accessing the basement and getting the explosives.'

'Tonight, I'm going back on my own,' Fred responded. 'I'll use a periscope to photograph the basement area, and I'll put the spy camera in place. It'll be undetectable. If access to the basement is possible without triggering an alarm, and if Zelda and her team are the only ones who come and go, I'll order the explosives.'

The photos taken with the periscope showed that it was possible to get into the basement area without triggering an alarm. It meant crawling on one's belly to the steps down. Heavy bars meant there was no question of entering the basement floor itself.

'Well done, Fred,' said Julia. 'Now I'm ready for bed. It's been quite a day!'

'Me too,' said Sue.

'I won't be far behind you,' George added.

'I have to make a phone call,' said Fred, 'to contact my link to the local hackers' network. Hackers tend to be nocturnal creatures. Then it's bed!'

By dark the next day, Julia and Sue had finished their task of studying the images relayed by the spy camera. Only Zelda and one of her team, a woman, had left the brownstone, returning after about three hours.

At breakfast the next morning, Fred was elated.

'Last night, after we got the all-clear, I messaged my contact. I explained the situation and what we needed. He asked no questions and promised to transmit my request to carefully selected hackers. Less than an hour later, I got a message asking what kind of explosive I wanted, and how much. I explained in detail what I needed it for. The contact suggested C4 because its blast profile is more suited to destroying buildings than that of Semtex. It's also more malleable and easier to detonate. I'd need seventy pounds to be sure of total destruction. This would cost thirty-five thousand American dollars, cash on delivery. He can get it by tomorrow afternoon. He'll text the location and wait for me in his car. I can't risk a cab, so I'll get a rental. We'll need a car anyway.'

'It seems a lot of money', said Julia. 'Well within out budget,' Fred replied, 'And he said he'd throw in the detonators.'

The seventy pounds of C4 – the seller still used pounds and ounces – had a volume of about thirty litres. It had been divided into five portions of fourteen pounds.

'Place these at equal intervals against the wall of the basement floor,' the seller explained. 'Although the blast will be directed inward, it will bounce back off the wall of the basement space, causing maximum damage.'

At four in the morning the following day, Fred and George exited the hire car and walked to the cul-de-sac. The C4 just fitted into a backpack. Geroge was to act as lookout while Fred placed the explosives and detonators which would be triggered remotely. Pushing the backpack ahead of him, Fred crawled on his belly past the front steps and climbed down into the basement area. He carefully placed each block of C4 as instructed and attached the detonators. Pushing the empty back-pack ahead of him, he got back to George without mishap. The maximum range of their remote trigger was three hundred metres. When they had reached that distance, Fred looked at George.

'Ready?'

'Now or never. Press the button.'

The explosion wasn't as loud as they had expected, but a subtle vibration beneath their feet told them of its power. They waited twenty minutes before walking back to the cul-de-sac.

'My God,' explained George. 'How on earth is any of it still standing?'

The basement and garden floors had been totally destroyed, but the other two floors were still relatively intact. They had simply collapsed on top of the wreckage of the two lower floors. Two fire trucks and an ambulance had already squeezed into the cul-de-sac. The area was floodlit, and two firemen were entering through what was left of the door at the top of the steps. One of them called out from a shattered fourth floor window:

'Three bodies on the third floor, one still alive but only just. Safest to get her out through a window.'

'Zelda?' asked George, 'or one of her team?'

A safety cordon stopped the pair getting close enough to see the face of the woman as she was stretchered into the waiting ambulance.

'Somehow,' said Fred, 'we need to find out.'

He called Sue and Julia to update them and let them know they were coming straight back to the apartment.

CHAPTER SIX

'It's on the early morning news right now,' shouted Julia as Fred and George entered the apartment. They all sat down to watch. The two fire trucks remained but there were no more attempts to enter the remains of the brownstone. As the team had hoped, there was little damage to the adjacent brownstone.

'There must be two double brick walls between them,' said George. 'They knew how to build houses in those days.'

'The two other members of Zelda's team must have been in the lower two floors,' said Sue. 'Squashed flat as a pancake.' No one laughed.

'I see that my attempt at light relief has fallen just as flat.' This time there was a murmur of amusement.

'But now it's time to get serious,' said George. 'Even if we find out which hospital the woman was taken to, she'll surely be under police guard. She's the victim of a crime that was clearly intended to kill her. Of course, she may not survive.'

'Perhaps my NIDA training will help here,' said Sue. 'I can impersonate a doctor, use my status to get inside info, and maybe even enter her room.'

'It's a plan,' said George, 'but first we need to locate the hospital, confirm it's Zelda. Then we'll need to find out how you'll prove your status, whether it's a badge or an identity card.'

'I can find out the woman's name and where she's being cared for through the hackers' network,' said Fred. 'It shouldn't take long.'

Just before three that afternoon, Fred got a message telling him that the victim's name was Zelda. She'd been admitted to the Mount Sinai Hospital on Madison Avenue.

After breakfast the next day, Julia and Sue went by cab to the hospital. Julia took photos of the identity cards worn by the staff. They discovered where Zelda was being held. But when the lift opened on the correct floor, a police woman barred their way.

As soon as they got back to the apartment, Fred examined the photos. 'I can get an identity card within twenty-four hours, but that may not be enough. The police will be alert to impersonation. You'll need cast-iron authorisation as well.'

'I can help here,' said Julia. 'I've had to create many such documents as part of my work.'

Fred had collected the identity card by noon the next day. With his help, Julia concocted a letter signed by the hospital's CEO stating that Dr J. Andrews was authorised to examine the woman identified as Zelda, essential from a medico-legal perspective.

Julia insisted on going to the hospital alone. Her cab arrived just before three. She went straight up to the right floor. The policewoman at the lift did not recognise her from their previous encounter. She read the letter and told Sue the room number. Two policemen were sitting either side of the door. After reading the letter, they agreed to let Sue into the room, accompanied by one of them.

The woman was not intubated. Sue pretended to take her pulse, even though its rate and rhythm were shown on the monitor. As she did so, the woman stirred, but did not open her eyes. Sue then managed to photograph her face without being seen by the policeman.

'I'm finished here,' Sue said with authority.

The policeman opened the door, and after thanking him, Sue strode back down the corridor.

'So that's what Zelda looks like,' Fred said, as soon as he saw the photo. 'Now I'll know who to watch out for.'

'She wasn't intubated, and she stirred when I pretended to take her pulse. But she didn't open her eyes.'

'She'll survive,' said George, with the authority of his medical background, 'and the absence of head bandages suggests no significant brain injury.'

'Fuck it!' Fred exclaimed. 'We've failed!

'Nonsense,' countered George. 'Our brief was to destroy Zelda's organisation, and we've done that. If we all agree, Fred can send a full report to his government contact. Our reputation will reach stellar proportions.'

'I see all that,' Fred responded, 'but if Zelda survives, killing me will be at the top of her to-do list.'

'Not necessarily,' said Julia. 'She wanted to stop you trying to destroy her business. Now that you've done that, she may have better things to do.'

'If you got another chance, would you kill her?' asked Sue.

'Only if she was a real threat to my own life. I've done her enough damage already.'

They were all in bed by nine-thirty.

At breakfast the next day they decided to stay for the full two weeks of their rental. George loved jazz and booked two of their four remaining evenings at the Lincoln Centre, renowned for hosting top-flight performances. The team spent the rest of the day wandering around the city, with Central Park their first port of call. The next morning, they all went to the Metropolitan Museum of art.

'Just so you know I'm not a complete barbarian,' said Fred, when at the last minute he'd decided to join them.

Sue's passionate interest in art took her, on the remaining days, to the Museum of Modern Art, the Guggenheim, the Frick Collection and several lesser-known galleries. She was ecstatic to find that two of Whistler's life-size portraits of women were hanging in the Frick. She had long dreamed of seeing them in the flesh. The others were happy to explore, take in a couple of shows, and eat and drink too much. They chose Qantas for the return flight because it was non-stop. George couldn't resist the free booze in business class and got slightly drunk, becoming over-friendly with some of the other passengers.

'I admit,' he said, when he'd sobered up, that I've got a bit of a problem. I can go for weeks with no more than a gin and tonic or two. Then I find myself on a bit of a bender. But this has never interfered with my work. I'm sure Fred can vouch for that.'

'Some mornings he looks like death warmed up,' said Fred, 'but he always delivers the goods.'

Once they were back at HQ, Sue asked to take a few days off. She needed a rest and wanted to catch up with her parents and a few friends. Julia and George also needed to rest. Apart from each other, they had no close friends. When George was struck off the medical register, he'd been ostracised, even by those he thought would stand by him. His parents, while not exactly disowning him, distanced themselves. He saw very little of them. Julia's obsession with work left little time for friendship, and she rarely saw her mother, who had married a man whom Julia heartily disliked. Fred's friends were exclusively online, a result of his reliance on the hacker's network in the pursuit of his crusade against evildoers. This suited Fred. Since his parents' murder, he had been unable to make close real-life relationships.

Four days after their return, the team met for breakfast at HQ. There were four job offers waiting for them. Two involved money laundering, the third a group of very sophisticated scammers. 'I've managed,' said Fred, 'to persuade my favourite aunt to let me give her the thirty thousand dollars she lost to scammers, so she no longer wants me to track them down. This means I've rather lost interest in doing that kind of work.'

The fourth job offer involved forgery. 'One particular group of forgers has become such a problem,' said Fred, 'that the Federal Government is determined to eliminate it. Because of our success with the last job, they've chosen us for this one. I'm not sure exactly what this group's into but let me outline the possibilities.

In the realm of art, they create replicas of famous paintings and sculptures and pass them off as originals. They do the same with valuable manuscripts and books. Fake documents are a real money-spinner: driving licences, academic degrees, professional credentials, property deeds, even genealogies to justify inheritance.

Also very lucrative are forged bearer bonds, even government ones. These bonds are anonymous, and there is no central register of them. Corporate bonds are especially seductive. Now that bitcoin has soared in value, it and other cryptocurrencies have become a favourite target. Skilled hackers can manipulate the bitcoin blockchain without detection, and digital currencies used by banks and financial institutions are also susceptible.

Fake goods such as designer handbags can be quite lucrative, depending on the skill and location of those who make them. The most sophisticated of these forgers are moving into impersonation, using deep fakes. These have the potential to seriously disrupt global harmony and wellbeing.'

'I had no idea!' exclaimed Sue. 'Why aren't we told about this?'

'Maybe,' replied Fred, 'It's because the targets are so wide ranging and disparate. There are no obvious links between, for example, digital currency manipulation, fake handbags, and forging old masters, so the targets don't communicate with each other. If they did, the true extent of the problem would be exposed.'

'What do we know about the structure and aims of this particular group of forgers?' asked George.

'Very little. If we decide to accept the gig, that's where we need to start. Shall we go ahead?'

As soon as the others agreed to do so, Fred brought the meeting to a close.

'We'll need to work out a division of labour, once I've done enough research. Give me twenty-four hours. Then we'll begin.'

CHAPTER SEVEN

Two days later, the team gathered at HQ for breakfast.

'I'm managed to discover what this particular group specialises in,' said Fred. 'Document forgery. World-wide, this branch of forgery costs hundreds of billions of dollars each year, and I'm not exaggerating. Our own government is concerned, amongst other things, about forged passports, visas, work permits, residence and citizenship certificates, and government bonds. Apart from the bonds, all these require marriage and birth certificates and other identity documents. Just as Donald Trump is concerned about the criminal element of illegal immigrants, so are our security chiefs. These criminals are often involved in human trafficking, a huge problem worldwide. Our government is also very worried about forged business contracts, land titles, and court orders.

Some forgery groups have internet connections in several different countries, which makes it very difficult for law enforcement agencies to coordinate and act effectively. Often these sites offer specialised services such as fake designer clothes and accessories, especially handbags. The one that we are targeting has few such overseas connections. Its main site is on the dark web. The group is highly centralised and has assembled a team of hugely sophisticated hackers and programmers. This team can meet almost any requirement in their area of specialisation.'

'Surely,' said Julia, 'there's a central record of many of these documents, so detecting forgeries should be relatively easy.'

'Often people assume the document is genuine, and don't bother to check. But even if they do, the best hackers can often get into the relevant data bases and manipulate them.'

'My God!' Julia exclaimed. 'They seem unstoppable.'

'It's very difficult to shut down the most sophisticated groups, but law enforcement agencies are constantly improving their efficiency, and they've had some successes overseas.

Now there's one other area that our group of forgers specialises in: art forgery. Dealing with that is not a top priority for the government, but it could be of great interest to us. Forging valuable art works, especially old masters, requires skills that may take years to fully acquire. Marketing them requires extensive documentation. A convincing provenance is essential. Often, the forgers concoct a story. A favourite one claims that the painting was inherited from a wealthy family member. Detailed genealogical data must be created to make the story watertight, so there is an intimate link between document forgery and art forgery.

Serious buyers of forged items will access our forgers' dark web site to check them out, and if they are satisfied, to initiate transactions. The site is so well protected that I haven't been able to get in. Access requires a password that is given to clients once they've been checked out. I don't even know the physical location of the business. I was losing hope until I suddenly realised that engaging them in a real-life transaction was the way to go. Buying documents from them is too risky. Penultimate because the end user can be identified. But buying valuable works of art, doesn't have that drawback. The buyer can remain anonymous. And your knowledge of art, Sue, makes you the best person for this gig.'

'It can't be any riskier than the casino job, or blowing up Zelda's HQ,' said Sue, 'but I'll need all of you to help me.'

Two days later, the team met to discuss what they had learned about art forgery.

'We've established,' said George, 'that some Sydney art galleries are almost certainly involved in art forgery. The extent of this ranges from turning a blind eye to active participation. A well-known overseas example is the Knoedler gallery in New York. For over fifteen years it sold more than eighty million dollars' worth of fake art. The works were supplied by Glafira Rosales, who claimed they came from a very wealthy collector who wished to remain anonymous. The fraud was exposed in 2011, and the gallery closed after trading for 165 years.'

'So, we know that shitloads of money can be made,' said Sue. 'Very tempting, especially for galleries struggling to survive. But there are over twenty significant art galleries in Sydney, and many more minor ones and artists' spaces. How on earth can we identify the crooked ones?'

'I've asked my hackers' network to explore this,' Fred replied. 'But art doesn't seem to be of much interest to this community, and I got mixed results. Out of the twenty or so established galleries, eight were identified as possibly or probably involved in counterfeit art. But there was no certainty about this. Sue, I think you'll have to visit all eight of these. The auction houses can be left out unless the trail takes us to them.'

'I knew I'd have to do some legwork, and I've sketched out a strategy. I need your feedback.'

'We're all ears,' quipped Julia.

'I think old masters are out. Too rare and expensive. I believe we should focus on Impressionists, including our own Heidelberg school. Art historians have finally decided that it fits well within Impressionism. For me, that's a no brainer. A Tom Roberts painting went for $976,000 in 2014. An Arthur Street sold for over three million dollars in 2021, and a Fred McCubbin fetched 2.3 million way back in 1998.'

'What about the French Impressionists?' Julia asked.

'Different ballpark. Claude Monet's *Haystacks* got 110 million American dollars in 2023. A still life Cezanne sold for over one hundred million in today's money in 1999. Camille Pissarro's works sell for over thirty million, and if you want to buy anything well known by Eduard Manet, you'll be stung between twenty and fifty million.'

After a brief discussion, the others agreed to support Sue's proposal.

'I'm less certain about how to approach the galleries,' Sue continued. 'I thought I'd introduce myself as a passionate lover of Impressionism who has recently received a very substantial inheritance.'

'I can't fault that,' said Fred, and the others agreed. 'If a gallery offers to help,' he continued, 'how can you tell if they're talking about fakes or the real thing?'

'I've thought a lot about that. I'll tell the gallery that my favourite Heidelberg artist is Arthur Streeton, and that I'd like to focus on him, at least to start with. I've found out exactly which of Streeton's over five hundred paintings have been sold or are owned by public art museums and galleries. Any art gallery seriously into art forgery will have the same data, or obtain it when necessary. That means they'll offer a painting from a fictitious private collector. They can claim that it was recently unearthed, or that it has been held only in private collections and has never been documented.

In reality, private collectors almost always document their holdings, mainly to facilitate trades or swaps with other collectors, some of whom they may not have heard of. With Fred's help I can assemble a list of Streeton's works held by private collectors. It may not be fully accurate or comprehensive, but it will be good enough. If the gallery deals in fake art, they will not offer to buy a painting on this list, because they know I can contact the collector myself if I have any doubts. Instead, they'll offer an undocumented work, a painting unknown to the public. If I agree, they'll create an unshakeable provenance of a fictitious work by Streeton, a work that will be irresistible.'

'Before the gallery goes ahead with anything,' said Fred, 'they'll have to be sure you are what you say you are. They'll insist on seeing bank statements and perhaps details of the inheritance. This will have to be of a member from a very wealthy family that has insisted on privacy. Let me know how much you inherited, and with the help of my hacker's network, I'll create the documents.'

'Six million dollars,' Sue replied. 'A not outrageous sum that will allow me to buy a Streeton, or at least the one they concoct. How long will the documents take?

'You'll need a forged passport to prove your identity. We can't afford to make any mistakes, so give me two days. What name shall I give you?'

'Same Christian name. Surname Roberts, and two days will give me time to revisit the Heidelberg school and make sure I'm up to speed.'

CHAPTER EIGHT

Sue began checking out the eight galleries that were under suspicion. The first five were legitimate. Entering the sixth, she approached an attractive woman in her thirties siting at the reception desk.

'Hello. I've fallen I love with the Heidelberg school and especially Arthur Streeton. I want to buy one of his paintings. A friend recommended this gallery.'

The woman smiled and introduced herself as Janine. 'What sort of price range?'

'Well, I've recently come into an inheritance. I want one of his finest landscapes.'

'Hold on.' Janine tapped her keyboard and peered at the computer screen.

'We're talking at least three million dollars, according to the most recent sales. Is that within your budget?'

'Absolutely.'

'You'll need to talk to my boss. He's in the rear gallery. I'll take you down.'

The boss was a plumpish man of medium height who looked to be in his fifties.

'Sue, meet William, owner of this prestigious establishment.'

They shook hands. William's palms were a little clammy, but his grip was firm.

'Sue wants to buy a Streeton landscape, one of his finest. She has the funds.'

'Before we start,' said William, 'we'll need to establish your credentials. There's a lot of work in setting this up.'

'That's what I thought. I've got everything with me. Bank statement, records of fund transfers, my passport.'

'Let's go to my office,' said William'. 'Would you like tea of coffee?'

'Coffee would be great. White with no sugar.'

'We have a small kitchen,' said Janine, 'and a large and very expensive coffee machine. I'll be back in a mo.'

William's office was bare apart from a dozen or so paintings stacked against the walls. An antique table served as a desk. He placed the documents on it and invited Sue to sit down on an antique chair.

'It's a Windsor,' he said proudly. 'Very robust design. and not uncomfortable.'

Sue smiled in response.

'Well, everything seems in order. No relation?'

'I wish. But no. Tom Roberts is a hero of mine, but we're not related. Up to now, I couldn't afford an original Streeton. Just prints, so I'm new to this. Can you explain how you'll go about the purchase?'

'I won't directly approach any private collectors. Even if they have the right paintings, they rarely want to part with them. If they do, they nearly always go to auction. I have a contact who should be able to track down the right painting at the right price. Leave it with me.'

Sue thanked him and gave him the number of the untraceable mobile that Fred had given her.

Back at HQ, the team assembled to hear Sue's report.

'So far, she concluded, 'the gallery meets all the criteria for art forgery. William will ring me when he's found the right painting, so we'll have to wait.'

'When he calls,' said Fred, 'try and keep him talking. I'll hack into his phone so we can track his calls.'

The call came that evening.

'Sorry to ring so late,' said William, 'but I've just got some really good news. My contact has an extensive network of dealers and collectors. He's located a Streeton landscape that has somehow escaped documentation. It's not on any register of Streeton's works. He'll arrange for it to be shipped here. Once you've seen it, you can decide whether or not you want to buy it.'

'That's wonderful! I'm so excited. How long before it gets here?'

'We must negotiate a price, then arrange insurance and a specialist courier to be certain it's not damaged in transit. All this will take four or five days.'

'I can hardly wait. Can you tell me a bit about the work?'

'You'll know his iconic *Golden Summer, Eaglemont.*'

'Of course. One of my favourites.'

'Well, this was painted three years later. It's a similar landscape, but there is more detail. To me, it's an even finer work.'

'Thank you so much William. You've done an amazing job.'

'Sue, I should thank you. Without your request, we would never have discovered this undocumented painting. Like you, I can hardly wait to see it. I'll contact you as soon as it arrives.'

'What a salesman!' said Sue after William ended the call.' Did we talk long enough?'

'Just. His phone had some protection, but I got into it. We can intercept his outgoing calls, but not those he receives. That should be enough.'

Fred updated the team the morning after next.

'William contacted an artist whose expertise includes forging paintings of the Heidelberg School. Specifying the exact requirements for the forgery required lengthy conversations between them, so I was able to hack into the artist's mobile. He's based on the outskirts of Melbourne, and he has a website. This shows a modest reputation as a landscape painter, a reputation that totally obscures his work as a forger.'

'Should we pay him a visit?' asked George.

'Too risky. We might arouse suspicion given that he's just got William's commission. Maybe a visit later, but he's small fry. Let me tell you about the other phone calls that William made.

He contacted the document forgers to arrange the fake provenance. They've done this kind of work many times, but William had to give them precise details, and this took enough time for me to hack into their dark web site. Cybersecurity detected the intrusion and shut me out. I'm sure they can't trace me, but I'll have to be careful when I try to get in again. This is a real breakthrough.

I'd thought that the forgers' dark web site was impenetrable.

I also learned more about William's operation. He has quite a network. I'll learn more over the next day or so, but already it's clear that he sends forgeries overseas, especially to Europe and America. His strength lies in the painters he's recruited, and his close links with the document forgers. Most of the artists are located in and around Adelaide. There's a huge pool of talent out there, but even the most talented artists struggle to make a living from their paintings. Forgery is very lucrative, very tempting. He also has two or three artists based overseas, and he uses them if the locals can't deliver a specific forgery. He also owns a local auction house.'

'We've got enough already to shut him down,' said Julia.

'It would be crazy to intervene before we've got enough to shut down the entire forgers' set-up,' said George.

'Agreed,' said Fred, 'the document forgers are the main game.'

Two days later, Sue got a phone call from William. 'It's arrived. Come and see it.'

The painting was truly amazing. It captured perfectly Streeton's style: his ability to capture the luminosity and vibrant light of the Australian landscape, and his mastery of atmospheric effects such as the haze of a distant horizon or the shimmering heat of summer.

'It's way beyond my expectations,' Sue exclaimed. 'I feel I don't deserve such a wonderful work of art. But of course I'll buy it, subject to an independent verification of the provenance. How much am I up for?'

'Four million dollars. This makes it the most expensive painting of his ever sold, though not by much. It's possible, I'm afraid, that someone else may try and buy it. The vendor will accept the best offer, so there's some urgency in settling things. I strongly advise you go ahead without taking the time and trouble to get an assessment of the provenance.'

'My inheritance has been placed in a trust. The trustee insists on authentication.'

'Perhaps I can help you by putting you in touch with a curator at the Art Gallery of New South Wales, who checks the provenance of potential new acquisitions.'

'Thankyou. Once he's given the okay, we'll go ahead.'

Sue gave a full account of events at the next team meeting.

'If the curator confirms the validity of the painting and its provenance, we'll know he's a crook. He may be part of a network. Something to investigate later.'

The following afternoon, the curator arrived at the gallery, where Sue and William were waiting for him. After studying the painting, he carefully went over the provenance, which was quite extensive.

'I have not the slightest doubt that this is a genuine Streeton. It is a truly remarkable find. You are most fortunate to be able to buy it.'

'This sounds crass,' said Sue to William, once the curator had left after signing a document confirming the painting's authenticity. 'But is the vendor open to negotiating the price? Could we bring it down a little?'

'Out of the question. Any delay creates the risk of another buyer. Four million it is.'

'How shall I transfer the money?'

'Directly to my bank account. I'll give you the details.'

'I'll need a bill of sale to show to the trustee. Once he's okayed it, I'll transmit the funds.'

Back at HQ, Sue updated the team.

'We need to work out a way of cancelling the sale without arousing suspicion. Any ideas?'

'Yes,' said Julia. 'Tell him that your bequest has been challenged by a sibling, and that the trust has been frozen. Sorting it out could take years. I think this is convincing and foolproof.'

Later that day, Sue rang William with the bad news. He was outraged.

'That's totally unacceptable! With a good lawyer, surely you can find a way around the problem.'

'Maybe, but that will take time, and money I no longer have. I'm sorry William, but I can't go ahead. I'm sure you'll find another buyer.'

'You'll be hearing from my own lawyer.' He ended the call.

'Well done, Sue,' said Julia, who had listened in to the conversation. Don't worry about the lawyer. It's an empty threat, made out of anger and frustration.'

'Thank God it's all over,' Sue replied. 'Now we can get on with the real business. The document forgers.'

CHAPTER NINE

George reviewed the situation at the next team meeting.

'We know pretty well everything about William's operation, including his auction house, which must be where he sells many of his paintings, both fake and legitimate. We could trace the buyers, but at this stage it doesn't seem necessary. I think we can move on from art forgery to our main target, the document forgers.'

The team agreed, and Fred took over.

'Our original plan was to trace the art forger's connection with the main group in the hope of hacking into their system. We know that didn't work. Their cybersecurity is too effective. I've decided not to try this again. It might invite retaliation.'

'Does this mean we're stuck?' asked Julia.

'I don't think so. Our group of forgers has recently expanded its services to those who want to commission deep fakes. We could place an order for a deep fake of such size and complexity that to deliver it the group might reveal some of its inner workings. Maybe even suggest a real-life meeting. As well, the project might help us access other deep fake operations.'

'This will cost serious money,' said George,

'We have the funds. Even if we don't succeed in shutting down the main group, we'll get well paid for exposing the art forgery side of the business. That should cover it.'

Julia looked uncomfortable. 'This is a bit too close to the bone. I'm still recovering from the trauma of my own deep fake catastrophe. But it makes sense. Count me in.'

Sue and George added their assent.

'Why just one deep fake?' asked Sue. 'Maybe three. A short one for Elon Musk's X, longer ones for the other platforms.'

'All this needs thorough research and careful planning,' said George. 'Let's meet again tomorrow and share our thoughts.'

Julia was the first to speak at the next team meeting.

'The social media platforms are very concerned about deep fakes, and there is increasing public awareness of them. To be effective, our deep fakes must be plausible as well as disruptive. If they are too racy or shocking, they'll be censored, but if we get them right, they'll be actively promoted. The platforms prioritise sensational material.'

'Thanks Julia,' said Fred. 'Now we need to decide what kind of deep fake best suits our purposes.'

'We need ones with a global impact,' said Sue. 'I'm thinking Donald Trump and some of his senior cabinet members. We know from Zelda's deep fake of Robert F Kennedy that these productions can have a huge impact.'

'Only a well-funded group could afford these big commissions' said Fred, 'We're talking hundreds of thousands of dollars, maybe over a million for a fake of major political significance. We'll have to find a group driven by hatred of America, The Big Satan, and of course Israel, The Little Satan. I have a contact in MOSSAD who owes me a favour. He may know of such a group. I'll get onto him right away.'

At the next team meeting, Fred had good news.

'The MOSSAD agent was really helpful. There's a rabidly anti-American group funded by both Iran and Russia that includes a loose coalition of high-ranking Iranians and others dedicated to the destruction of American influence worldwide, and to the elimination of Israel. When I've created a convincing cover story, I'll join the group.'

Once his membership had been approved, Fred contacted the forgery group using the alias of Kamran, a common Iranian name. In response, he got an email from a woman called Tessa, who said that his credentials had been confirmed. Fred outlined what he wanted and Tessa switched to voice mode.

'We can do it,' she said, 'but our fee will be nine hundred thousand dollars American for each one. We need to be sure you have the funds.'

'I can send you the necessary confirmation.'

'For something this complex, we might want to meet you in person. Is that acceptable?'

'In principle, yes.'

'Send a down payment of two hundred thousand dollars and we can get started.'

The team had originally decided to commission three deep fakes. The short one, designed for Elon Musk's X, was shelved. It took two weeks for the forgers to create a draft of the Trump deep fake. Trump's persona was captured perfectly, and what he said was totally convincing.

'We believed that our use of bunker-busting bombs during the Iran-Israeli war of mid-2025 had destroyed Iran's capacity to build a nuclear bomb. We were wrong. Today the CIA discovered that Iran is only days away from completing one. This greatly increases the threat that this rogue nation poses to Israel, which its theocratic dictatorship has sworn to destroy. To prevent this, I have ordered the bombing of a deeply buried site that escaped destruction. Our Airforce does not have the capacity to do this successfully, even with bunker-busters. We must therefore deploy a nuclear weapon to ensure the elimination of this acute danger, a threat not only to Israel, but to the whole world. I will keep you, the American people, informed of developments. God bless America!'

'Imagine,' said Sue, 'what would happen if this fake was actually released. Total chaos. Is there a chance the forgers could release it without our go-ahead?'

'Our agreement prohibits that,' Fred replied, 'and I can't think of any reason why they would, but I'll ask them to put the finishing touches on hold until we see the second fake.'

The second fake concerned J.D. Vance, Trump's vice-president. The draft was ready ten days later. It was just as convincing as the Trump fake, and in it, J. D. Vance said:

'My fellow Americans, it is no secret that I am strongly against abortion. The Federal

Government does not have the authority to ban or restrict termination of pregnancy. I am therefore asking the Supreme Court to legislate a nation-wide ban of all abortions except where there Is a serious risk to the mother's life. With the recent appointment of another Trump nominee to the Court, I am confident that the legislation will be passed. Our administration will ensure that it is fully enacted. Thank you. God bless America!'

'This will cause as much chaos as the Trump one,' said Julia. 'It must never be released.'

Later that day, Fred was contacted by Tessa.

'We have a problem. One of our other clients has illegally accessed the drafts of the Trump and Vance videos. This client is a very powerful pro-American who has threatened to publicise our work and shut down our business if we release the fakes. He certainly has the ability to do so. This threat put us in an almost impossible position. Our reputation will be destroyed if we cancel your deep fakes, but our whole business could be destroyed if we release them. This situation is so critical that we have arranged to meet a key member of the pro-American group in person. If you attend this meeting, a compromise may just be possible.'

'Where will the meeting take place?'

'Our whole team insists on being present, so it has to be at our operations base in Perth, Western Australia. We know that you are based in Sydney. The meeting is scheduled for noon next Thursday, three days from now. It's vital that you attend.'

'Let me know your location. I'll be there.'

'They're panicking,' said Julia when Fred updated the team. 'Revealing their location makes them acutely vulnerable to any hostility. What extraordinary luck for us!'

Fred arrived at the designated location fifteen minutes before noon. It was a large modern house in Cottesloe, one of Perth's most exclusive suburbs. Tessa introduced him to three of her team and the pro-American activist. They settled around a small conference table, and Tessa opened proceedings.

'We all know what's at stake. I'm praying that we can resolve this matter amicably.'

'My group and I have made a decision,' said Fred. 'We've decided not to publish the fakes, subject to compensation. We don't want to risk exposure.'

Tessa breathed a sigh of relief. 'What sort of compensation?'

'Reimbursement of our expenditure so far, with an additional three hundred thousand dollars.'

'Is that manageable?' Tessa asked her team.

After a brief discussion, all three agreed that it was and that the offer should be accepted. The money was to be transferred before Fred left. The pro-American group insisted on proof that the videos had been destroyed, and this was agreed. Tessa closed the meeting.

Fred notified his government contact of the base's location as soon as he left the building. He was back in Sydney by late evening, in time to join the rest of the team for a few celebratory drinks.

By then, he'd heard from his contact that the Federal Police had already acted. They had arrested all the deep fake producers, and at the same time discovered their links to the document forgers. All of them had been arrested also.

At breakfast the next morning, they all looked a bit worse for wear, especially George.

'Let's hope our luck stays with us for our next gig,' he said.

'I don't want to spoil the party,' said Julia, 'but what if the forgery group work out that it was us who dobbed them in? Could they retaliate?'

'I hadn't thought of that,' Fred replied. 'It's possible. We don't know what will happen after their arrest. They've almost certainly got fail-safe procedures that delete all incriminating evidence in the event of exposure. It may be very tricky to prosecute them successfully, so prison sentences aren't guaranteed. Some may remain at large. I just hope they've got more pressing issues to deal with than getting revenge, but it's something we need to watch out for. Let's hope that good luck continues to bless us. Not just to keep us from harm, but to help us beat the baddies. We're going to need all the help we can get.'

'Let's take the rest of the day off,' George suggested. 'I'm too hung over to do any serious work, and you lot look a bit jaded, to put it mildly. Tomorrow we can look at job offers and decide if any are of interest.'

The others needed no persuasion.

CHAPTER TEN

'I'm disappointed,' said Fred at the next day's team meeting. 'Only two job offers, both about money laundering. Given our recent triumph, I'd expected offers to flood in.'

'Maybe,' said Sue, 'the Government has put a lid on it because they didn't want to reveal their vulnerability to document forgery.'

'Here's what might be a third option,' said Julia. 'I've just got a message from an old colleague, Emma, who must think I'm still practicing. She's American, worked in Sydney for two years. I helped her with her passion, human rights. She's deeply concerned about illegal organ harvesting.

A woman, an illegal immigrant, approached Emma after two of her friends, also illegals, disappeared. This woman felt unable to approach the police, but a friend told her it would be safe to contact Emma. After a few enquiries, Emma suspected that a highly sophisticated organisation was, amongst other barbarities, abducting illegal immigrants and killing them in order to harvest their organs.

Emma approached me in desperation. She found that her attempts to find out more were obstructed. The operation is based in Clark County, Nevada. There are many illegal immigrants there, servicing the casinos, infrastructure building, the tourist industry, and agriculture. The disappearance of an illegal is unlikely to be investigated. I'm afraid I told Emma I couldn't help, but now I'm thinking this could be our next project.'

'My first thought,' said George, 'is that we won't get paid.'

'Let's not forget,' Fred replied, 'that our goal has always been to take down the baddies. Our bank balance now stands at just over eleven million dollars. We can easily afford a pro bono project.'

'I stand corrected. Julia, how committed are you to helping Emma?'

'I hugely admire Emma and her passion for human rights,' said Julia, 'I'll do pretty well anything to help her.'

'Human organ trafficking horrifies and disgusts me,' said Sue. 'I'm with Julia. So, let's all do some research. Then we can decide.'

Two days later, George offered a summary of their efforts.

'About 180,000 organ transplants were done worldwide in 2024, yielding a revenue of around twenty billion dollars. Kidneys make up about twenty percent. Heart, lung, pancreas and intestines make up the rest. Corneas aren't included because, along with skin, they are classified as tissue transplants. Hospitals usually turn a blind eye to the origin of the organs, and here's why. In America a kidney transplant costs about 450,000 dollars. Livers cost about 900,000, hearts 1.8 million, and a single lung about 950,000. Some twenty percent of documented transplants used illegally harvested organs.'

'I had no idea,' Sue interjected, 'that the industry was so extensive and lucrative. It makes illegal harvesting very tempting.'

'That takes me to Nevada,' George continued. 'The state hosts about one hundred and fifty fully equipped casinos, and many more smaller ones. Revenue has been falling quite steeply because of online gambling and the opening of new casinos in other states, which find the revenue hard to resist. So new sources of income are required to keep government services functioning. Emma found it impossible to get any information about organ transplants in the state, and I've also struggled to do so. To go further, I think some of us have to go there.'

'In the scheme of things,' asked Sue, 'how big is the Nevada operation? This is important. If it's just one of many similar set ups, exposing it won't have a globally significant impact.'

'To be honest,' George responded,' we just don't know. But it's well established that China had an extensive industry based on killing imprisoned dissidents or members of persecuted groups such as Muslim Uyghurs. Worldwide outrage forced China to close the industry in 2015, but there's a suspicion that they haven't fully shut it down.

In the context of the fall of the Assad regime in Syria, the liberating forces released thousands of political prisoners. So far, they've been unable to access some of the most deeply buried parts of the biggest prison. It's likely that these dungeons were the site of organ harvesting from thousands of political prisoners, whose deaths would never be exposed. This industry yielded substantial revenue for the Assad regime. The absence of what was a regular and probably large supply might cause a shortage of organs. This could be an incentive for the creation of new harvesting operations.

If we're successful in Nevada, public awareness of the industry will be increased, and new players might perceive a greater risk of detection. I think this is more important than the actual size of Nevada's operation.'

'I hope you're right,' said Julia, 'but what if our success drives the illegal operations further underground?'

'If that happens,' George replied, 'Their costs will increase and distributing organs will be more challenging. I'm not too worried about it. Now, have I said enough for us to make a decision?'

The whole team agreed to plan for the trip but wanted more research into Nevada's Las Vegas County Division. Sue volunteered to do this.

At the next team meeting, Sue outlined what she had learned.

'I've looked at Clark County as a whole. We won't have any trouble finding a place to stay. The County has 150,000 hotel rooms! Although it's basically a desert, it has an interesting and varied terrain. There are tours to numerous canyons and wilderness areas. The hotels are clustered around the casinos, which also have staff accommodation. There are five cities in the County. They host nearly all the casinos, but most of the dozen or so small towns and villages have them also.

Las Vegas has a population of about 660,000, and three of the other cities have populations of between 280 and 340 thousand. Any of these cities are big enough to house and hide the organ harvesting site. There's one area that isn't desert, Mount Charleston. It's 12.000 feet high and in the northwest of Clark County. It has some forests and is one of the tourist attractions.'

'So, where's the best place to stay?' Julia asked.

'Probably Las Vegas. We'll need a cover story in case we're suspected of prying. We can pose as tourists looking for a mixture of gambling and sight-seeing. Staying in a central hotel will add plausibility to the story, although it will be pricey.'

'Money isn't an issue,' said Fred. 'Should we book in advance? And when's the best time to be there?'

'If we leave in a day or two, we'll arrive towards the end of their high season. It will still be very busy so we should book ahead. I suggest two rooms for two weeks.'

The team gave Sue the go ahead to book the flights and the hotel.

CHAPTER
ELEVEN

Their room was part of the casino complex, and they could access the casino without going outside. They agreed not to play at any of the numerous card tables. Instead, they wandered around the slot machines, of which there were a huge number and variety.

Sue put fifty dollars into a machine called Buffalo Grand. She found herself mesmerised by the spinning wheels. It took about fifteen minutes for her to lose the money.

'I could get hooked on this,' she thought to herself.

Wanting to look the part, the team put a total of eight hundred dollars into a variety of machines. Only Julia and Fred came out ahead, getting their money back and a few dollars more. The team knew that overhead cameras were everywhere, and that they were already in the casino's data base. When they'd played the slot machines long enough to pass as affluent tourists, they returned to the hotel.

Sue suggested they hire a car.

'We can explain to the hotel receptionist that we don't want to go on guided tours but will explore by ourselves.'

'Good thinking,' said Fred. 'That way we can investigate without raising suspicion.'

After booking a 4WD and paying for a parking spot, the team decided it was time to contact the illegal immigrant who had alerted Emma to the abduction of her two friends. With her permission, Emma had given them the woman's phone number.

'Martina here. Who's calling?'

'We're friends of Emma,' Julia replied. 'We know she told you we might be coming over to help you. We're in Las Vegas. Can we meet?'

'Let me double check with Emma. I'll get back to you when she's given the go ahead.'

Mid-afternoon Julia got a call.

'Emma says it's okay. I finish work at half past six.'

The address was in a Las Vegas suburb about two kilometres from their hotel. Martina's dwelling was a granny flat in the rear garden of a large house. After welcoming them, Martina introduced the team to two other women, Renata and Lucia. 'We three are all from Mexico. We made our way across the border and managed to get to California. That's where I met Renata and Lucia, also illegals. When Donald Trump started to get rid of illegal immigrants, we moved here. We were told that Nevada is friendly to illegals and that we'd be safe there.'

Drinks appeared, and everyone sat down in the one main room.

'There are four of ius here,' Martina continued. It's cramped but there's a bathroom and kitchen, and it's not too far from the town centre. The rent is outrageous, but the landlord asks no questions.'

'Who is the fourth?' asked Sue.

'Maria. She works as a casino hostess in the evenings. From seven.'

Subtle glances between Martina and her two friends suggested that Maria's work might involve a bit more than persuading gamblers to buy drinks.

Martina's English was nearly flawless, but that of her friends was heavily accented.

'I work as a waitress in a café. Lucia and Renata are cleaners. It's safe to include them in our discussions.'

'Have any more of your friends mysteriously vanished?' asked Julia.

'No, but the grapevine says it's still happening. Only to us illegals, it seems.'

'I know that one quarter of Nevada's population is made up of immigrants.' Julia continued. 'Without them, the state's economy would collapse. How many are illegals?'

'Nearly forty percent. That's about 350,000.'

'You're obviously well informed.'

'I've done as much research as I safely can. I've discovered that many of the abductions, perhaps most, take place in California, which is only a three-hour drive away. The organ harvesters know that if they rely on Nevada alone, the numbers would be too big. The danger would be recognised, and illegals would start taking precautions.'

'Do you know where the harvesting takes place?' asked Fred.

'Yes, on the northwestern side of Mount Charleston, well away from the tourist areas. The base is on an elevated plateau. They've been very, very clever. The front part of the site is occupied by a small rehab facility, funded in part by the Federal Government. It specialises in psychiatric care, especially PTSD. Soldiers are about a third of the patients. The rest are sent by insurance companies.

The facility is legitimate, but behind it is a large building supposedly devoted to research. It is strictly out of bounds to patients and staff. Nobody seems to know what kind of research is done there, but there are rumours about viruses and nerve gas. Enough to keep people well away. There is a separate entrance through a tunnel which is always guarded. I've no idea how deep the buildings go into the mountain.'

'That really is clever,' said Julia. 'The rehab facility diverts attention from what's behind it, and accounts for much of the increased traffic in the vicinity. It must have cost megabucks to set the whole thing up.'

'I haven't been able to find out anything about who paid for it,' Martina replied, 'but the state of Nevada must be a major shareholder.'

Once Martina had told the team everything she knew, they went back to the hotel. They'd assured the three women that they would do nothing to endanger them, and that they would keep them informed of developments.

'Well, we've found where it is,' said Fred, 'but how do we get in?'

'We know they don't just extract organs but transplant them as well.' George replied. 'Could we pose as potential transplant recipients?'

'Let me look into it,' said Fred. 'And I need to buy a couple of things. This could take a day or so. Meanwhile, you three can do the tourist thing.'

Two days later, Fred outlined what he'd learned.

'Even for those who can afford it, or who are insured, arranging a transplant is very difficult. Hospitals have very long waiting lists. The organ supply meets only a small fraction of demand. In search of a short cut, many of those desperate for organs end up on the dark web, usually through an agent. This Mount Charlston site is listed on the dark web. I've posed as a middle-aged man urgently needing a liver transplant. I was told that a liver would be available within a week, but extensive documentation would be required before surgery could be offered. I didn't provide that. Instead, I told them I've made other arrangements. Now we know how to get in.'

'Getting in as a fake candidate sounds very dangerous,' said Sue.

'Not if two of us apply. Each can insist on being accompanied by a support person. I suggest that Julia requests a liver transplant, and Sue a kidney. I can pose as Sue's husband, and George as Julia's. I'm not being sexist, but if it comes to violence, George and I have some experience in dealing with it.'

Sue's kidney transplant would cost 400,000 American dollars and Julia's liver 900,000, fees slightly below those generally charged in legitimate venues. Payment was to be made once the procedures were successfully completed. After Fred's fake documents had been approved, surgery for both women was scheduled for three days later. They would have to be admitted the day before surgery.

The four were picked up early the next morning. They entered the facility through the tunnel, and each couple was shown into a comfortable suite. They planned to postpone pre-operative tests by claiming incapacitating gastrointestinal symptoms from contaminated food. They would cancel surgery once they had gathered sufficient data to force the police to act.

Later in the morning they went separately in search of incriminating evidence. Julia managed to get into an office with a computer. She booted it up and started downloading data into a flash drive. She was about to remove it when a man entered. He pushed Julia into a chair and pocketed the flash drive.

'I'm acting on my own,' she said, 'the others know nothing about this.'

'We'll see about that. Meanwhile, come with me.'

The man took Julia down a long corridor to a large room, where they were joined by a man and a woman. Julia was strapped to a chair, and the woman punched her hard in the face. Julia's nose poured blood.

'Who are you working for?' the woman demanded.

'A lawyer. Nothing to do with the Feds. Or the CIA. I swear.'

Another blow, this time from one of the men, then another, harder. Julia briefly lost consciousness.

'I'll give you the lawyer's number. She will confirm my story.'

Emma had agreed to be contacted in the event of extreme danger.

'You're lucky,' said the woman, 'on two counts. First, the lawyer confirmed your story. We'll deal with her later. Second, we'll give you an anaesthetic.'

'But I'm not ready to go ahead with the transplant.'

The woman laughed. 'You will be the transplant. We 're going to remove all your innards. What's left of you will be incinerated. You will disappear without trace. Your husband will meet the same fate.'

Julia was unceremoniously strapped to an operating table. A mask was put over her face. As consciousness faded, she saw a golden light at the end of a tunnel, felt her body rising, and was totally at peace.

CHAPTER
TWELVE

Julia was woken by a sharp crack. She opened her eyes. Two more cracks. She raised her head and saw two bodies on the floor. Fred was standing in the middle of the operating theatre, holding a pistol. George was applying plastic zip-ties to the wrists of a woman lying face down.

Sue came to her side.

'Get up Julia. We have to get out of here.'

Stepping over one of the bodies, Julia recognised the man who had pocketed the flash drive.

'Wait!' Julia reached into his jacket pockets and quickly found the drive. She followed the others out. George pushed the woman ahead of him. Fred walked by her side. He put his mouth close to the woman's ear.

'I've already shot two of your men. I'll shoot you if you don't get us out of here. Go by our suites so we can grab our gear.'

Cases in hand, they entered a garage and climbed into a large 4WD

'Let's go straight to police HQ,' said Fred, finding its location on the car's GPS.

'If the cops are in on this,' said Sue, 'they'll arrest us and let the woman go.'

Her attempt at humour fell flat: the police could well be complicit. George removed the plastic ties from the woman's wrists.

'We need to see your chief,' said Fred to the police officer at the front desk. He'd left his gun in the car. 'It's a matter of national security.'

Fred held up an FBI badge. The officer at the desk jotted down the number. They were taken to a conference room and seated round the central table. The Chief of Police, a grey-haired woman in her fifties, joined them about ten minutes later.

'This meeting will be recorded,' she said by way of introduction.

Looking at Fred, she said 'Please proceed.'

Fred outlined the situation but omitted mention of the flash drive or the shooting. He pointed to Julia's face as evidence.

'We've known about this facility for some time,' the Chief responded. 'The Governor and the County Commissioner have reassured us that it is legitimate. Without a lot more evidence, there's nothing I can do. And you seem to have kidnapped this woman, whose silence so far suggests intimidation, to say the least. If you want to escape prosecution, I suggest you withdraw your allegations. You can all sign a document to that effect before you leave. I will overlook your fake FBI badge,' she said to Fred with the hint of a smile. 'Yes, we checked the number.'

Back at the hotel, stiff drinks were needed.

'It's obvious the police are in on it,' said Sue, 'or at least their top dogs. They may think we'll cause trouble. They know who we are. Should we be worried?'

'Before we talk about that,' said Julia, 'tell me how you rescued me. How you saved my life.'

'I was worried there might be trouble,' Fred replied. 'I got into the local hackers' network and arranged an automatic pistol and a fake FBI badge. When you didn't come back to the suite, we went looking for you. I tracked your phone's location and that took us to the operating theatre. We burst in just as the surgeon raised his knife to cut into you. He came towards me with it. I had to shoot.

The other man tried to run out. I shot him too. The rest you saw.'

'I'll never be able to repay you all.' There were tears in Julia's eyes.

'You would have done the same for any of us,' said George

'Now that I have the full picture.' Julia continued, 'I want to call Emma. The woman who beat me up said they would deal with her later.'

Emma told Julia that she would contact the police and the FBI about the situation in Nevada. She would request police protection until any threat to her wellbeing was eliminated.

'Congratulations to all of you,' she concluded. 'I know you'll finish the job.'

'So, are we in danger?' Sue asked for the second time.

'I don't think we're in any physical danger,' Fred replied. 'They'll threaten us with kidnapping charges if we cause any trouble, or with homicide if any of my shots were fatal.'

'Will the FBI act on Emma's allegations?' Sue asked.

'Probably,' Julia replied, 'but given the extent of corruption in Nevada, their investigations will almost certainly be thwarted. We can't rely on their involvement, so it's up to us. But only if we're willing to take the risk. We have the flash drive. Let's see what's on it.'

The drive listed the names of the illegal immigrants who had been abducted and eviscerated, together with the names and dates of birth of those who had received their organs. Relevant financial data were included.

'We've got them!' exclaimed George. 'If we take this to the media, all hell will break loose. They are finished. Let's make copies of the drive, carry one each, and get out of here. If they discover the download, we're in real danger. We can go to the media when we're somewhere safe.'

They checked out immediately, using the excuse of a family crisis. They were able to get on a flight to Los Angeles, where they booked into an airport hotel. There were daily flights to Melbourne, so they delayed making reservations until their tasks in Los Angeles were completed.

The next morning, the team went to the office of the Los Angeles Times. It took time for them to be taken seriously, but finally a reporter agreed to look at the flash drive. Before they handed one over, the team secured a promise to protect their identity. The reporter was shocked by the drive's contents but insisted on making further enquiries before taking any action.

'This will take a while,' he said. 'I suggest you go back to your hotel and wait.'

The call came just after midday.

'It all checked out. My editor wants me to draft a background piece. It will go to the press tonight. Front page in tomorrow morning's edition. I'd like to acknowledge your achievements, your heroism, but I'll respect your wish for complete privacy. Thank you for trusting the Los Angeles Times.'

'Well, that wraps it up,' said Fred. 'If we book a flight for tomorrow morning, the paper should be out before we board'

The team grabbed four copies of the Los Angeles Times which got to the airport only minutes before their flight was called. The story occupied most of the front page and a full page inside. It summarised the contents of the flash drive and added a comprehensive account of the entire Mount Charlston operation.

Their names were not mentioned, but their identity was hinted at in the acknowledgements. The team understood that any talk about what they'd read must wait until they were safely home. The flight took fifteen hours and is was past eleven before they got back to HQ. Exhausted, they agreed to postpone discussion until breakfast. Then they all went to bed.

After breakfast, the team was surprised at how much they needed to ventilate.

'How do you feel about shooting those two men?' Sue asked Fred.

'I had no choice,' replied Fred, 'but I feel some guilt. I hope they both survive.'

'The man I searched for the flash drive,' said Julia, 'stirred a little There wasn't a lot of blood. He'll probably pull through. But the surgeon? Who knows?'

'I hope he's dead,' spat Julia. 'He was about to gut me.' Then she began to sob, shoulders heaving. She wept for a long time before saying anything more.

'When they put me on the operating table and applied the anaesthetic, I began to drift off. Then I saw this golden light at the end of a tunnel. I felt my body rising. The last I remember is a profound sense of peace, of total acceptance.

I'm sure that was what they call a near death experience. I've been an agnostic all my adult life. No longer. There was a divine presence at work. It's the only explanation for the miracle of my survival. This divine presence spared my life for a reason. I'm not sure what that is, but meanwhile I'm very happy to go on with our work together.'

There was a silence, broken by Sue.

'How extraordinary that after all we've been through together, we've talked so little about our ideas of the transcendental, of that which lies beyond. You all know that my father is a Lutheran pastor. I've absorbed his passion for fighting evil, though I'd rather think of it as righting wrongs. But not his unshakeable belief in God. Like you used to be Julia, I'm agnostic.'

'I'm an atheist I suppose,' said Fred, 'but I'm not wedded to it. I'm open to other possibilities.'

George paused before he spoke. 'I can't accept that this amazing world we inhabit arose purely by chance. I'm sure there's some kind of agency at work, but whether this agency is divine, or part of some deep corporeal mystery that we can't fathom, well I just don't know.'

'Enough of the theology,' quipped Fred. 'We need to think about our next project. But I have an idea. What if I call my government contact and let him know, in the strictest confidence, about our recent success. I know that the Government is deeply concerned about human trafficking, independent of organ harvesting. What we've learned will greatly help us if we decide to look at the broader picture: the whole human trafficking industry. I'll ask my contact to tactfully explore the possibility of a government commission in this area.'

'I've already told you all,' said Sue, 'That human trafficking is, to me, one of the very worst of evils. I'd welcome a project on it.'

Geoge and Julia agreed to allow Fred to make his call.

CHAPTER THIRTEEN

The team spent the next two nights at HQ. There were four beds in the two bedrooms, a bathroom and toilet. Fred, of course, was still homeless but in no hurry to buy another dwelling. He complained about George's snoring but was otherwise happy to share a bedroom with him when he had to.

There had been no discussion of such arrangements, they had just happened. Sue decided to raise the issue.

'I haven't been back to my flat for over three weeks. It's a bit of a fleapit. How would it be if I moved in here?'

She had addressed all three of the others, but the question was really directed at Fred, who thought for a moment before replying.

'It's no secret Sue, that I find you very attractive. I understand that you don't feel quite the same towards me. Anyway, we know that intimacy between us might jeopardise our ability to work together as part of the team. Given all this, I'm happy for you to move in, to the other bedroom of course!'

She smiled at Fred's attempt at levity. 'But what if you did meet someone who wanted a relationship?'

'I'm not looking for that. My work's enough.'

'George and I have been lovers, of course,' said Julia. 'I know we're still attracted to one another, but we've learned that a sexual relationship no longer works. I'm happy to keep my flat. No mortgage. What about you George?'

'Same as you. Happy to keep my townhouse, and to stay here when it makes sense.'

'All this raises another issue,' said Sue. 'I haven't a boyfriend, and as for sex, I'm pretty good at looking after myself.'

Fred's face turned bright red, but he said nothing.

'So far, our work together has left no time or energy for me to think about a boyfriend. If this changes, I'll discuss things with you all before I make any decisions. Any intimate relationship will be tricky because I won't be able to talk about our work together. I'd have to invent something, and I hate that idea. That pretty well rules out any new relationship.'

'You and I are on the same page Sue,' said Julia. 'I can't add to what you've said.'

'It's pretty well the same with me,' said George. 'I don't have a girlfriend. I'd put the team's needs ahead of my own if intimacy beckoned. I know that the ordeals and challenges we've faced have united us, but I find it incredible that we all put our work together ahead of our personal needs. If it stays that way, we can do anything.'

'Which takes us back to business,' said Fred. 'I still haven't heard from my contact. If it's no go with the human trafficking, we've still got three offers, all to do with money laundering or document fraud. We've been there, done that, but should we take one on?'

'I'd rather go freelance with the human trafficking,' Sue replied. 'We've got the funds.'

Julia and George agreed.

'We'll wait then. Meanwhile let's continue Sue and Julia's lessons on the world of computers and hacking.'

The call came just after lunch.

'It's on!' Fred exclaimed. We'll get full details of the contract later today. While we wait, let's share what we've learned so far about this very nasty business.'

CHAPTER FOURTEEN

While the team waited for the details of the government contract, Julia outlined what they'd learned so far.

'Because of climate change, increased poverty and global conflicts, more and more people are vulnerable to exploitation. The number of identified victims has risen by over fifty percent in just the past two years. Total numbers trafficked are reliably estimated at fifty million or more last year.'

Julia paused. 'I can hardly bear to say this, but forty percent of these were children, nearly all girls, most of whom were sold to be sex slaves. Another twenty percent were adult women, evenly distributed into forced marriage, domestic slavery and prostitution. The men are trafficked mainly for forced labour, but increasingly to run online scams and cyberfraud. Boys are used to facilitate crime, to beg, and for sex.'

'It's even worse than I thought,' said Sue, on the brink of tears, 'And it's obviously getting worse. Why don't governments do more to stop it?'

'We know,' Julia replied, 'that our own Government is deeply concerned about the problem. It has a National Action Plan to Combat Modern Slavery, with a National Policing Protocol to back it up. Overall policy is set by the National Human Trafficking Coordination Team.'

'Then why the hell do they need us?' demanded Sue.

'The traffickers are getting more and more sophisticated, especially online. We already know about the huge extent of document fraud, which is a crucial part of human trafficking. The traffickers are outpacing the government, which recognises that it needs help from the likes of us. We aren't constrained by red tape or political correctness. We'll do anything to get results.'

The contract arrived an hour or so later. Fred downloaded it and printed four copies. It was very detailed. They were to be paid a total of three million dollars, half up front, the rest on fulfillment of the terms of the contract. Because it was full of legalese and bureaucratic jargon, Julia, with her legal background, offered to summarise it.

'The traffickers they want us to eliminate have a site in the dark web. They have an extensive online network of agents and operatives, and their physical activities are based in Java, mainly in areas where poverty is still widespread, and missing persons are rarely the subject of official investigation.

They've added a supplement which gives more information. The full extent of the traffickers' human exports is unknown, but many come to Australia. Entry is through the docks, where victims are hidden in specially designed shipping containers. Probably, corruption facilitates this. Forged documents allow many victims to enter by air or sea. Intimidation or false promises ensure their silence. That's about it. Should we accept the deal?'

All four agreed without hesitation. Fred alone was required to sign the contract, which he did immediately.

'So where do we start?' Sue asked.

'I see three options,' George replied. 'One, find out who's behind the use of shipping containers to smuggle people through the ports. Two, trace the origin of false passports, visas and other documents used by the smugglers. Three, do what we did in our last gig: pose as customers.'

'Targeting the ports will be very hit and miss without inside info,' said Fred. 'I could ask for help on the hackers' network, but that's not guaranteed. Tracing the origin of forged documents may lead us only to the forgers, not the end users.'

'The third option,' said Sue, 'will be risky, probably dangerous. I suggest we look at it only if the other two are dead ends.'

'That makes sense,' said Julia.' 'Both the other options rely heavily on you Fred. What do you think?'

'I think the ports are our best bet. I'll make a start with Port Botany. It's local, and I think it handles nearly all the state's container traffic. This could take a while. I've taught the three of you a fair bit about hacking, enough to know what's safe and what isn't. Why not sharpen your skills by looking into the document forgery side of things?'

At next day's team meeting, Fred outlined his progress.

'Port Botany handles over ninety percent of the state's shipping containers, nearly three million last year. About sixty percent of these are imports, mainly consumer goods, vehicle parts, building materials, chemicals, plastics, machinery, and food and drink. Such a variety makes it easier to design containers that hide human beings.'

'There must be a way to detect these victims,' said Sue.'

'X-rays and gamma-ray scanners can reveal objects not declared on the manifest, but only if they aren't shielded by dense materials or structures. Thermal imaging relies on the temperature difference between living beings and the container's interior. If this is elevated artificially or otherwise, detection fails. Carbon dioxide detectors are easily fooled and are notorious for false positives. Movement detectors work only in quiet environments. The small number of sniffer dogs makes them of use only when suspicion is aroused. Routine physical inspection is impossibly time-consuming.'

'Which makes our job seem impossibly difficult,' said Julia.

'Not necessarily. Each shipping container must have a manifest detailing its contents. These are recorded in a central registry. I can hack into this. So can any competent hacker.'

'How will this help?' Sue asked.

'When I asked for help on the network, I was lucky enough to be contacted by a fellow hacker with a particular interest in this area. One of his aunts in Indonesia mysteriously disappeared, and he suspects human traffickers. He's created two amazing programs which analyse the manifests held in the central registry. One identifies the chances of a particular container having people hidden inside. It incorporates a huge range of data about the container's origin, its contents and probable destination. Even within a time frame of, say, two weeks, the number of suspicious containers runs into thousands, with the likelihood of their actually imprisoning people ranging from two or three percent to about twenty.

The second program is pure genius. It identifies containers that are very likely to have been designed for people smuggling. Ahmad, the creator of the programs, claims an accuracy of between thirty-five and fifty-five percent, but he has never tested his programs in real life. They may not work as well as he hopes, or not at all. He's asked me to help him with the next step: trying it out in the real world of Port Botany.

The others urged Fred to go ahead with the collaboration as soon as possible.

'Why not ask Ahmad to meet us all?' asked Sue, 'either at HQ or a location of his choice.' Julia and George backed Sue's suggestion. Within half an hour, Fred had arranged for Ahmad to meet them at HQ the next day.

Ahmad was a slightly built man of Eurasian appearance. He looked to be in his early thirties. Initially nervous, he relaxed quickly after a warm welcome from each of the team.

'Tell us a bit about yourself, Ahmad,' said Sue.

'Well, I was born in Melbourne. My father is Australian, my mother from Indonesia. That's why I have relatives there. I've always loved Information Technology, or IT, and I've been lucky enough to work in the industry since I left uni. I confess I spend a fair bit of time chatting with other hackers on the network, but never to do bad things.'

Each of the team then told Ahmad a bit about themselves. Then it was down to business.

'With my government authority,' said Fred, 'I can contact the Harbour Master at Port Botany and ask him to support a trial of the program. About five thousand containers are imported each day. We won't know which, if any, of these should be targeted until Ahmad runs his program. If he identifies targets, the authorities will have to act quickly. All this will take a while to organise. I'll visit the Harbour Master in person to make sure he gives the project top priority.'

There were no hits on the first three days of the trial. On the fourth day, three containers were identified as valid targets. Fred had insisted that the team and Ahmad be present when the inspections took place, and that the containers would be guarded until then.

The first two containers were empty of human cargo. Sue noticed that in the third, one of several large wooden boxes had holes drilled in the side, near the top. The lid was loose, and she and Julia lifted it easily. It was empty except for a dozen or so muesli bar wrappers, and a puddle of what smelled like urine.

'There were people inside,' Sue exclaimed. 'How did they get out?'

The Harbour Master had just arrived, and Fred asked him how long it had taken to place guards after the alert.

'With three containers in different parts of the dock, nearly an hour.'

'So, it was possible for the container to be opened the moment it was landed, before the guards arrived.'

'Theoretically, yes.'

'This implies,' said George, 'that the traffickers somehow knew they had to get their human cargo out of the containers as soon as possible. But how?'

'There's only one way,' Fred exclaimed, 'and I should have thought of it. I'll explain when we get back to HQ.'

'If Ahmad can hack into the registry of manifests,' said Fred, when they were all seated around what had become their conference table, 'then so can the traffickers. They must have traced Ahmad back from the registry and then hacked into his programs. They know, as soon as we do, which containers are targeted.'

'It never occurred to me that this might happen,' said Ahmad. 'I was obsessed with creating the program and gave little thought to security. Now we must find a way to block their access. If we can't, we're totally screwed.'

CHAPTER FIFTEEN

Ahmad's pronouncement added to the team's despondency and uncertainty about what to do next. Fred tried to reassure Ahmad that all was not lost. He knew they all liked him and would welcome his continued involvement. On this basis, Fred asked him to join the team, at least until they had done all they could to eliminate the people smugglers.

'That would be an honour,' Ahmad replied with sincerity. 'As you know, almost all my paid work is online. It will be easy to fit it around the work that I do with you.'

'The team would like you to join more permanently. We all like you, and you have skills that will add a great deal to what we can achieve together. It's a bit cramped when we are all here, but we can organise things to give you a bit of comfort and privacy when we really need to stay together overnight. Sometimes this is necessary for an extended period.'

'If I become a fully-fledged member of the team, will it be a full-time commitment?'

'Absolutely, but you won't have to worry about money as we are very well funded. So far, we've all chosen to share equally the payments we receive for commissioned work. If you join us, you would be an equal partner in every respect. We can arrange a salary if you don't want to share the profits.'

'Let me think about all this. I'm lucky enough to own a comfortable apartment in Redfern, but I'm happy to stay here overnight when necessary. I can bring stuff over that will let me work from here.'

Ahmad then went home. The team decided it was time to turn in. They all wanted to stay at HQ.

Ahmad arrived just after breakfast the next day. There was small talk while Julia made him a cup of coffee. Then they all sat around the conference table.

'I've been up half the night,' said Ahmad, 'thinking about the offer to join you on a long-term basis. I have a good life doing what I love, and getting paid for it. Of course, I want to work with you until the end of our current project, but a permanent place on the team is a different matter. My decision is based partly on the idea of ridding the world of those who prey on the weak and vulnerable, like my aunt who disappeared. But it's not just human trafficking. It's the whole world of evildoers. I didn't realise how much I hated them until I started to work with you. I seem to have absorbed some of your beliefs. After thinking it all through, I'm absolutely sure I want to go on working with you, become part of the team.'

Sue started clapping and set off a round of applause. Ahmad's face showed a mixture of pleasure and embarrassment which highlighted his good looks.

'Thank you. Now there's no time to lose. I'll go to my apartment and bring back the equipment I need to connect my technology with yours.'

'Like some help?' asked Sue

'If it's not too much trouble.'

The pair set off at once. They came back in the early afternoon carrying boxes, the contents of which Ahmad and Fred connected to HQ's technology.

'That should be it,' said Fred. Ahmad booted up his computer. A message appeared on the screen: 'We know who and where you are. If you don't back off, you're dead.'

'It could be a bluff,' said Fred.

'I don't think so,' countered Ahmad. 'My lack of security will have given them access to core data, including my identity. This isn't a bluff.'

The team reassembled at the conference table.

'I'm sorry,' said George, 'that we've put you in danger, Ahmad. If you change your mind, decide to leave the team, we'll totally understand.'

'It's made me more determined than ever,' Ahmad replied. 'Now we need to decide what to do next.'

'We have to back off, at least for now,' said Julia. 'Fred, can you explain things to the harbour Master?'

'Not a problem. I'll reassure him that the traffickers won't use Port Botany, at least until they're sure their containers won't be targeted.'

'Are we totally fucked?' Julia asked.

'I don't think so,' Ahmad replied. 'We know the traffickers are physically based in Java. It'll be difficult to find out where, if not impossible. Fred and I have only just started working together. We don't know what our combined skills can achieve, but I'm hoping for miracles.'

'How often do two of the world's best hackers work together?' asked Sue.

'Both security agents and those they target online have teams of hackers. These hackers collaborate almost exclusively online. Because of hackers' fiercely competitive nature, physical proximity yields both positive and negative results. Fred and I will not compete. We will work together harmoniously. If we do locate the traffickers, we'll have to decide what to do next. We may have to go to Indonesia, but all this will take time. Meanwhile, can I suggest that you mug up on Java? The island hosts over half Indonesia's population, and also its capital, Jakarta.

The other four were taken aback by Ahmad's assertiveness. He had seemed so shy and retiring. Passion had transformed him. After lengthy discussion, they backed his suggestions.

Fred and Ahmad started immediately.

'Our first problem,' said Ahmad, 'is to identify their IPS. They'll have back door protection, probably Imperva's cloud WAF.'

'Let's make sure we share the same acronyms,' said Fred. 'IPS means Intrusion Protection System. WAF stands for Web Application Firewall. Right?'

'Right, and we know the WAF can be customised, which will make it much trickier to bypass it without being detected.'

'The traffickers will be most concerned about highly skilled hackers,' said Fred, 'so let's aim at a lower level, one they may not have considered.'

'You mean looking for network infrastructure vulnerability?'

'Exactly. The cloud has only recently become a crucial part of this infrastructure. It's possible that the traffickers haven't optimised their infrastructure protection in the cloud. This could give us a way in.'

The pair worked well into the night without a break.

'We're on the right track, I'm sure,' said Ahmad, 'but my brain hurts. Let's turn in.'

They started again mid-morning the next day, working so closely that they were almost a single entity. Just after two the next morning, Fred shouted, 'we're in!'

They started downloading data, constantly fearful of being detected.

'Let's analyse it in the morning, with the others,' Ahmad suggested. 'I can't keep my eyes open. It's long past my bedtime.'

After breakfast, the team settled round the conference table. Fred displayed the downloaded data on a large screen. It was not as helpful as they had hoped. The traffickers had created a back-up security system that made it impossible to access much of their website. There was no information about their extensive network of agents and operatives, but the data made it possible to approximate the traffickers' physical location. Fred worked for half an hour on another computer before outlining what he'd found.

'The traffickers are based somewhere in an industrial area adjacent to the Kanjung Priok port, which is the largest port in Indonesia. It's on the Java Sea about ten kilometres up from Jakarta's city centre. There are twenty-seven terminals and over eighty berths, including three berths for passenger ships. Eight million shipping containers were exported through the port last year.'

'So, it's perfect for the traffickers,' said Julia. 'The passenger berths mean they can send some of their victims by sea. They can enter Australia using forged documents. The huge volume of container traffic makes it a challenge to detect those used to smuggle people, even if we're somehow able to set up Ahmad's program.'

'Perhaps we'd be better off trying to pinpoint their physical base,' Fred responded. 'Give Ahmad and I another few hours. We'll see what we can do.

'We've tried everything,' said Ahmad later, 'but we don't have enough data. The base is within an industrial zone of about five square kilometres, but we can't place it more accurately than that. I assume it's disguised as a factory or warehouse from which containers can be transported to the docks without raising suspicion. Unfortunately, I've no idea how we might find it. There will be hundreds of possibilities. Any ideas?'

'We could hand the search over to the local police or Interpol,' said George, 'but they won't know what to look for any more than we do, and our own government might not want to involve them in the search. They'd probably want to involve ASIO. If ASIO did find the base, would we still meet the terms of the contract?'

'That's a grey area,' Fred replied. 'They might try and reduce our fee, but we're all just speculating, trying to avoid the elephant in the room.'

'What elephant?' Ahmad asked with a puzzled look on his face.

'The elephant about whether or not we go to Java ourselves, and whether we all go or just some of us.'

'There's no point in going unless we have some way of pinpointing the traffickers' base,' said Sue. 'I have an idea. Ahmad, we've discounted the notion of using your program at Kanjung Priok. But could you set it up if the harbour master agreed?'

'Certainly, if the Port keeps a central register of container manifests, but I'll need the full cooperation of the Harbour Master, and it'll take a day or two before we can test it in real life.'

'So, what's your idea Sue?' asked Julia.

'If we can locate a container with people hidden inside, the manifest will detail its origin and contents, so we can trace it back to the traffickers' base. It's also possible that the victims may know of its whereabouts.'

'Sounds like a plan,' said Ahmad, 'but it assumes the Harbour Master will support it. What if he's corrupt, and getting a rake-off from the smugglers? I'm afraid this is all too possible. Corruption is rife in Indonesia.'

He paused and then exclaimed: 'I have an idea. My mother has four sisters, now three since my aunt disappeared. One of them lives in Jakarta. She's a successful and well-connected businesswoman. I could explain our plan to her and ask her to discuss it with the Harbour Master. If he supports it, we can go over and set it up. I think the whole team will need to go. All hands on deck for this one!' Ahmad's pun was clearly unintended.

'But what about the threat to kill you if we don't back off?' asked Julia

'The best way to handle that,' Ahmad replied, 'is to destroy their whole operation. Then they'll have more to worry about than killing me.'

Ahmad's aunt Kirana acted quickly. As a woman of influence, her extensive social network included other movers and shakers. She used their network to assess the likelihood of the Harbour Master being corrupt. It seemed that he was an honest man. Using that same influence, she got him to support the use of Ahmad's program.

Kirana's home was large, but not large enough to accommodate all five of the team. Ahmad booked an apartment close to the port for two weeks. On leaving Sydney, both he and Fred had to pay for extra baggage. Ahmad's program needed their custom-built software, and the hardware to activate it.

CHAPTER SIXTEEN

The three-bedroom apartment had a sea view, according to the booking agency. George, the tallest of the team, caught a glimpse of the Java Sea by standing on tiptoe.

'We're not here to sightsee,' quipped Sue, 'you can have a swim when we've finished the job.'

'Haven't brought my budgie smugglers,' George quipped back.

They unpacked and then sat round the kitchen table to start planning

'I'd like to visit my aunt Kirana as soon as possible,' said Ahmad, 'and I know she'd like to meet all of us.'

'Why not give her a call?' George asked. 'It's only one thirty, so we could see her this afternoon if she's available.'

Kirana was free and keen to see them. Although it was only about fourteen kilometres to Kirana's house in one of Jakarta's inner suburbs, the cab ride took nearly an hour. The trip was a nightmare of dodging in and out of endless lines of traffic.

Kirana welcomed them warmly and ushered them into a spacious lounge. 'Have you had lunch?' Her English, though accented, was quite fluent.

Kirana summoned a servant and asked her to prepare a light lunch. They chatted while waiting for the food, which was served at a large mahogany dining table.

Serious talk began when they had settled back into the lounge.

'Thank you so much for getting the Harbour Master onside,' said Ahmad in English, 'and for checking him out.'

'I'm so pleased I could help, and I'll do anything else you might need to fix these evil people.'

'It would help a lot if you arranged for us to meet the Harbour Master, and if you came with us. Are you free tomorrow morning?'

'I've put my schedule on hold. I'm at your disposal.'

Kirana made the call at once. A meeting was arranged for ten the next morning.

Kirana wanted full details of the team's plan, and this took up the rest of the afternoon. The team got back to their apartment just after seven. Rush hour meant that the journey took nearly ninety minutes. They all had mild sore throats from the air pollution.

'That'll wear off soon,' Ahmad assured them.

Fred and Ahmad spent the rest of the evening setting up their equipment. After a takeaway supper, they were all in bed by ten.

The Harbour Master was a slender man of middle height who looked to be in his forties. He was deferential towards Kirana and polite to the others. His English was poor, so Ahmad detailed their plan in Indonesian. He stressed the need for absolute secrecy, adding that they may need to contact him any time of the day or night. The Harbour Master granted them full access to the registry of manifests.

'We've modified the program so that our access to the registry is almost impossible to be detected,' Ahmad explained when they were back in the apartment. By five in the morning they had identified four containers with a strong likelihood of harbouring people. They roused the harbour

Master at half past five. He immediately ordered guards to be placed on the targeted containers, with strict instructions to wait until he and the team arrived.

The first container was empty of people, as was the second. The third contained nine large metal boxes. One of those, squeezed behind the others, had small holes near the top of one side. The sealed lid was not locked, and they were able to prise it up. Inside were four young women, dressed only in bras and panties. There was no food or water.

Helped out, the women were able to stand and walk unaided. They were taken to the Harbour Master's office and provided with what clothing could be found. Ahmad began a gentle interrogation.

Each woman was abducted from a different part of Java. All these were impoverished, isolated areas. Their captors had been careful not to bruise or scar them, knowing that this would reduce their value. The container's manifest showed that its destination was Australia. The sea journey took ten to twelve days, so Ahmad assumed that once the container was loaded on board, the women would extract themselves from the box and access enough hidden food and drink to sustain them until they reached their destination. Reluctantly, the women confirmed this, but Ahmad was unable to extract any further information of value. He thought that they were fearful of repercussions

'Please order a careful search of the entire container,' said Ahmad to the Harbour Master, once he had finished his interrogation. 'Finding food and drink will confirm the women's story, and there may be other clues of value.'

Before the start of Ahmad's interrogation, the Harbour Master had traced the origin of the container, a warehouse close to the centre of the adjacent industrial district. With Ahmad's agreement, he had notified the local police, who dispatched a unit to the building. One of the officers drove the team to the warehouse in a police van.

The unit commander explained to Ahmad what they'd found.

'You can see that the warehouse is used to store containers. We've counted twenty-three of them. Preliminary inspection shows that some of them are specially designed to hide people, with false floors and hidden compartments. There were no people in the warehouse, nor in the office.'

'Can we see the office?' asked Ahmad.

'Of course, but please don't touch anything until we've finished our search for fingerprints and other clues.'

The office, which was connected to a toilet and shower, had clearly been left in a hurry. Half full coffee cups were on a large desk, the drawers of which were empty. So rushed was their exit that the traffickers had left behind a row of six filing cabinets. All were locked.

'Someone must have tipped them off,' said Ahmad to the unit commander. 'I know the Harbour Master alerted you immediately after we found the women, so the tip off must have come from someone at the scene or watching it from elsewhere. I assume you'll look into this as part of your investigation.'

'Of course.'

It occurred to Ahmad that the tip off may have come from the police themselves. Wisely, he kept his mouth shut.

'It's crucial that my team has full access to the contents of the filing cabinets.'

'That may be impossible,' replied the commander. 'Access to such evidence is restricted to our own investigation. We cannot risk contamination.'

'Who will make that decision?'

'The Chief of Police.'

With Kirana's help, Ahmad was able to see the Chief just before noon. He argued his case, stressing the involvement of the Australian government, but the chief was adamant.

'My team of investigators will start searching the filing cabinets at once. You will be fully informed of their findings.'

He then politely ushered Kirana and Ahmad out of his office.

Back at the apartment, the team agonised about what to do next.

'Can we tell your government contact that it's mission accomplished?' asked Julia.

'I think so,' Fred replied. 'We've eliminated the traffickers' infrastructure and admin centre. This means the port will no longer be their exit point, but I think we should wait to see what data comes from the filing cabinets. If it allows identification of the traffickers' agents and operatives, we can claim complete success. Meanwhile, let's try and relax. Maybe do a bit of sightseeing. Kirana will have some ideas about that.'

Two days later, the Chief of Police contacted Ahmad.

'I haven't been able to find the source of the traffickers' tip-off,' he said, 'but the filing cabinets have revealed a great deal about the smugglers' operation. Most importantly, the names and locations of many of their agents and operatives. We have already started rounding them up. Congratulations, Ahmad, to you and your team. I will send confirmation of all this so you can prove to your government that your mission has been fully successful.'

'Can we trust them to do what he says?' asked Sue.

'Kirana,' replied Ahmad, 'is fairly sure that the Chief is honest, but who knows about the lower ranks? We have to take him for his word. Now, I want to go and see Kirana. I have a small gift for her, which I've taken the liberty of saying is from all of us.'

Inside a box was a beautifully crafted glass vase decorated with exquisite floral motifs.

'That is so beautiful,' gasped George, 'I think it will adorn her lounge to perfection. We will share the cost of course. No argument!'

When the others had finished admiring the vase, Ahmad carefully packed it back into the box.

'While I'm with aunt Kirana,' Ahmad suggested, 'why don't you book the flight home? There's nothing more we can do here.'

CHAPTER
SEVENTEEN

As soon as they were back at HQ, Fred told his government contact about their success and later emailed a full report. There were three projects waiting for them, none very appealing.

'Shall we take the least unattractive?' Fred asked, 'or create a project of our own? We can afford it. The three million for the trafficking job will be in our account shortly. Or we could look at past job offers in case some are still open.'

The team gathered around the big screen and watched the list unfold.

'That's it!' Ahmad exclaimed. 'The one on hitmen. I'm a bit worried about being a target myself after the traffickers' threat. They won't all be rounded up. Killing me is not likely to be at the top of their to-do list, but I'm still a bit anxious. If we do this project, we should learn enough to ensure my safety, and of course with Zelda above ground, she's still a threat to you, Fred.'

'We didn't have this incentive when we rejected the project,' Fred responded, 'let me find out if it's still on.'

The offer had come through Fred's government contact, who confirmed that the problem had not been resolved. If anything, it had got worse. The contact sent an update which Fred summarised.

'In 2003 the Australian Institute of Criminology published a report titled *Contract Killing in Australia.* It reported on sixty-nine completed hits and ninety-four unsuccessful ones between the first of July 1989 and the thirtieth of June 2002. Almost all the completed hits were connected to organised crime. All of those were successful, and firearms were used in eighty percent, as against only fourteen percent in other homicides. Most gangland hits were fuelled by inter-gang rivalry, failed business agreements, and the elimination of police informants or witnesses in upcoming trials. Only about fifteen percent were directly connected with drugs. Less than half were solved by the police.

The unsuccessful hits were totally different. None were linked to organised crime. Motives included getting rid of intimate partners or ex-partners, ending custody or property disputes, cashing in on insurance or super policies, or revenge.'

'Has there been any systematic review since 2003?' asked Julia.

'No, but the available data shows a significant increase in the use of contract killers by organised crime.'

'Is that why the government has become more worried about the problem?' asked Sue.

'In part. Collateral damage is a major factor. As the number of gangland hits increases, so does the number of unintended victims. The killing or wounding of innocent bystanders often raises a public outcry for more to be done to stop these hits and what fuels them, but there's an even more worrying reason.' Fred paused to take a sip of diet coke. 'Since the fall of the Assad regime in Syria, the new Islamic government has appointed radical Islamists to key positions in its military and elsewhere. There is growing anxiety in the West about the re-emergence of the Islamic State of Iraq and Syria, or ISIS, and similar groups such as Islamic Jihad. ASIO has detected an increase in radical Islamic activity in Australia. ISIS and similar groups have become increasingly sophisticated. They now regard suicide bombings as counterproductive. Instead, they're aiming at individuals and small groups. These will become the victims of what the Jihadists call 'Targeted Assassinations'. ISIS and others have mastered the use of the dark web and use bitcoin as their currency. This makes it extremely difficult to discover their plans. These radical Islamists are driven by an unshakeable belief in their mission: to create a world-wide caliphate.'

'Are they linked to organised crime in Australia?' asked George.

'Almost certainly. ASIO suspects that they have already paid a gangland hitman to kill one of their most outspoken critics. The coroner's verdict was accidental death. Top hitmen are brilliant at creating a scenario that leads coroners to the false conclusion of death by accident, suicide, or natural causes. They often work in small teams to achieve this. Sometimes they simply abduct the victim and then dispose of the body. Success is of great importance to them, not just for the money, but for their reputation.'

'These hits must be expensive,' said Julia.

'The 2003 report found the average payment to be sixteen thousand five hundred dollars. This would be about forty thousand in today's money. The highest payment was one hundred thousand for a double hit. Today's top hitmen would charge at least that for a single hit. ASIO thinks ISIS is paying gangland hitmen to train some of their operatives in the art of contract killing. Then ISIS will do their own targeted assassinations.'

'All this is pretty scary,' said Ahmad

'It will only get worse,' Fred responded. 'Imagine ISIS and similar groups with the capacity to eliminate their enemies in Australia and elsewhere, and to obscure the true cause of their deaths. None of us would be safe.'

'Any involvement by us will be dangerous,' said George. 'Perhaps very dangerous. What has the government offered us?

'Four million dollars for the elimination of the ISIS threat and those directly connected, including any gangland facilitators. As before, they've acknowledged our willingness to do anything to complete a project, even such a dangerous one. This can't apply to government agencies, who are constrained and accountable in ways that we aren't. As well, ASIO believes that ISIS HQ is based in Sydney.'

There was a long discussion, at times very animated.

'It seems,' said Ahmad, 'That we need to come up with a decisive plan of action, one that minimises danger to the team. Only if we can do that should we accept the contract. Fred, can you ask your contact to wait a day or so for our decision?'

'He's already allowed for that. He understands the level of risk. That's why our fee is four million. So, let's start planning.'

As genius-level hackers, Ahmad and Fred had finally achieved a long-cherished goal: hacking into some dark web sites without being detected. The ISIS site was so well protected that accessing it proved impossible, but they were able to hack into another site that was connected to ISIS. This site, one of those used by organised crime, enabled them to monitor communications from gangland to ISIS, but not the other way round.

'The gangland contact,' said Ahmad, 'has told ISIS that because of increased surveillance by ASIO and the Federal Police, they could no longer provide hitmen, but they would continue to train ISIS operatives to do their own assassinations. This gave me an idea: one of us could pose as a hitman.'

'Aside from the risks involved,' said George, ''How can we get ISIS to choose our fake assassin?'

'Easy,' responded Fred. 'We can create a convincing message from gangland extolling his skills. Most hitmen have their own dark web site. We can create one that will convince ISIS to use our man.'

'Why not our woman?' asked Julia rather petulantly.

'In spite of the movies,' Fred responded with great patience, 'female assassins are unknown, at least within gangland.'

'So, it's George, Fred or me,' said Ahmad.

'You and Fred will need to be glued to your computers,' said Geore. 'It has to be me. It can't be more dangerous than what I went through with the Iranian disc saga.'

After more discussion, the team agreed to go ahead with the plan.

Just after eleven the morning after next, ISIS contacted the dark web site set up by Ahmad and Fred.

'You have been highly recommended for a targeted assassination that we require urgently. Please let us know if you are available. We will then send details.'

'Bingo!' exclaimed Ahmad. 'I'll reply at once.'

'The target,' said the ISIS representative, 'is a dangerous Rabbi based in Sydney. Here is his name and location. We will leave the rest to you. What is your fee?'

'One hundred and fifty thousand dollars,' Ahmad replied. 'Because there is no guarantee of success, I do not charge an upfront fee. I require payment only if I am successful. In bitcoin, of course. There is one other thing. I insist on meeting one of you in person, with absolute proof of your ISIS membership. Only in this way can I be sure you are not undercover police or ASIO.'

'That's possible. Let me make the arrangements.'

The meeting was scheduled for ten the next morning in the concourse of Central Station, at a designated point. The ISIS agent would be wearing a small yellow backpack. He would prove his identity with a tattoo that was exclusive to ISIS operatives. This exclusivity had been confirmed by Ahmad.

'We have to attach a tracking device to the man,' said Fred. 'We can use the one we've developed ourselves, based on Star Chase technology. It's fired from a device disguised as a biro. It's tiny, and once lodged in clothing, is undetectable. I'll let the government agent know exactly what's planned, so the Federal Police can move as soon as we've attached the tracker.'

George arrived at the meeting point ten minutes early. At exactly ten, a man wearing a yellow backpack strolled into the concourse. George approached him cautiously and identified himself as the hitman. The ISIS agent showed his tattoo, and they shook hands. George took out the biro.

'Is there anything to sign?'

'No. Your handshake is enough. Are you satisfied that I am an ISIS operative?'

'Yes. I will now go ahead with the project. I will contact you once it is completed.'

As the ISIS agent turned to leave, George fired the biro at the side of his jacket. Spring-loaded, it made no sound. The tracker stuck. He knew that Fred and Ahmad had already started monitoring and would relay the data to the Federal Police.

Back at HQ, the team waited for news. The call from Fred's government contact came just after three.

'We've done it!' Fred exclaimed, 'the ISIS agent went straight back to ISIS HQ. The occupants have all been taken into custody. Their local operations have been completely eliminated, and the Feds have gathered enough evidence to arrest several gangland members suspected of working with

ISIS. We've helped them in this by sharing our access to the gangland site on the dark web. This means we've fulfilled all the terms of our contract with the government. We'll get our four million.'

'In retrospect,' said Sue, 'it seems like money for old rope.'

'We were incredibly lucky,' said Fred, 'as seems to have been the case ridiculously often. It could have taken far longer and been far more dangerous. Or failed.'

'Since my near-death experience,' said Julia, 'I know that there's a higher being, a divine entity that some call God. I believe that he, she or it, is looking after us. In fact, I'm sure of it.'

'Amen to that,' said Fred irreverently. 'Time to celebrate.'

CHAPTER EIGHTEEN

Julia's invocation of the divine had muted the previous evening's celebrations. At breakfast the next morning, hangovers were less evident than on previous occasions. Even George, though a little bleary-eyed, was good to go.

'There are a couple of new offers,' said Fred, when the team was seated at the conference table. 'One seems promising. It's from the Art Gallery of New South Wales. They want us to recover a stolen painting. I assume we're on their radar because of the art forgery we uncovered as part of the gig on document fraud.'

'It's a no-brainer,' Sue exclaimed. Anything to do with art, I'm in. Tell us more.'

'The painting was to be part of the gallery's exhibition of Impressionist works from the Musee d'Orsay. When the paintings were unpacked, one was missing. It was Manet's *Berthe Morisot with a Bouquet of Violets*, painted in 1868. The thief probably chose it because at only fifty-five by forty centimetres, it's easy to conceal.'

'It's one of his best-known portraits,' said Sue. 'It's exquisite. I'd say it's worth between forty and fifty million American dollars.'

'Because it was stolen in transit,' Fred continued, 'there's no coverage by closed circuit cameras. The gallery has no idea of how or when the theft took place.'

'If we take the gig,' said Julia, 'how on earth will we get started? The thieves will want to sell it at the best price, but obviously they won't want to put an advertisement in the media. There must be a dark web site they can use, but it's just possible the theft was commissioned by a wealthy collector, or a dealer acting on his or her behalf. That would make the painting much more difficult to track.'

'What fee has the gallery offered?' Julia asked.

'The painting was insured, of course, so the fee will be paid by the insurance company. The gallery has negotiated with it on our behalf. A fee of seven and a half percent of the value of the painting will be paid on its recovery. The value will be determined by an independent expert.'

'That's at least four million dollars,' gasped Julia. 'Even more than we got for our last gig. Any ideas Fred?'

'I've studied the details of transit provided by the gallery. This has convinced me that the painting was stolen during its passage through Australian Customs. This involves the corruption of at least one staff member. It also requires inside information about the precise location of the painting. Thinking about the overall logistics of the theft has convinced me that this heist wasn't commissioned by a wealthy collector. The painting was stolen for the thieves' own purposes.'

Fred paused briefly.

'Now let me back up my theory by sharing with you what I've learned about the paintings' transit. The works were placed in custom-built crates that are insulated and cushioned. These crates were taken under armed guard to the airport and put into the hold of a cargo plane. On arrival in Australia, they were examined by customs under the ATA Carnet, a temporary admission scheme that waives import duties and other fees. Our Customs are notoriously strict. They will have insisted that each crate be opened for inspection. This is when the paintings are most vulnerable to theft. A corrupt customs official could create a diversion that allowed a single work to be removed from a crate without detection. This scenario supports the choice of a small painting.'

'Because we can't prove any of this,' said Ahmad, 'we probably won't be able to argue for an inquiry into probable corruption at Customs.'

'I doubt if this would help anyway,' Fred replied, 'a crime of this magnitude comes with a very high price for betrayal. No-one involved will risk talking.'

'So where does this leave us?' asked George.

'We have to assume that the painting will be advertised on the dark web,' Fred answered. 'Ahmad and I will investigate. If we find such sites, we can try and hack into them without detection. Give us the rest of the day.'

'We've found only one site that meets all our criteria,' said Fred at the next morning's meeting. 'This was a real surprise. We assumed there would be several at least. It suggests that this site has evolved over time to become the main dark web access to stolen art and those involved. Because of its importance, it is impenetrable, with one of the highest levels of security that we've ever come across. If we tried to hack into it, we would certainly be identified. This could put us all in danger.'

'Does this mean we're fucked?' asked Sue.

'I hope not,' replied Ahmad. 'Access to the site requires a special code. We think that a personal code is given to carefully selected people or organisations. These would include art dealers who specialise in stolen works, collectors who are willing to pay for them, and criminal organisations. A theft like this requires a specialised team. There can't be many such teams, even world-wide, but I'm sure they account for almost all successful thefts. Their expertise helps to explain why only ten percent of stolen art is ever recovered.'

'Only ten percent?' asked George. 'Is that an accurate figure?'

'It's the one published on the Interpol Stolen Works of Art data base,' Ahmad replied. 'We'll come back to that later, as part of our plan to create a fictional team of art thieves that will be given access to the dark web site.'

'A clever idea!' Sue exclaimed. 'But it sounds very risky.'

'It's our best bet,' said Fred. 'Ahmad and I are fairly confident about achieving it. Confident enough to recommend that we accept the job.'

After a brief discussion, the team agreed.

'Out first step,' said Fred, 'is to access the Interpol data base. It contains descriptions and images of more than fifty thousand stolen items.

All the information is police certified, and the works must be fully identified. That includes provenance when it's available. Once we've accessed the site, which is open to the public, we can select some high value works and claim that our fictitious team has stolen them. This should be enough to get access to the dark web site. If it isn't, we can pose as a private collector who has obtained a valuable work and wishes to sell it. Sue, we'll need you to help us chose the paintings from the Interpol data base.'

'I can start on that right away. I'll be looking at a price range of ten to twenty million. High enough to get the attention of wealthy collectors and high-end crooked dealers.'

It took Sue much longer than she'd expected to choose the paintings. It wasn't until late morning the next day that she had finished.

'Here are my suggestions,' she said to the assembled team. 'The Interpol data base has good images of them and some provenance on all four.

First, *Landscape with an Obelisk* by the Dutch painter Govaert Flinck. Worth about fifteen million American dollars. Second, *The White Duck* by Jean-Baptiste Oudry, a seventeenth century French painter. It's worth about twelve million. Third, *Two Laughing Boys with a Mug of Beer* by the

Dutch painter Frans Hals. About fourteen million. Finally, *Chez Tortoni* by Manet. It's very small, so worth only about twenty million. I've chosen it as a possible link to the Manet stolen from the gallery's exhibition. I'm hoping that these four will be enough to convince the operators of the dark web site that our fictitious team of art thieves should be given access.'

'Well done, Sue,' said Ahmad. 'How long will it take you to create a convincing provenance for each work?'

'Give me the rest of the day. I can elaborate on what data are provided on the Interpol site. I'll make it convincing and attractive.'

The whole team assembled after breakfast the next day. A PDF had been created that included images of the works, and the provenances that Sue had created. This was dispatched to the dark web site. They waited anxiously. Nothing. The team were on the point of giving up their wait when a message appeared on the large screen.

'Thank you for your PDF file. We are checking the authenticity of its contents. This will take some time. We will contact you with the outcome of our enquiries.'

Rather than continue waiting, the team dispersed to go about their various tasks. Just after midday, the big screen flickered to life with another message.

'We've authenticated your details. It's always a pleasure to welcome new entrants to our business. We will send you a code allowing direct entry to our website. Please keep it secure. We look forward to doing business with you.'

Sue was the first to speak. 'Now we're in, what next?'

'We offer one of our paintings for sale,' Fred replied. 'Any buyer will insist on seeing it in real life before parting with the cash. He or she will almost certainly employ an expert to verify that the painting is not a forgery.'

'This means,' George added, 'that we can take it to the buyer in person. This creates the chance of phone hacking and bugging,'

'The buyer could insist we use a fine art transport service,' said Sue.

'We can insist on a face-to-face meeting,' Fred countered. 'Say that we want to make sure that the buyer is a genuine collector and not a member of a crime syndicate, or an undercover agent.'

'Which painting?' asked Julia.

'*Chez Tortoni,*' Sue responded. 'It's only twenty-six by thirty-four centimetres. Small enough to be hand luggage. I know an artist who would be able to create a copy. I'll give her a sanitised version of why we need it.'

'Good thinking,' said Ahmad, 'let's get things moving while we wait for the copy.'

The Manet was offered for sale on the dark web site for seventeen million dollars. Three potential buyers emerged within twenty-four hours. Two offered less than half the asking price. The third offered ten million, an offer which the team agreed to accept. After extensive negotiations, the buyer, a Mr Rogers, agreed that the painting would be handed over to him by a member of the team. He gave an address in San Francisco.

'It's my home and my gallery,' Mr Rogers explained. 'Once I show you round my collection you won't have the slightest doubt about my true identity as a passionate collector. I will have with me an expert who will examine the painting and, I hope, authenticate it. As soon as she does, I'll transfer the ten million to your designated account. Let's meet as soon as possible.'

The whole team insisted on going to San Francisco. This wasn't strictly necessary, but the arrangement had been hard wired into the team's way of working. A meeting with Mr Rogers was proposed for five days later. Sue, who had become the team's spokesperson, explained to him that they would need this time to arrange insurance for such a valuable item.

'Here it is!' Sue announced two days later, holding up the copy. It depicted a stylish gentleman seated at a café table. He wears a top hat and holds a pencil in one hand, sketching or writing on a piece of paper.

'I asked her to do her very best work, so that Mr Rogers will ask his expert to authenticate it and not reject it as an obvious fake. She's done a brilliant job, as you can see.'

The other four all nodded wisely. No-one wanted to admit that they had no idea how to make the necessary judgement.

'Of course,' continued Sue, 'we won't actually insure the painting, but to be totally convincing, we'll need to obtain a custom-built container that's insulated and padded. It's unlikely any art supplier will have one of the right size in stock, so they'll need to make one up. This could take a day or two. Luckily, we've got the time.'

On arrival at San Francisco International Airport, the team took a maxi taxi to the nearby hotel they'd booked for three nights. The flight from Sydney had been direct, and they had been able to sleep for much of it

The meeting with Mr Rogers was scheduled for ten o'clock the next morning. Sue rang the number he had given her. He answered at once and Sue was able to confirm that they would arrive at his house as arranged. Sue and George would deliver the painting.

At the appointed time, Sue pressed the bell of a stately mansion in Presidio Heights, San Francisco's poshest district. The middle-aged man who opened the door introduced himself as Paul Jackson. He apologised for his use of the alias Mr Rogers.

'You'll understand the need for circumspection,' he added before taking them through the mansion to an extension large enough to fill a third of the sizeable back garden.

'The expert has been delayed. She'll be here in about twenty minutes. That will give me time to show you round the gallery.'

Beyond the foyer and an office, the gallery was a single huge room. The collection was breathtaking, even to George, who was not particularly arty. Impressionists and neo-impressionists dominated, but there were some wonderful British paintings from the nineteenth and twentieth centuries. Paul pointed to three works by Manet: 'The *Chez Tortoni* will compliment them perfectly.'

He took the trouble to comment on some works by American artists with whom Sue was not familiar. Although Paul claimed to be legitimate, it was clear to Sue that several of his paintings must have been stolen.

The expert entered the gallery just before the tour was completed. Paul introduced her as Sonia. Back in the office she carefully removed the painting from its crate and inspected it closely. She then placed it carefully on a transparent platform attached to another piece of equipment. Sonia then pressed a button. There was a buzzing noise, and a text appeared on a small screen.

'I'm so sorry,' Sonia said, 'this is a forgery. It's very well done, but I'm afraid there is absolutely no doubt.'

Sue and George managed to look gobsmacked. Paul Jackson's face showed a mixture of astonishment, disappointment and rage.

'I know you'll never forgive us,' said Sue, 'but we're just as shocked as you are. Our expert passed it as the original. Please keep the painting. It's the least we can do.'

'Just leave. Just get the hell out!' Paul shouted. Fearing fisticuffs, they left at a trot.

Back at the hotel they told their story.

'Were you able to plant a bug?' asked Fred.

'Two actually,' George replied. 'While Paul and Sonia were waiting for the machine to pronounce judgement. One in the office and one in the gallery itself. They are well hidden and won't be detected unless the room is swept for them, but I can't see Paul suspecting us of spying, just as bumbling idiots.'

'We've tapped into his phone,' said Ahmad. 'I suggest we extend our stay for a day or two. Let's pray that we learn enough to lead us to the thieves we're chasing.'

CHAPTER NINETEEN

The tapping of Paul Jackson's phone yielded a major breakthrough. When he'd shown Sue and George his three Manets and explained that the *Chez Tortoni* would complement them perfectly, they assumed that his Manet collection was complete. They were wrong. Paul had heard about the theft of Manet's Berthe Morisot portrait, and he was very keen to get hold of it. As a trader of stolen art, he had full access to the dark web site. He assumed that the work was for sale and offered to buy it. A call from one of the thieves confirmed that it was on the market. The price was thirty-five million American Dollars.

The bug in Paul's office allowed the team to monitor the transaction. Paul offered one of his paintings in exchange, but the thieves insisted on cash. After prolonged haggling, a price of thirty million was agreed. The thieves wanted the sale to be completed as soon as possible. They offered to send the work by a reputable fine art transport service, but Paul insisted that it be handed over in person. The thieves' physical base, and the painting, were in New York. The handover at Paul's gallery was scheduled for two in the afternoon of the day after next.

'The maximum size of hand luggage allowed on domestic flights in America is fifty-five by thirty centimetres,' said Ahmad. 'With packaging, the portrait will be about sixty by forty-five, only a little above the limit. The thieves will be able to get permission to take it on as hand luggage. I'm guessing there will be two of them, for security. Assuming one of them calls Paul to confirm their arrival, we can hack into his phone. We'll need to extend our stay for three days. There's still plenty to see and do in San Fran.'

Two hours before the scheduled handover, one of the thieves called Paul.

'His phone was well protected,' said Ahmad, 'but we managed to hack into it. So now we can monitor his location. Perhaps track him back to the thieves' base.'

The bug in Paul's office revealed that Sonia had confirmed the authenticity of the Morisot portrait. As soon as the money was transferred, the thieves left.

'We should be able to pinpoint their location in New York through the hacked phone,' said Ahmad. 'Then we can fly there ourselves, or hand things over to the Feds.'

The hacked phoned stopped moving just after eleven that night.

'They've flown straight back to New York,' said Fred. 'It's late. Let's go to bed and decide what to do in the morning, when we're fresh.'

After a late breakfast, the team struggled to decide whether or not they should fly to New York.

'Let's check on Paul,' Sue suggested. 'That might help us decide.'

The bug in Pauls' office revealed the presence of three men. They had clearly just arrived. The team gasped when Paul introduced the men to each other. Two of them had met previously. They were among the richest men in America.

The team continued to listen in silence as the four men moved into the gallery. It became clear that the two wealthy men were involved in buying and selling stolen art. The tour had been arranged with this in mind. After about an hour, a light meal was served in the office. It took another hour or so for the transactions to be completed.

'So, two of the richest men in America are hooked on stolen art,' said Sue. 'Can we identify the third man?'

Ahmad worked on his phone. 'He's a senior member of the American Mafia. He's there to facilitate their financial transactions, all in bitcoin.'

'The two collectors wield enormous power,' said Julia. 'I assume they can access the dark web site and have direct contact with art thieves like those we're pursuing. If they discover our involvement, they may fear exposure. Are we in danger?'

'I think you're worrying too much,' George replied, 'There may be no connection between our thieves and the two collectors, and the dark web guarantees their total anonymity. But we need to be alert, so let's add the collectors to Zelda and the organ harvesters as possible threats. Quite a collection. This means we have to fly to New York.'

The team had settled into their New York hotel suite by late afternoon the next day. Fred and George set off at once to check out the thieves' location, which they had now been able to pinpoint. Their cab took them to a quiet street in West Harlem. They strolled past the location, a large four storey brownstone near the middle of a row. Fred double checked the position of the hacked phone to make sure it was the correct building.

'It has to be the thieves' HQ,' he said, 'So, let's inform the local police of what we've unearthed.'

Fred was able to prove his connection to the Australian government to the officer at the Police Station's front desk before outlining the situation. The station chief saw them at once, and Fred convinced him of the need for urgent action. The chief contacted his federal counterparts who, after a brief enquiry of their own, set things in motion. The Federal police decided to observe the building before acting further. Once they had confirmed that it was the thieves' HQ, they would go into action.

Two days later, a SWAT team, together with local police, surrounded the brownstone. Six of the SWAT team smashed through the front door. Shots were heard. More officers entered the building. Five men and two women were taken into custody. No-one was injured: the SWAT team had fired warning shots when one of the thieves appeared to be reaching for a weapon. A search of the brownstone confirmed that it was the base of a sophisticated group of art thieves. Several stolen paintings were found, although none of them approached the value of the Berthe Morisot portrait.

Before the start of the New York operation, the San Francisco police had been informed of the location of the stolen portrait. They had raided Paul Jackson's studio, arrested him, and recovered the stolen work.

Fred was sent a document that confirmed his role in what was described as a resoundingly successful operation. The police would contact the Art Gallery in Sydney and make arrangements for the safe return of the portrait.

The day after their return to HQ, the fee for the successful return of the painting was settled. The portrait had been independently valued at forty-eight million American dollars. At the prevailing exchange rate, this equated to seventy-five million Australian dollars. Seven and a half per cent of this was just over five and a half million Australian dollars. This largesse yielded yet another celebration, this time with the best French champagne.

CHAPTER
TWENTY

'Industrial espionage,' said Fred at the start of the next meeting. 'IE for short. The request, with background details, comes from the Federal Government. IE is a huge problem worldwide. It's reliably estimated to have cost the US alone six hundred billion dollars last year. More than the five hundred billion that the country spent on research and development. Worldwide, IE comprises one third of all cybercrimes.

Many countries opt for IE as an alternative or supplement to research and development. China has achieved much of its industrial and scientific advances through IE, especially on America. A major focus is microchips. China has an emerging microchip industry thought to lag behind those of America and Taiwan. But the launch of DeepSeek tells us they've caught up. Google has recently created a chip called Willow which, when linked to a quantum computer, will allow processing speeds infinitely faster than those achieved by digital devices. This enormous power and speed will allow all current encryptions to be broken in minutes, if not seconds. Such innovations are prime targets for IE. The stakes are high.

A group specialising in IE is causing problems. It has already hacked into the Australian Submarine Corporation, based in Osborne, South Australia. This company has started building infrastructure for the nuclear submarine project sponsored by America. If it can't foolproof its cybersecurity, the Americans will have to move the project elsewhere, a disaster for the South Australian defence industry. The Federal government has asked us to identify this IE group and shut it down. We'll be paid two million dollars for a successful outcome.'

'How does the group operate?' asked Julia.

'About half of IE is between businesses,' Fred replied. 'We know that the group is involved in this. The remainder of IE is almost entirely State sponsored. You'd expect the attack on the Submarine Corp. to come from one of these states, presumably a hostile one. The fact that it was done by a private group is very concerning. It implies that the group has links with enemy states such as North Korea, Russia and Iran.

Almost two thirds of corporate IE is done by insiders. Existing employees are bribed or coerced. Insiders are placed as new employees. Rival businesses poach key staff and bribe ex-employees. The corporate world can't risk direct involvement in these often illegal activities, hence the need for groups specialising in IE.

All this requires some physical contact. Doing it entirely online is risky and cumbersome. Our IE group must have a physical base. They couldn't use drones, now crucial to IE, without one. The Federal Government hasn't been able to pinpoint their location, but they are fairly sure it's in Sydney. That's one reason we've been chosen for the gig.'

'What businesses has the group targeted?' Julia asked.

'They've tried hacking into BHP and Fortescue Metals, our two biggest resource companies. Their cybersecurity was good enough to block the attack. Fortescue metals managed to trace it back to a site on the dark web. Naturally, after alerting the authorities, they left it at that.

The group had two successful penetrations, one on a biotech company and the other on a financial services group. Both are still assessing what, if any, data has been stolen.'

'What's our brief?' asked Sue.

'Find their physical base and shut them down. But before we accept the gig, we need a viable plan. Any ideas?'

'We could pose as a client,' Ahmad suggested, 'contact them through their dark web site.'

'That's one option,' Fred replied. 'Any other ideas?'

'We know that the attack on the Submarine Corp. must have been ordered by a foreign power,' said Julia. 'So, the IE group has links beyond Australia. Perhaps it's limited attacks on businesses are designed to obscure its real purpose: to act as an agent for enemy states.'

The others quietly absorbed Julia's suggestion.

'If you're right,' said Sue, 'and I think you are, what might their next target be?'

'I've just discovered what's called 'store now, decrypt later,' said Fred. 'When data analysis is blocked by encryption, the data are stored for decryption by quantum computers. These will be available within three years, four at the most. Where do we store data most valuable to enemy states?'

'Data centres,' Ahmad replied. 'They provide storage for vast amounts of data, some of which could be of strategic value.'

'Where is our biggest repository of strategic data?' asked Julia.

'Pine Gap of course,' Sue replied.

'Exactly. I think that will be the group's next target. It's near Alice Springs, and employs about eight hundred people, half American and half Australian. Run by the CIA and America's National Security Agency, it is absolutely crucial to signal intelligence. Detecting missile launches is a vital part of this. Let me find out a bit more about what they do there.'

Next morning, Julia outlined what she had gleaned.

'There are currently forty-five satellite dishes at Pine Gap. The volume of data collected is so huge that advanced filtering and processing programs are essential to isolate relevant material. The sheer complexity of Pine Gap's operations makes cyber-security a challenge, but we can be sure its defences are impenetrable. Our IE group might be happy to wait for quantum computers, but I don't think so. They will want real-time data.'

'If Pine Gap's cybersecurity is impenetrable, how will they get access?' asked George.

'There's only one way,' Julia replied. 'They will need an insider. If we can identify one, we might be able to shut the IE group down.'

'I'll explain all this to my government contact,' said Fred. 'I'll suggest that ASIO contact security at Pine Gap. Their focus, I'll argue, should be on checking out recent employees and monitoring the activities of anyone who raises suspicion.'

Fred made the call. 'It's on! Now we just wait and see.'

The government contact called Fred in the late afternoon of the following day. Ending the call, Fred was pumped.

'We've done it! Working together, ASIO and the CIA identified the insider. She had been placed over six months earlier, and had achieved some status, so all this has been quite long in the planning. The insider was actually a member of the IE group itself, and interrogation yielded it's physical location. The base was raided by the Federal Police. Five people were arrested, and all their equipment impounded for analysis. This should reveal their contacts and operatives. Our crucial role has been certified. We'll get our fee of two million dollars. Let's celebrate!'

CHAPTER TWENT-ONE

The following afternoon, Sue heard from her mother that her father had been admitted to hospital after a fall. He'd fractured his left hip and needed surgery.

'Let me take a couple of days off. I'll be back as soon as he's recovered from the op.'

The rest of the team used her absence for tasks they'd neglected while on mission.

On the morning of Sue's return, Fred convened a team meeting. 'How's your dad?' asked Julia.

'Out of hospital already and in good spirits. I'm happy to leave him in my mum's care.'

'A new project came up yesterday,' said Fred. 'I'm really not sure about taking it on. It might be too dangerous. Would you like me to explain it anyway?'

'Give us the chance to decide,' said Julia.

'It's about a group of hackers who call themselves *The Mob*, although they have no connection with the Mafia. They are self-styled anarchists, determined to create mayhem with the ultimate goal of overthrowing democracy. To show how dangerous they are, I'll tell you about a similar group in America called *The Con*.

This group was headed by a man called Sharkie. It caused massive problems in the five years or so before Sharkie's location was discovered, and he was arrested. *The Con*'s hacking skills were of the highest order. They managed to penetrate NVIDIA and Musk's X, selling valuable data to China and elsewhere. These data helped China to catch up on chip development, allowing them, for example, to launch DeepSeek. *The Con* hacked into major retailers and stole the details of tens of millions of customers which they either sold or ransomed. Worse, they hacked into AT&T's wireless service and stole fifty million call records, including those of FBI agents.

They were particularly good at SIM swapping, which allows control of the victims' phone numbers. *The Con* then changed passwords and accessed financial accounts, including cryptocurrency wallets. Emboldened by their success, they hired third parties to raid houses at gunpoint, using the victims' computers to transfer funds and steal bitcoin.

They were so dangerous that the FBI agents erased their names from their reports to protect their identities. Sharkie's arrest would not have been possible without the efforts of a cybersecurity researcher called Enoch, who devoted over five years of his life to exposing him. *The Con* threatened to kill Enoch, so he surrounded his house with security cameras and made it impossible to enter without authorisation.

The Con then tried 'swatting'. Swatters make fake emergency calls to the police that endanger those targeted. For example, they report domestic violence, home invasions, or other dangerous situations. This allows police or SWAT teams to force entry and arrest or injure innocent people. But Enoch successfully countered these attempts.

Because of Russia's central role in hacking, Enoch learned Russian. He hacked into a Russian site and discovered a plan to post him heroin and then inform the police, The heroin was posted, but Enoch had informed the police of the plot, and escaped prosecution. That's about it. Since Sharkie's arrest, *The Con* has ceased to operate.

'Is there a link between *The Con* and *The Mob*?' George asked.

'Yes. Sharkie has a key colleague called Wolfie, who is based in Turkey. The FBI are arranging his extradition. They've told ASIO that he's liaised with *The Mob*. It's unlikely that he's moved to Australia, but it's very likely that he's arranged for other ex-members of *The Con*s to do so.'

'Irrespective of any links with ex-members of *The Con*, *The Mob* seem just as dangerous. Have they got started yet?'

'They're still setting up. We know of their activities only through hackers who have been contacted by them. The vast majority of hackers deplore groups like *The Con,* but there are always a few willing to sell their souls for money, or cooperate out of fear. I'm sure they've attracted some local recruits.'

'If we decide to go after them,' said Julia, 'now is surely the time. Before they've finished setting up.'

'It's still very dangerous,' Sue responded. 'What's in it for us, apart from the fee, of course? How much has the Government offered?'

'Four million,' replied Fred. 'That's a measure of their concern, and of how much danger might be involved. But there's one thing I haven't shared with you all. *The Con* was paranoid about other hacking groups trying to copy them or expose them. They were utterly ruthless in eliminating perceived threats. When online intimidation didn't work, they used real life tactics, sending enforcers to threaten or beat up adversaries. It's possible that some were killed, their deaths disguised as accident or suicide. If we take the project on, they might identify me. Their hacking skills, perhaps linked with AI, may allow them to identify our physical location. This could put you all in danger as well.'

There was a silence

'We've always worked as a team,' said Sue. 'It's in our DNA. We've faced many dangers together. We won't let you face this one alone.'

'Hold on a moment Sue,' said Ahmad. 'Before I can agree with you, I need to hear Fred's plan.'

'Enoch and the Feds were able to track Sharkie down because he made an online error. Combined with their other information, this mistake was enough. I plan to trick *The Mob* into such an error. It's the safest way to go. I'll need your help Ahmad, but I'll make sure this doesn't put you or the others in any danger. Let me give it a try.'

Reluctantly, the rest of the team agreed.

Fred's plan was impressive

'I'll ask my government contact to approach the FBI and request them for all they have on Sharkie's Turkey-based contact Wolfie. Then I'll masquerade as Wolfie and send a message to *The Mob*'s dark web site. The message will say: 'The danger of extradition is now so great that I must leave Turkey. I'm coming to Australia to join you. I'll book a flight as soon as I've got a fake passport. For security, don't reply to this message. I'll contact you with my flight details. Meet me at Sydney airport. I'll be wearing a fez, with appropriate clothing. The password is Goliath.'

'That's brilliant,' exclaimed Ahmad, 'but it hinges on two things. First, locating their dark web site. Second, that *The Mob* don't know what Wolfie looks like.'

'I'm sure that between us we'll locate *The Mob*'s dark web site. We can't be certain that Wolfie was involved in creating *The Mob*, but it's likely. Even if he wasn't, *The Mob* will certainly have heard of him. I'm sure they'll accept my fake message from him as genuine. They'll do what he asks. Wolfie will have kept his true identity secret from the other hackers. They can't know what he looks like.'

'Before we start,' said George, 'let's wait to hear what the FBI told Fred's government contact.'

It wasn't until the next morning that Fred's contact provided the information.

'The extradition process is not yet complete,' said Fred, 'the Turkish authorities are not being particularly cooperative, but they've allowed the CIA to monitor Wolfie's activities. He doesn't seem to be aware that his extradition is imminent, although he knows it's on the horizon. He may or may not have informed *The Mob* about this. Either way, it won't affect our strategy. So, let's get going.'

It took Fred and Ahmad nearly a whole day to find the Mob's dark web site. Knowing that the fake Wolfie would need time to make the necessary arrangements, they waited a day before sending the second message with his flight details. He was scheduled to arrive at Sydney airport at three twenty the next day.

Fred informed his government contact of the plan. The contact alerted the Federal Police. George insisted on being the one to go to the airport.

'It's a no brainer. I've done this sort of stuff before, but I'd like one of you to come with me, just in case things go pear-shaped.'

Julia volunteered. George would wear a tracker so that the Federal Police could follow him to *The Mob*'s base.

George and Julia arrived thirty minutes before the fake Wolfie was scheduled to land. George positioned himself so that he could enter the concourse at exactly the right time. Holding a carry-on case and wearing a red fez, he cautiously walked out. Almost at once, a young man approached him.

'Goliath?'

'That's me. No real names. Let's go.'

The Mob's base was a warehouse in Strawberry Hills, a near city suburb. As soon as George and his contact arrived, it was surrounded by local and Federal police. A SWAT team forced entry. Inside were four men, none looking older than thirty. They were arrested and their equipment impounded. George was arrested also to maintain the fiction that he was Wolfie.

'I've said this before,' smiled Sue, when the team assembled at HQ that evening, 'but it seems like money for old rope.'

'You all know what I think,' Julia responded, 'so I won't go on about it. We were incredibly lucky, as always. If it wasn't for the grace of God, so many things could have gone wrong. We could all have been put in real danger, but we wrapped the whole thing up quicker and safer than we could possibly have imagined. As always, we worked together. If

I had to single out a pivotal moment, it would be Fred's brilliant suggestion that we impersonate Wolfie. Well done, Fred!'

'I'll admit it was a good idea, but it was just an idea until the rest of you worked with me to make it happen. So well done to you too.'

The team was elated but very tired. As usual, they celebrated their success, but fatigue took them all to bed after only two bottles of French champagne.

CHAPTER TWENTY-TWO

'Here's a new one,' Fred announced at the team's next gathering. 'Wildlife smuggling. It seems that criminal gangs have recently moved into it because it uses the same strategies and techniques as drug smuggling. It's very lucrative and penalties are relatively light. The Federal Government has become concerned about a crime gang that has combined wildlife and drug smuggling. This group alone has created a measurable increase in wildlife smuggling out of Australia and the import of illicit drugs. They want us to shut it down. The Government hasn't been able to pinpoint the gang's physical base, but they believe it's in Sydney.

This will be a complex and risky gig, which is why they've offered payment of four million dollars. As usual, they've provided a great deal of background info.'

'Let's hear it,' said Ahmad.

'Wildlife smuggling worldwide is currently worth about fifty billion American dollars a year. It ranks fourth behind firearms, drugs and human trafficking. In Australia, about eighty percent of the trade involves reptiles, amphibians, insects and arachnids.'

'Arachnids?' asked Ahmad.

'Spiders and scorpions mainly but also ticks and mites. We have over nine hundred reptile species, nearly all found nowhere else. Shingleback lizards are highly prized and fetch around fifteen thousand dollars, more if they have distinctive colouring. A mating pair would fetch up to fifty thousand. Because of their small size, lizards and other reptiles, such as turtles and snakes, are nearly always smuggled out through airports. Experienced smugglers immobilise them by taping their limbs and then put them in socks.

They carry then through customs in specially designed vests, the same as those used for drug smuggling. Lizards can survive for days without food or water by entering a state of torpor called brumation. This allows some to be sent overseas by mail. The same vests work for insects and arachnids, even crustacea such as crayfish and lobsters. Blue lobsters are very rare and can fetch up to ten thousand dollars, would you believe!

Small birds such as finches, budgies and lorikeets can also be smuggled in vests. Larger birds can sometimes pass customs through the use of false documents, but most are transported from remote landing strips by light aircraft, which are flown very low to avoid radar surveillance.

This market is the most lucrative for wildlife smugglers. A glossy black cockatoo could fetch fifty thousand dollars. Red-tailed and black-tailed cockatoos are priced around thirty thousand. A Major Mitchell, with its beautiful pink and white plumage, is worth about fifteen thousand. Palm cockatoos, with their striking red patches and unusual drumming behaviour, cost about twenty thousand.

Although the trade is less lucrative, light planes are used also to transport marsupials such as koalas, sugar gliders, quokkas, bettongs, potaroos and bandicoots. Bettongs and potaroos, which are quite rare, can fetch up to fifteen thousand dollars.'

'Is there more information about the link between drug and wildlife smuggling?' asked Julia.

'Crime gangs can use wildlife as collateral for drug deals or exchange it for drugs. In one well documented case, planeloads of Australian birds were transported to Bangkok in exchange for heroin. False documents are another link. Crime gangs have the know-how to forge the kind of paperwork that allows customs to be bypassed.'

'How are the birds and animals actually collected?'

'Regular smugglers use well equipped camper-vans to go to remote areas. They may spend weeks collecting enough product to meet demand. For birds, they travel to their known habitats. Some have the expertise to net birds themselves, but for the most valuable species, they pay locals to find and trap them.'

'Any ideas about how we might start?' George asked.

'I think we should focus on birds, especially the very high value ones. I suggest we choose a partic-ular species, research its habitat, and then go there ourselves, posing as twitchers.'

'Twitchers?' asked Julia

'It's what we call dedicated birdwatchers. The nickname distinguishes then from casual or less obsessive observers. If we ask the locals to help us, we can suss out if any of them have links with wildlife smugglers. If we find the right person, we can tell them that our real purpose is to capture a bird on behalf of a wealthy Australian collector who wants to stay anonymous.'

'I assume the gang has a site on the dark web,' said Sue. 'If we can access it, we might be able to track some of their orders. It's possible they'll have placed one with the same bird- netter who we'll ask to help us. If so, when the smugglers arrive, we can follow them or at least place a tracker on their vehicle. Perhaps even on their clothing. This will allow us to follow them back to their base.'

'What if our bird-netter doesn't have an order?' asked Sue.

'We can wait until they do,' replied Fred, 'or we can arrange one ourselves, although this may be impossible. I imagine that anyone ordering a bird worth upwards of thirty thousand would be a collector who already has access to the smugglers' dark web site. Without this access, we can't place an order. The site will be well protected. We may not be able to hack into it.'

'Fred's plan doesn't sound too dangerous,' Julia continued, 'but it relies on good luck. We've been blessed with it since we've started our work together. I'll pray that this blessing continues. I think we should go ahead.'

The others agreed and the team began detailed research and planning. Their first task was to select a particular bird. All this took a full two days but yielded a unanimous choice: the glossy black cockatoo. Sue offered to summarise their research.

'The glossy black cockatoo is listed as vulnerable but not endangered. There are at least eight thousand throughout their native habitats. The bird has deep significance for First Nations people. The town of Nowra in New South Wales is named after the Yuin name for the bird, which features prominently in local creation stories. It nests in hollow eucalypts and feeds on she-oak seeds. The species has evolved large bulbous beaks which allow the birds to extract the seeds from the trees' cones. Recently discarded cones suggest they may be nearby. They don't fly in flocks but in twos, threes or small groups.

We've chosen to go to Nowra because of the bird's local significance, and because the town is close to the Booderee National Park, a known habitat for the glossy black cockatoo. Nowra's population is around twenty-two thousand. It's about twenty kilometres inland from Shoalhaven, which is one hundred and sixty kilometres south of Sydney. Because we haven't been able to access the gang's dark web site, there's no question of placing an order. But it's still possible one will have been placed with the bird-netter we employ.'

The next day they drove to Nowra in an eight-seater Land Rover Defender, hired in case they needed to go off-road. Their three-bedroom apartment was close to the town centre. Once settled in, they enquired about bird watching in Booderee, stating an interest in the glossy black cockatoo.

It took much of the day, but by early evening, they were given the name of a First Nations man. Directed to the local hotel, they found a man of his description drinking at the bar.

'Excuse me,' said Julia, 'are you Jarli?'

'Who wants to know?'

'We're twitchers from Sydney, very keen to photograph a glossy black cockatoo. We were told you could help us.'

'I'm your man, but it'll cost you. How keen are you?'

'Very. Name your price.'

'It could take a day or two. Five thousand up front. Another five when we find the bird. I can guarantee that we will.'

'It's a deal. When can we start?'

'Pick me up from the Zest café tomorrow at eight. I'll have my nets. We'll go to the Booderee National Park.'

Jardi was waiting for them at the café. It took only forty minutes to get to the park entrance.

'It's run mostly by First Nations people,' said Jardi. The board of management has a majority of us blackfellas. I'm not on the board, but they know me and give me free reign.'

'What if we want to buy a glossy black cocka-too?' asked Sue.

Jardi stopped in his tracks.

'Are you serious? I thought you were twitchers after photographs.'

'We'll be honest with you.' Sue continued. 'We're not twitchers. Not that interested in bird watching at all. We've been offered fifty thousand dollars to bring one back to a collector in Sydney.

'I'll be honest with you then,' said Jardi. 'I've worked with some people who pay me five grand for a bird in good condition. I had no idea what a glossy was really worth. They've cheated me.'

'Has anyone ordered a bird recently?' asked George.

'Not a glossy black cockatoo, but they're coming to get two gang-gangs and a yellow-tailed black cockatoo. Arriving in two days. When I've trapped the birds, they'll go straight into their campervan, well hidden.'

'Given that you've been cheated, do you feel loyal to them?' asked Julia.

'No. I'd like to screw them like they've screwed me.'

'I've got another confession,' Julia continued. 'We're not really here to get a glossy black cockatoo. We're here to catch the traffickers who buy and sell them. Will you help?'

'If I do, it will mean the end of my business, but talking to you lot, I realise I've never thought things through. I just wanted the money. Helping these people, these traffickers as you call them, means supporting the whole nasty business. I don't want to go on doing that, but I really need the money. I've a few debts to pay off.'

'How much would you need before you stopped working with them?' asked Fred.

'I've paid off some of the debt. I'd need at least forty thousand to clear it all and set myself up doing something else.'

'We can offer you fifty thousand. Half now, and half if everything works out. On top of the five grand we've already paid you. But we're asking you to take a few risks'

'What risks?'

'We want you to phone us when the traffickers arrive at the bird's habitat. We can track your phone's exact location. We don't want to meet them, just put a tracker on their campervan. We can't risk putting the tracker on their clothing, but you could do it. We'll show you how.'

Jarli agreed to do all that they asked. Although he was in many ways unworldly, he had a bank account into which Fred transferred twenty-five thousand dollars. He was given a lesson in using the pen-like device that shot a tiny tracker into the target's clothing.

Jardi knew the time that the traffickers were due to arrive at the park, and so the team were ready for his phone message. While the traffickers – two men – followed Jardi into the dense scrubland, they placed a tracker on their campervan. Jardi was able to fire a tracker. into the clothes of both men

All three birds were captured by late evening, The campervan left as soon as they were hidden safely inside. After they had settled up with Jardi, they followed its course. It entered a warehouse in Mascot, a suburb about seven kilometres south of Sydney's CBD. Fred had already alerted his government contact, and as soon as the team were sure that the warehouse was the smugglers' HQ, they informed the Federal Police. Aided by a SWAT team, the police entered the warehouse, arrested five men and two women, and impounded all the equipment. No birds were found other than the ones in the campervan,

'This time,' said Sue, when they got back to HQ in the early hours of the morning, 'I won't say it was money for old rope. We earned our four million.' There was no celebration. Everyone just wanted to get to bed.

Late the next afternoon, Fred's contact told him the preliminary investigations had confirmed that the gang were, as suspected, both drug and wildlife smugglers. They had close links with a small group of document forgers who were also located and arrested. This meant that the team had been more than fully successful. The four million would be paid.

CHAPTER
TWENTY-THREE

lthough none of the team was Jewish, they were united in their loathing of antisemitism. When Fred revealed a new project that concerned a group of neo-Nazis, the others were keen to hear more.

'The gig refers to a combined ASIO and Federal Police operation. Based in Melbourne, this particular group of neo-Nazis has extensive overseas connections. If the group was closed down, it would be impossible to trace any of those, so ASIO introduced an undercover agent, hoping that he would get these and other crucial data before the authorities moved to eliminate the group. He was exposed and murdered.'

'So, they are totally ruthless,' said Julia. 'Did they try and disguise the murder as an accident?'

'On the contrary, the body was dropped off at a Melbourne hospital. Burns on the feet suggested that the agent had been tortured. We have to assume that he revealed all that he knew about ASIO's strategy. There's a suspicion that an ASIO or Federal Police insider may have leaked information about the agent to the group, which has now melted into the background. Given all this, it's no surprise that neither ASIO or the Federal Police want to risk the lives of any more undercover agents. The Federal Government wants us to find the group's physical location, infiltrate it, and shut it down.'

'What?', exclaimed Julia, 'that's ridiculous. 'Why should we risk our own lives?'

'That was my first reaction,' Fred replied, 'but there's more. When we exposed *The Mob* and the authorities entered their HQ and arrested those present, some key members were elsewhere. They escaped arrest. As committed anarchists, they wanted to regroup, but doing this as *The Mob* was clearly impossible. Instead, they joined the neo-Nazis in Melbourne. Both groups share a wish to undermine democracy, although *The Mob* has never mouthed explicitly antisemitic views

Before he was murdered, the undercover agent discovered that we ourselves are one of the group's targets. *The Mob's* remaining members have discovered our role in exposing their organisation. Using their network of hackers and programmers, they managed to identify George as the fake Wolfie. They then identified Ahmad and me. So far, Julia and Sue have escaped detection, but we are all in danger. *The Mob's* surviving members want revenge, and they are as ruthless as the neo-Nazis, perhaps even more so.'

'We're between a rock and a hard place,' said George. 'If we don't go after them, they'll go after us.'

'Exactly. It's possible that ASIO has exaggerated the danger, but I don't think so. Unfortunately, it all makes sense. So, what do we do?'

'We could focus on boosting our security,' suggested Ahmad.

'HQ is already as well protected as it can be,' Fred responded. 'The danger lies outside. Whenever we leave HQ, especially to go to our own homes, the threat is real. We can't ignore it. We have to act.'

Faced with this stark reality, the team agreed to start planning.

'Let me outline the background info provided by my government contact,' said Fred. 'Neo-Nazi's have created a worldwide network, made up of a wide range of groups who share a culture of radical opposition to mainstream society and idealise a revolution in the name of the Aryan race. They constantly share ideas and are inspired by each other's activism.

The Melbourne based group is part of a group called Australian Resistance, or AR, founded in 2016. It's web site states: "Our goal is to gather all young National Socialist Australians into a single youth movement, one that embodies our National Socialist worldview. We will urge them to be socially and politically active. We're the Hitlers you've been waiting for."

Australian Resistance claims to have at least four hundred activists spread throughout Australia. They are linked to the website Fascistforge.com, which has worldwide connections. Its main page has the banner "Gas the Kikes, Race War Now, 1488 Boots on the ground."

'What's 1488?' asked Sue.

'It's the equivalent of a Masonic handshake. Neo-Nazis use it as a code to greet each other and to judge loyalty. The 14 is from *The Fourteen Words*, a white nationalist slogan coined by David Lane: "We must secure the existence of our people and a future for white children." The 88 stands for Heil Hitler, 'H' being the eighth letter of the alphabet.'

'The code implies violence,' Sue continued. 'How violent are the members of Australian Resistance?'

'Most acts of violence are carried out by people on the fringes, usually because of mental instability. They generally perform these acts impulsively. The group leaders tend to downplay the use of violence but those in AR must have felt they had no choice but to murder the undercover agent. This may lower their threshold for extreme violence.'

'That threshold may be important later,' said Julia, 'but right now it's irrelevant. If we go undercover and they rumble us, they'll kill us for sure.'

'What if Julia and I go undercover together?' Sue asked. 'If we play our cards right, we can get away with it. AR hasn't identified us yet.'

'We do have to go undercover,' said George, 'and I am clearly the best candidate. But I will go in alone.'

'That won't work,' Julia replied, 'they know who you are. The same is true of Fred and Ahmad. But they don't know of Sue and I.'

'That clinches it,' said Sue. 'Julia and I will go in together. Fred and Ahmad can concoct a convincing cover story, including fake documents and clips from Facebook and Instagram.'

Reluctantly the team agreed to Sue's suggestion. Fred and Ahmad spent the next two days creating a convincing basis for the women's wish to join Australian Resistance.

'We've done our best,' said Ahmad. 'Here it is. We can fine tune it if necessary. Your parents, Sue, are Lebanese. You were born in Australia, but you and your family have kept close ties with your many relatives in Lebanon. Your parents were visiting Lebanon when the Israeli Defence Force raided the country as part of their campaign against Hezbollah. Tragically, they were killed by an Israeli bombardment. This has left you with a deep hatred of Jews. You Julia, hate Jews because your family of origin is rabidly antisemitic. This hatred was drummed into you from an early age and remains a core part of your identity. You and Sue met each other at a demonstration against Israel's invasion of Gaza. You have been close friends ever since. We've created documents that confirm all this. We've even created a false Facebook account of Sue's parents' deaths, and we've identified the website that will allow you to contact Australian Resistance.'

Julia and Sue examined the documents carefully and watched the Facebook clip.

'Well done you two,' said Julia. 'We can't fault what you've put together. So, let's move.'

Almost immediately after Julia emailed AR's website, she got a reply:

'We haven't many female members but we're willing to meet you and your friend. Although our HQ is in Melbourne, we have an active group in Sydney. One of us will meet you there. I'll send you details as soon as we've made the necessary arrangements. We'll take it from there.'

Sue and Julia arrived at Circular Quay twenty minutes before the scheduled time. Their contact would meet them at the entrance to ferry wharf number three. He arrived on time, introducing himself as David. Blonde, blue eyed, good-looking, mid-twenties.

'Let's sit out front of Penelope's,' he suggested. 'We can order drinks.'

All three ordered diet cokes. Sue and Julia pushed their credentials across the table. David studied them carefully.

'Can I keep them to show my Zug Fuhrer?'

'Zug Fuhrer?' asked Sue.

'Oh, sorry. The best translation is 'platoon leader', the soldier in command of a group of men, usually about twenty to thirty. We tend to use military jargon here in Sydney, but that's a bit unusual. HQ in Melbourne don't do it. For us, it's a sign that we are ready for combat.'

'You can keep the documents,' said Julia, 'we have copies except for Sue's birth certificate. We've kept the original.'

'That's okay. Now I need to ask you something important. How far are you willing to go in our crusade against Kikes, Muslims and the LGBTQ perverts?'

'We'll do whatever's necessary,' Sue replied.

'That's good enough for me. We'll be in touch.'

David shook their hands and strolled away, leaving them to pay the bill.

The following morning, they were invited to a meeting of the Sydney chapter of Australian Resistance, scheduled for seven in the evening two days later.

CHAPTER
TWENTY-FOUR

The meeting was held in a warehouse in Alexandria, a suburb four kilometres south of Sydney's CBD. The area had been gentrified, and property was expensive, suggesting that the Sydney chapter of Australian Resistance was not short of money. The warehouse was divided into three: a large meeting area, a smaller area for equipment and storage, and an office with adjacent toilets and a shower. The roof was insulated, and air-conditioning had been installed. It was clearly the group's HQ.

Some thirty chairs had been placed in a circle. Twenty or so were already occupied. David indicated two seats for Sue and Julia and then sat down next to Sue.

'We'll wait a few minutes,' he said quietly. 'There's always a few stragglers.'

When only three seats were still vacant, a tall, blonde, well-built man got to his feet.

'That's Albrecht, the Zug Fuhrer,' David whispered in Sue's ear. 'He used to be Albert.'

'Guten Abend. First, I want to welcome two new members. Julia and Sue, please stand up.'

They did so to a round of applause.

'Sue is the blonde one,' Albrecht continued. 'Let's all introduce ourselves, although if they're anything like me, they won't remember half our names.' There was a ripple of laughter.

As the names were revealed, Julia studied those around her, nearly all in their twenties or early thirties. There were four other women.

'I have some good news,' the Zug Fuhrer continued. 'We've attracted some new sponsors, and our financial situation has become even stronger. We owe this to Brigitte, who has done amazing work as an influencer on the social media. She sells our image in a way that offers both hope and security. At the latest count, Brigitte has over one hundred thousand followers on TikTok, and nearly sixty thousand on Instagram. Take a bow, Brigitte.'

A petite, pretty, brown-haired woman stood up to rapturous applause. She looked to be in her late thirties or early forties, perhaps the oldest in the group.

'Now I'll ask the planning sub-committee to report.'

The leader of the sub-committee, Karl, was a stocky black-haired man in his mid-twenties. He stood briefly, then spoke while seated

'You'll remember when we destroyed the Adass Israel synagogue in Melbourne back in December 2024. Burning it almost to the ground was one of our greatest victories against the chosen people, but this victory created big problems for us. The Government greatly increased security around synagogues and for Kikes generally. We haven't been able to repeat such an attack. Our demo's have been a disaster, with the Feds stitching us up with lies and false accusations. We've been restricted to posters and stickers. Not to downplay Brigitte's brilliant work in fund-raising and propaganda.

So, we've done some lateral thinking, both figuratively and literally. There are three synagogues in Adelaide. One of them is the Chabad. We think we can do to it what we did to the Adass Israel. Maybe do it better. Maybe burn it to the ground. We haven't done any detailed planning, and we won't start until you've given us some feedback.'

David immediately rose to his feet. 'It's a brilliant idea, but Australian Resistance hasn't got a physical base in Adelaide, although we've got quite a few members there. We'll have to move a team over. This in itself will take a lot of planning, especially to keep the project under the Feds' radar. Only when the team's in place can we start detailed planning. All this could take weeks, even months. Can we justify using our precious resources for such a remote and risky project?'

'We won't need to send a big team over,' Karl responded. 'Four will be enough, and accommodation isn't a problem. I've already had offers from several of our members in Adelaide.'

'How much did you tell them?' asked Albrecht. 'If the slightest hint of our plan gets out, we're fucked.'

'I'm aware of the need for absolute secrecy. I gave nothing away. I know that not a word can be spoken about any of this outside our circle. But we're ahead of ourselves. We need the whole group's support before we can go forward.'

There were more comments and questions. When no one else raised their hand, Albrecht said 'Ok. Let's vote. For?'

Everyone in the group raised an arm. There was no further business. Albrecht closed the meeting, inviting everyone to stay for drinks and snacks.

Sue and Julia were able to exchange a few words before lining up at the drinks table.

'Already a dilemma,' said Julia. 'We should alert the Feds, but as newbies we'll be prime suspects.'

'Agreed. We'll just have to wait. The whole thing may just stay an idea.'

'David fancies you, Sue. Both of you are blonde and blue eyed. I'll bet he has fantasies about fucking you stupid and having lots of beautiful Aryan offspring.'

'Yuck. He's a handsome creature, I'll admit, but I won't let him touch me with a barge pole.'

'He's near the top of the local hierarchy. If you play along you might get some inside info.'

'That's a point. I prostituted myself in the money laundering case. I can do it again if I have to.'

David made an effort to introduce them to as many people as possible. They were surprised at the warmth of the greetings, especially when embraced by two of the women. The last few members were ready to leave just before ten thirty. Julia and Sue left with them

Assuming that they'd be expected to offer hospitality, the two women had arranged Julia's apartment to look like a shared dwelling. It was obviously impossible for Sue to invite members back to HQ, where she now lived.

The fake documents that had secured their entry to AR membership had included their employment records. Julia was a stenographer. Her typing skills were good enough to back that up. Sue was a waitress in a café, a role with which she was, of course, very familiar.

Both Sue and Julia were tasked with placing posters and stickers. They were expected to recruit, but to do this very cautiously and carefully. Julia was asked to type AR documents after work once a week or so. She did this with enthusiasm, in the hope of gleaning inside information. Sue was asked to help with setting up drinks and snacks for the social gatherings that were usually held after the formal meetings.

As time passed, they could not avoid becoming involved in the group's social activities, which were frequent and intense. The group's leaders were very conscious of the need to ensure its members' commitment to Neo-Nazi ideology, and they mixed this into the social events that they organised. Aside from these gatherings, there was an overwhelming need among group members for shared companionship. Sue and Julia were embraced, and this embrace demanded that they entertain group members at their shared apartment. Although revealing their address increased their vulnerability, they played host with as much enthusiasm and enjoyment as they could muster.

The plan to destroy the Chabad synagogue in Adelaide was given top priority. Only six weeks after Sue and Julia had joined the group, the four-man team had established itself in Adelaide and created a plan of action. The attack was to be launched two weeks later. Sue and Julia knew that they had to alert the authorities. They knew also that this would expose their duplicity or at least make them prime suspects. This dilemma caused much anxiety among the rest of the team. Fred was so concerned about the safety of the two women that he insisted they come to HQ where he would upgrade the tracking devices that were currently hidden in their clothing.

Julia and Sue had avoided going to HQ throughout their time with Australian Resistance in case they were observed by chance or followed deliberately, but they yielded to Fred's concerns.

'If they kidnap you or otherwise put you in danger, they'll probably humiliate you with strip searches and replace your clothing, so your trackers will be compromised. I'm going to implant a tracker into the upper arm of each of you. They're our latest model and are self-charging. Once in, they work indefinitely. The implant technique itself is simple and reliable. You'll hardly feel a thing.'

Reluctantly, Sue had entered a sexual relationship with David. Within the culture of Australian Resistance, it was assumed that women would willingly agree to have sex with men in the group, especially those of high status. Using her NIDA training, Sue had feigned adoration of David and used the intimacy between them to subtly extract crucial information. In this way, she discovered the exact date for the synagogue attack. She also learned that the AR team was based close to the synagogue. Five days before the planned attack, Sue contacted Fred, who alerted his government contact. Close surveillance of the synagogue and the surrounding area led to the arrest of the AR team and the impounding of their equipment.

Sue and Julia knew that if they ceased attending AR meetings, their duplicity would be obvious. So they went to the next one. After the chaotic reaction to the news of the Adelaide team's betrayal, Albrecht demanded silence.

'Someone has betrayed us. Someone here. We think we know who. I'm going to close the meeting. I want you all to leave immediately.'

As Sue and Julia moved towards the exit, four men surrounded them. They were taken to the office where David joined them.

'I became suspicious Sue, after you kept asking me for information about the synagogue operation. When you and Julia left together, you were followed. We're good at that stuff. When you entered that basement, we were pretty sure it was your operational centre. We tried to access it but it's too well protected. We watched and waited. We know who you're working with. So, here's the plan. We'll take you both to a very secure location, and we'll ask Fred — yes, we know about him — for five million dollars for your safe return. We're pretty sure he has the money. If not, he'll just have to find it.'

CHAPTER
TWENTY-FIVE

As soon as Fred got the ransom demand, he contacted George and Ahmad. They were both at home as things had been fairly quiet while they waited for news from Sue and Julia.

'Please get round as soon as possible. It's an emergency.'

'Are they in real danger?' asked Ahmad after Fred had sat them down and told them the news.

'Yes. We know that the Melbourne chapter of Australian Resistance has already killed an undercover agent. The Sydney group will kill Sue and Julia if they think they have to.'

'We've got the money,' said George, 'Why don't we pay the five million?'

'These people are utterly ruthless. They'll do anything to achieve their goals. They won't stop at five million. If we pay it, they'll ask for more. And more after that. When we can't pay any more, they won't release the girls: they know too much. We'll never see them again.'

'Perhaps you're right,' said Ahmad, 'but I think we should pay the money and see what happens. Unless we can think of something else.'

Before Fred could respond, Fred got a message on his phone.

'It's them. They've given us a deadline. We have to transfer the funds to an offshore account within twelve hours, or the deal is off. They've given us enough time to put the money together. There's no time for anything else.'

'What about the Feds?' Asked George. 'Can you ask your government contact to get them involved?'

'Too risky. The exposure of the undercover agent told us that AR probably have an informant within the Federal police or ASIO. There's a chance that AR will be informed of any involvement of the Federal Police.'

'How quickly can you organise the money?' asked Ahmad.

'Almost immediately. I just have to move it to a different account.'

'So, we've got nearly twelve hours before the deadline. Time to check their location. Thank God you implanted the trackers.'

The trackers showed that both women were in the same place: Matraville, a suburb just inland from Port Botany, making it about nine kilometres south of Sydney's CBD.

'A clever location,' said George, 'heavily industrialised and busy with traffic to and from the port. Lots of development. Easy to find a small warehouse or a secluded house. A place where no questions would be asked about comings and goings. Let's check it out. That'll help us plan our next move.'

Matraville was, like many Sydney suburbs, being gentrified. The trackers pinpointed a pre-war house on the edge of a large redevelopment zone. There were no neighbouring dwellings. Even though darkness had fallen, they were fearful of detection. They studied the house from a distance, using powerful thermal binoculars

'I can see several closed-circuit cameras,' said George. 'They may have used the house before. We have to assume they've turned it into a fortress. Let's take our time photographing it from all angles. We might find a way in.'

Back at HQ, Fred transferred the five million an hour before the deadline. A response was immediate.

'We've received the money, but we forgot to tell you something. The five million was for Sue. We need another five for Julia.'

The message included a return phone number which Fred rang at once. He knew he had to stay calm.

'You've more than cleaned me out. I had to borrow to raise the five million.'

'If you want to see the girls again, you'll get the cash. We understand that this might take a while, whether you steal it or borrow it. So there's no deadline, but we'll expect regular progress reports.'

'Before we go any further, I want proof of life. Let me speak to Sue and Julia.'

Sue was put on the line

'So far, we've been treated quite well. I was frightened that David would punish me for betraying him, but he seems to have forgiven me. He's not here but ....'

The call was interrupted by a curt male voice.

'That's enough. Let Julia speak.'

'They've taken our clothes and put us in smocks. If we did manage to escape, we'd look ridiculous. But as Sue said, we've been treated okay so far.'

The male voice returned.

'You've got your proof of life. Don't forget to keep us informed about your fund-raising activities.' The call ended.

'I'll create a fictitious narrative about our fund-raising. We still have about twelve million, so we can pay the five if we must. But they'll go on asking for more. We just have to rescue the girls. I can spread out our fund-raising activities for days without raising suspicion, so we've got time to work out a plan. Let's start by setting up an observation post that can't be detected.'

The site renovation was proceeding slowly and was focussed on an area about four hundred metres from AR's safe house. There was a half-demolished warehouse about seventy metres away from the house. Under cover of darkness, the three men explored it. There was a small cellar, still dry. The following night, they put their equipment into it, with food, drinks, a blow-up mattress and a camp chair. This took several hours as their car was hidden behind the remains of a building over one hundred metres distant. One of them was to observe AR's safe house at all times.

'We'll have to minimise our comings and goings,' said George. 'We could be spotted, even at night. I suggest twelve-hour shifts, including one overnight. Put me down for the first one, starting at eight o'clock this evening.'

'I'll do the next shift,' said Ahmad. 'I'll arrive at seven-thirty to give time for a debrief, although you'll have told us if anything important happened.'

George sat in the camp chair. He'd placed it on a small platform, allowing him to see through one of the warehouse's windows, long empty of glass. He'd taken a Modafinil tablet, a mild stimulant designed for the treatment of narcolepsy but easily obtained without a script. It kept him wide awake, and slightly euphoric. Lights were on in the safe house, but drawn blinds and curtains made it impossible to see through the windows. The infrared technology of his thermal binoculars enabled him to detect movement within the house. Prolonged observation told him there were five people present. There was no way of picking out the two hostages. He detected no comings or goings.

Ahmad saw a lot of activity during his tour of duty. There was a double garage attached to the house, and all vehicles were driven straight into it. He counted two arrivals and one departure. The contents of the garage were half visible to him. One car was left inside at the time Ahmad handed over to Fred at seven thirty that evening. There had been no pedestrian activity.

Two days and nights of observation had enabled the vehicles to be photographed with enough definition to capture their number plates. Once these data had been obtained, it was decided that no further routine observation was needed.

'We know there's absolutely no way of getting into the safe house without being detected,' said Ahmad, 'but what if we hijack one of their cars? Get into the garage. Do whatever's necessary to rescue the girls.'

'Brilliant!' said George and Fred together. 'We know,' said Fred, 'that AR moved its HQ after the arrest and interrogation of its Adelaide team. But we haven't found its new one. We'll have to follow one of their cars back to their new HQ. They'll be alert for anything unusual, so we need to be very careful. I suggest we use two cars, swapping them strategically. As back up, we can fire an adhesive tracker onto one of the car's wheels, where it'll be almost invisible. They may not use the same route each time, so we'll have to keep following them until we can pinpoint the ideal place for an ambush.'

'We'll have to be armed,' said Fred. 'I've got a revolver and silencer tucked away. I can get two more with silencers from my hacker's network. I won't have any problem using mine. What about you two?'

'I won't hesitate to shoot,' George replied. 'To kill or injure. I know how to use a revolver.'

'You'll have to show me how to use one,' said Ahmad. 'Once I know, I'm willing to shoot any one of these evil bastards.'

It took them three days to decide on the ambush point. Only two cars visited the safe house regularly, and each followed a slightly different route.

'We'll target the black 4WD,' said Fred, 'use road spikes to stop it.'

The ambush point was on a little used road between a derelict warehouse on one side and a small factory on the other. The factory was being renovated.

'If anyone's in the factory, we'll have to make sure we don't injure them. Our whole operation will be over before anyone can raise the alarm.'

They knew that the target vehicle usually left AR's HQ at around noon. At eleven, Fred positioned himself on one side of the road, George and

Ahmad on the other. There was no sign of life in the factory.

The target vehicle came down the road on schedule. It screeched to a halt after the road spikes had torn into its tyres. To ensure they didn't shoot each other, the three men stood at different angles from the car. They all fired at its windows, rushing forward. Two men were inside, both bleeding heavily from wounds in head, neck and shoulders. They pulled them out. Neither was going to raise the alarm. Quickly they moved the two bodies inside the derelict warehouse.

Using the remote that they knew was inside the 4WD, they raised the door of the double garage and drove in. Guns drawn, they entered the house. They found themselves in a short corridor, at the end of which a young man started walking towards them. He stopped short. Before he could raise the alarm, Fred hit him hard on the side of the head with his revolver. The man collapsed unconscious to the floor.

'There'll be two more,' said Fred, 'Let's find them.'

The other two, both men, were sitting at a table in the kitchen-dining area. They had a light lunch before them.. One of them reached instinctively inside his jacket. Fred shot him twice. He fell face down on the table. The other man raised his hands.

'Take us to the women,' said George, 'and no funny business.'

The man led them upstairs and opened a door off a corridor. Inside were Julia and Sue. Overjoyed, they rushed towards their rescuers and embraced them. The noise of the greeting almost obscured the gunshot. George felt a hard blow on his shoulder just as Fred shot the man who had fired. In the excitement of the rescue, they had not checked him for weapons. He dropped his gun and sank to the floor. Fred kicked the gun away.

George was sitting on one of the two single beds, blood seeping through his jacket at the right shoulder. Julia's joy turned to fear and panic. She carefully removed George's jacket and shirt.

'You're lucky George,' she said, 'it's only a flesh wound. The bullet's gone right through. We just have to stop the bleeding.'

'I'll check on the man Fred knocked out,' said Ahmad. 'Meet me there when you've sorted things out.'

His expression told that the others that he was on the point of fainting or vomiting. He needed a moment's respite.

The man shot by Fred was semi-conscious, bleeding from a chest wound. Julia insisted that they lift him onto one of the beds. She was about to examine him when Fred said. 'Julia, we don't have time for this. Leave him.'

Ahmad was standing over the still unconscious young man when the rest of the team came down the corridor towards him. The bleeding from George's wound had been staunched with a towel and strips of torn bedding. He was able to walk unaided.

'Shall we just leave this guy?' asked Ahmad.

'Why not,' Fred replied, 'he can't tell them anything they won't work out for themselves.'

'Just a minute,' said George, 'Let's take him with us. We can ransom him for the return of our five million. There's plenty of room in the Toyota.'

The young man regained consciousness on the journey back to HQ. They tied his legs to a chair, leaving his hands free. Julia rebandaged George's shoulder using one of HQ's first aid kits. The wound had stopped bleeding.

'Take these,' said Julia. 'I found them in the fridge. Amoxicillin. They haven't expired. Take one three times a day to guard against infection. No need to go to hospital, so no awkward questions.'

Sue approached the young man. 'Are you worth five million dollars?'

'What the fuck do you mean, bitch?

'Swearing at me won't help you. Where do you fit into Australian Resistance?'

'Fuck off.'

Fred forced the barrel of his revolver into the young man's mouth.

'I've killed one of your group. Maybe two. I'll kill you if you don't get some manners and start talking.'

Fred removed the gun barrel. 'What's your name?'

'Alex. I'm part of the planning sub-group.'

'So, you're of some value. You will call Albrecht right now and tell him we'll release you unharmed as soon as he repays the five million we sent him.'

To everyone's surprise, Albrecht agreed to the deal at once, but he added a caveat:

'We have to come to an understanding. The Feds don't know the location of our HQ. If you agree not to tell them, I'll take you off our hit list. Is that a deal?'

'Give us a moment to discuss it,' said Fred. 'Hold the line.'

'We went into this to protect ourselves. Any benefit to the Feds is secondary. We owe them nothing. Let's make the deal.'

The rest of the team quickly agreed.

Albrecht transferred the five million later that day. Alex was dropped off at AR's HQ.

Back at their own HQ, the team speculated about Albrecht's rapid agreement to the deal.

'Perhaps he and Alex are lovers,' Julia quipped, raising laughter.

'That's not so far-fetched,' said George. 'We know there was a lot of homosexuality in Hitler's SS and other paramilitary groups. If it was a way of bonding, it might be a part of AR's culture. But strictly in the closet. Not that it concerns us. We've finished the job. Albrecht will stick to our agreement. He knows we'll inform the Feds of his location if he doesn't.'

'How are you feeling Fred?' asked Sue. 'You may have killed two men.'

'You all know that I killed one man, maybe two, during the Nevada organ harvesting gig. I said then that I had no choice. It was the same this time. I feel some guilt, to be honest, but I don't agonise. It's behind me. But I know I'll do it again if I have to.'

'And you, Ahmad?' asked Julia.

'When George was wounded and Fred shot the man who did it, I almost lost it. That's why I left. I used the excuse of checking on the man Fred knocked out. But I pulled myself together. By the time you all came down, I was ready to do whatever was necessary. I'm okay now, I really am.'

'You'll know exactly what I'm going to say,' said Julia, 'but I'll say it anyway. I know George was wounded, but the wound isn't serious and should heal quickly. The scar will add to his collection! Apart from that, we've had our usual extraordinary good luck. Thanks to the grace of God. I'm going to thank him in prayer. I'd love it if you joined me, but I'll totally understand if you don't.'

Julia knelt down, joined by George, Sue and Ahmad. She uttered a brief but poignant prayer of thanks.

'Amen to that,' said Fred, who had not joined them in prayer. This was his standard response to Julia's invocation of the divine. But this time, his usual cynicism was entirely absent. Julia noticed this change of tune.

'We'll wait for your conversion Fred,' she joked. 'We have all the time in the world.'

CHAPTER TWENTY-SIX

'Last night,' said Ahmad at the start of the next team meeting, 'I got a call from my aunt Kirina. You'll remember her from our work in Jakarta on the people smugglers.'

'Of course,' replied Sue, 'without her we couldn't have completed the job. We were worried that she might be exposed to harmful repercussions. Is that what the call's about?'

'Not exactly. Since her involvement with us she's been concerned about the smuggling trade popping up elsewhere in Indonesia. As you all know, she's highly respected in Jakarta and well connected throughout the social and business networks. She's heard rumours of both women and men mysteriously disappearing from isolated and impoverished parts of Java. She started to look into this. but got text messages telling her to back off. Typically, she continued her investigations, but then two men came to her house and threatened to harm her if she continued her enquiries. That was enough to stop her, but she'd already learned of the likely source of the abductions: an organisation developing bioengineering to enhance human attributes. She knows it was established quite recently, but has no idea of its whereabouts, except that it's in Java.'

'So, this organisation is abducting people for bioengineering experiments,' said Julia. 'That sounds more like science fiction than science.'

'It's called transhumanism,' said George, 'and it's very real. I got interested in it during my work as a psychiatrist. It's moving into the mainstream. Jeff Bezos has invested hundreds of millions setting up his Altos Lab. His aim is to slow aging by rejuvenating cells using cellular reprogramming.'

'What's that exactly?' asked Fred.

'It all stems from a ground-breaking discovery called "clustered regularly interspersed short palindrome repeats". CRISPR for short. It's best thought of as molecular scissors. It can cut out any gene from the many thousands in the cell's genome. Its accuracy is very high. A later development called CRISPR-Cas9 can insert DNA into the cell to create new genes. This technology is less reliable than CRISPR alone, but it is being developed in many labs around the world.

Recently Chinese researchers used CRISPR to change the genetic structure of beagle embryos. Specifically, they knocked out the myostatin gene which inhibits the growth of skeletal muscle. This created beagles twice the size of non-modified ones. They can run and jump far faster and higher, and they are very healthy. These are super-beagles! Consider what the same technology could do for humans!'

'Why stop with myostatin?' asked Julia. 'Surely the CRISPR-Cas9 technology allows many more genes to be knocked out or modified.'

'You're talking about one of the hottest topics in the field,' George replied. 'Designer babies. We're not there yet, but soon the technology will allow the blockage, elimination, enhancement or replacement of a great many genes with recognised functions. Perhaps within five years or so, parents will be able to order a child with precise specifications. One, for example, with an Einstein IQ, great physical strength and endurance, and an almost invincible immune system. Only the very rich will be able to afford this, at least in its early years. Imagine the social upheaval that this technology will create if it is used by all who can afford it. The American Food and Drug Administration, a very powerful body, has described the technology as a huge threat to society at large.'

'Does the FDA's position mean that the technology is likely to be regulated, at least in America?' asked Sue.

'Very much so. The FDA has already banned the technology. Many countries have already introduced similar legislation. It's likely that the use of CRISPR-Cas9 technology will eventually be made illegal worldwide, except for eliminating harmful genes, or for ethical research. This means, of course, that organisations will be created to circumvent or flout the law. It's highly likely that this is the aim of the transhumanist set-up that is abducting men and women in Java.'

'Are there any other technologies that we should know about?' asked Ahmad.

'Absolutely,' replied George. 'Jeff Bezos isn't the only tech titan investing serious money in transhumanism. Elon Musk has created a programme called Neurolink. Its aim is to connect the human brain directly to phones and computers. The programme has already allowed the installation of a brain chip called Telepathy into several volunteers.

This enables them to control selected electronic devices just by thinking. The programme is designed to help people with various degrees of paralysis and locomotor malfunction. But will it stop there?

There is one more technology of importance. It's used not in embryos, but in adolescent or adult humans. Viruses are modified to make them harmless and allow them to enter specific cell types. Carefully designed fragments of DNA are attached to these viruses. These fragments enter the cell's genome and modify its structure. Theoretically this should create changes in the targeted organs that could otherwise be made only by altering the genetic structure of embryos. The technology is at a very early stage. Once it is fully developed, the implications are profound. Ordinary human beings could be endowed with attributes otherwise achievable only through working on embryos. Imagine the military value of soldiers with superhuman powers! I'm sure that the organisations we're trying to target will be deeply involved in this type of research. Oh, and these almost invincible soldiers will probably have infra-red vision, allowing them to see in the dark. This has already been achieved in experimental animals by injecting nanoparticles directly into their eyes.'

'Research into transhumanism,' said Sue, 'is attracting big money, perhaps even more than illegal organ harvesting and transplantation. I'm thinking of our work in Nevada. You'll recall that the illegal harvesting and transplanting operation was fronted by a legitimate rehab facility. Behind it, mostly buried in Mount Charleston, was where their real activities were carried out. This largely hidden structure was said to be for research into viruses, a fiction that kept people well away.

Now I'm going to be outrageously speculative. Java is very mountainous. We know that the transhumanist facility was established recently. Could it have been set up in the same way as the Mount Charleston operation? Fronted by a rehab clinic or a health farm and built into a mountain, disguised as a research facility.'

'Your speculation isn't so wild,' said Fred. 'Consider what the transhumanists would need to set themselves up, in Java or anywhere else. The first thing would be a supply of experimental subjects. They would search the dark web for an organisation with a track record of successful abductions. Top of the list would be the illegal organ harvesters. We know they were responsible for the mysterious disappearance of hundreds, perhaps thousands, of people over at least fifteen years.'

'Why the organ harvester?' asked Julia. 'Why not the people smugglers?'

'Because abductions are a relatively small part of the people smugglers trade, which relies mainly on false promises of a better life. Let's speculate. Suppose that the transhumanists approached the illegal organ harvesters on the dark web. Given that the harvesters are based in America, it's unlikely they could offer a service in Java. Instead, they would have offered to share their expertise. This could not be done on the dark web alone. The harvesters would have sent their own people to Java, to train some of the transhumanists to do their own abductions. As part of this, the organ harvesters would have described their Mount Charleston setup. The transhumanists realised that a similar setup would be perfect for them. The organ harvesters then sent another team over to help in the construction of the transhumanist base.'

'This is highly speculative,' said Ahmad. 'How can we test Fred's hypothesis?'

'We can start', said Julia', by looking for newly established rehab clinics or health farms in Java. If we find any, we can check their location. Those adjacent to mountainous terrain will justify further exploration.'

The team's research found four rehab clinics in Java, all of long standing. It discovered several health farms, including one that Ahmad already knew about because one of his Indonesian relatives had been there.

'It's called Amantjiwo,' he said excitedly, 'and it overlooks the famous Borobudur temple in central Java, the biggest Buddhist temple in the world. Oh, sorry if I got carried away.'

'Don't apologise,' said Sue. 'We understand your love for Indonesia, and your wish to share it with us.'

All except one of the health farms had been open for some time. The new one was located in the mountainous province of West Java, which was, said Ahmad, relatively unpopulated. Its web site showed it to be in a forest clearing at the foot of a steep upland. The forest was described as an attraction in itself, with an extraordinary biodiversity that included teak, oak, maple, ironwood, eucalyptus, juniper, banyan and rhododendron. Clients were assured of peace and quiet because the area had been relatively inaccessible and was not a tourist attraction or used for logging. A sealed road had been built to ensure ease of access. The farm was about sixty kilometres from Bandung, the provincial capital, and close to the small village of Wae Wae.

'A brilliant choice of location,' said Ahmad. 'Relatively isolated, but not far from major roads that support the local economy. There's agriculture, sheep and poultry farming, and quite extensive manufacturing, mostly in industrial precincts. Once we've pinpointed the farm's position, we can view it on google maps.'

The team agreed to let Ahmad contact the health farm directly, ostensibly to check on availability, but in reality, to determine its exact location. Google maps confirmed that it was built at the base of a steep upland. Immediately behind it was a structure that extended into the upland. It was impossible to know the size of this subterranean extension.

'Well, Sue,' said Fred, 'it looks as if your outrageous speculation was spot on. I think we can be fairly sure that we've found the transhumanist's base. Now we've got to decide what to do next.'

'We have to go there,' said Ahmad. 'It's the only way of confirming that it's our target. If it is, we'll need time to study it and create a plan of action. There are plenty of vacancies in the health farm, perhaps because it's so new.

We must think carefully about how we book,' continued Ahmad. 'Let's assume we all arrive together. Anything else would be too messy. I suggest we explain to the health farm that although we are friends, we need separate accommodation. There's a choice: an eco-tent, a cabin, or an apartment in a small block. The eco-tents and most of the cabins are designed for two people. We can book one eco-tent for George and Julia, one for me and Sue, and another for Fred.'

Fred turned red and looked very uncomfortable, but Sue spoke before he could say anything.

'Fred, I know you've been wondering about Ahmad and me. We're not in a relationship, although we'd be in one if it didn't compromise the integrity of the team. And that won't change while we're sharing an eco-tent. Or any time soon.'

'Thanks for explaining that,' said Julia, 'George and I had also been wondering. We're much the same. As you know, we had a sexual relationship that we agreed to stop. Since then, nothing changed until quite recently. We're not in a sexual relationship, but our mutual physical attraction has been rekindled. Rest assured though, that there will be no sex in the eco-tent, or for as long as we all work together as one.'

Fred's equilibrium had been restored. 'You all know that I fancy Sue. I've pretty well come to terms with the situation, although there are moments when my feelings leak out. But they won't ever get in the way of our work together. Let's go ahead with the bookings.'

CHAPTER
TWENTY-SEVEN

The booking was made for three days later. From Sydney, the team flew direct to Jakarta. Ahmad wanted to visit his aunt Karina, and so the team decided to stay two nights before flying to Bandung airport, where they had booked a 4WD for the sixty kilometres to the health farm.

By late evening they had settled into a three-bed apartment near Jakarta's city centre. They arranged for pizzas to be delivered and went to bed straight after eating them.

'I'll go and see Aunt Karina right away,' said Ahmad at breakfast the next morning. 'I know she'd love to see you all, but I want to spend time with her alone. I'm still worried about her safety, and she's more likely to be honest about how she's feeling if it's just me. You can join us in the afternoon.'

'That works for me,' said Fred. "I've got a lot to do. We'll need to be prepared for anything when we get to the health farm, so I want to buy a gun. I can't risk taking it on the flight to Bandung, so I'll arrange to pick it up after we arrive. There'll be English speakers on the local hacker's network, and I've learned some Indonesian. If I get stuck, I'll ask you to help me, Ahmad.'

'There's a lot to see in Jakarta,' said Julia. 'Why don't Sue, George and I do some sightseeing? Ahmad, will you phone me when it's okay for us to visit Karina?'

'No problem. Now I must go.'

Ahmad spent the whole day with Karina. By the time he got back to the apartment, the rest of the team were there.

'Aunt Karina's a tough cookie,' said Ahmad, 'but the threats to harm her have taken their toll. She has bronchitis and is quite unwell. I was with her all day because she needed help with quite a few things, both domestic and business, and she had to sleep for two hours after lunch. Sadly, she didn't feel well enough to see you all, but she sends her love.'

'Perhaps we can see her on the return journey,' Sue suggested. 'let's hope she's feeling better by then.'

Mid-morning the next day the team boarded a Garuda Indonesia jet for the forty-five-minute flight to Husan Sastrenegard airport, just eight kilometres from Bandung's city centre. They all had International Driving Permits, but Julia took the wheel of the 4WD. The gun had to be collected from a car park on the city's outskirts. The vendor would be waiting in a blue Honda Civic hatchback. The transaction went smoothly, and Fred pocketed a Sig Sauer P938 micro-compact pistol, together with a small box of rounds.

The sixty-kilometre drive to the health farm took just over an hour, and they arrived at a quarter to two. The last two or three kilometres had been gently uphill.

'I know we grumbled about paying seventeen thousand dollars each for two weeks,' said Ahmad, 'But just look at this place!'

The google maps image of the health farm had been partly obscured by forest cover, so they saw its full extent for the first time. As they followed signs to reception, they saw a thirty-metre swimming pool at the edge of a large central area. This circular space was obviously designed for big gatherings. It was occupied by many chairs and couches, placed strategically around a central fountain. There was retractable roofing.

'That fountain's a bit over the top,' exclaimed Sue, as she gazed at the three-meter-high structure. Water gushed from the mouths of two intertwined figures, a man and a woman, their embrace falling just short of an overtly sexual one.

'I rather like it,' said Fred, 'Perhaps,' he added hopefully, 'It's a sign of things to come.'

After checking in, they were led by Nina, an attractive young Indonesian woman, into the surrounding tropical forest. She took them to an eco-tent.

'This one's for Julia and George,' she said in good English. 'Forgive my use of Christian names, but we are very informal here.'

She pointed to an adjacent eco-tent.

'That's for Sue and Ahmad., and the one just over there is for Fred. We have a total of twenty-three eco-tents, and ten cabins for those who prefer them. There's also a small apartment block behind reception. The number of guests is a maximum of eighty, though at present there are only about sixty. Our guest to staff ratio is about two to one when we're full, so you'll be well looked after.'

'So, we're talking around forty staff,' said Ahmad. 'How many live on site?'

'All of us. It's a condition of employment. We have our own apartments in blocks a little deeper in the forest, well out of sight. Most of us think of our employment here as a privilege. This may sound trivial, but we don't talk about our centre as a health farm. We call it a wellness retreat. Oh, they're bringing your luggage over now. I'll leave you to settle in.'

'Hold on a mo,' said Gorge. 'What about mosquitoes?'

'Because we're about three hundred metres above sea level, they're not a huge problem You'll notice mosquito repellent plants in tubs and strategically placed electronic deterrents. We don't have malaria here. If you're worried about being bitten, we have an excellent lotion that repels for up to six hours. It's not strictly necessary in the centre itself, but I suggest you apply it if you go deeper into the forest. We also have an excellent sunscreen which we recommend if you spend any time out-of-doors.'

All their baggage had been delivered, and so Nina excused herself once again.

'I feel slightly patronised,' said Fred. 'All that lotion stuff is just common sense. It didn't need micromanagement.'

'Perhaps it was Nina's way of telling us how much the centre cares about our wellbeing,' said Sue. 'Anyway, let's explore our tents.'

They started with the one allocated to Julia and George. The canvas covered structure was supported by bamboo poles. It had a high ceiling and transparent panels set into the walls. These could be curtained at night. In one corner was a queen size bed next to a small wardrobe. A lounge was set against the opposite wall, and there were three bamboo chairs. A bench on the inner wall had a small wash basin and an expensive looking coffee machine. Underneath was a small fridge. Through a heavy curtain were a toilet and shower. When the entrance was closed, the tent would be fully mosquito proof.

'No TV,' said Sue. 'I'll miss Antiques Road Show, but a TV detox will be good for me.'

'Interesting that there's been no mention of a digital detox,' said George, 'They haven't confiscated our smart phones. I wouldn't let them anyway.'

The two other eco-tents were virtually identical. The team was about to walk up to the registration office when Nina reappeared.

'Are you ready for a tour? There's a lot to see and quite a few things to explain. You'll notice as we walk that the centre is built on a natural plateau. When the buildings were constructed, soil dug out for the foundations was spread out to create a level surface and for flower beds and grassed areas. We are careful with water use, but there's a huge artesian basin deep underneath. Rainfall is very heavy during the monsoon season, which keeps the basin topped up, so we extract as much as we need without causing any problems. And we're connected to the electricity mains, although we have generators for back up. The mains supply isn't the most reliable.'

'Your landscaping is breathtakingly beautiful,' said Ahmad. 'You've been here for only three or so years, yet some of the trees are already quite tall. Everything's so well looked after. You must have a small fleet of gardeners!'

'For us, the environment is crucial. It's the context in which personal healing and development take place.'

The tour took nearly an hour. The spa had a plunge pool and a steam room. There was even an oxygen booth. A room was dedicated to mud baths. Another was used as a sound bath which, Nina explained, was a meditation experience where guests lie down while immersed in the soothing sounds of singing bowls, gongs, chimes, and other instruments.

'This,' Nina continued, 'promotes deep relaxation, reduces stress and anxiety, and balances energy in the body.'

The next room was large, and used for Tai Chi, breathwork, Pilates, Qigong and dance fitness.

'Qigong?' asked Fred.

'It's a Chinese practice that combines movement, meditation and breath control to enhance and balance energy within the body. It's been used for thousands of years.'

There was a large, well-equipped gym, and several smaller rooms for massage and individual treatments.

Nina then handed them over to the dietitian, an Indonesian woman in her thirties.

'Let's go to the dining area.,' she suggested, 'you're probably a bit hungry by now. It's nearly five.'

The dining area was large enough to house the full complement of eighty guests. It was slightly elevated, giving views of the centre and the adjacent forest. There was only a handful of other guests: the evening meal would not start until six.

'We don't grow our own food,' the dietitian explained, 'unlike some wellness centres. That's partly because local agriculture produces just about all we need, and we'd have to clear more of the forest, which we absolutely don't want. My regime isn't strict. I have a vegetarian bias but there's plenty of meat on the menu. Our chefs are all highly skilled. You won't be disappointed. Guests serve themselves from the tables over there. There's plenty of variety, and always some fresh fruit. But now, just a little snack.'

The final meeting of the day was with the Therapeutic Programme Manager, an American woman named Joan who looked to be in her early forties. Ahmad established that she spoke good Indonesian.

'I'll want to meet with you all one-to-one, to work out a programme. Here's a booklet outlining what we offer. I suggest we arrange the meetings for tomorrow morning, starting at nine. I'll need about half an hour with each of you. Is there anything you want to know before then?'

'Yes,' said Ahmad. 'It's not connected with your programme though. We've been wondering about the fenced-off structure immediately behind the centre. There's just a front wall and entrance door visible, but we assume the structure goes into the upland behind.'

'It's entirely separate from the wellness retreat. I confess we don't mention it unless we're asked. We've been told it's for research into viruses and other pathogens. There's another entrance accessed by a sealed road. We keep well away!'

'So will we!' Ahmad exclaimed. 'Don't worry about that. I'll see you at nine tomorrow. The others will follow every half an hour.'

The team gathered in Fred's tent.

'How seriously do we take our programmes?' he asked.

'Seriously enough to avoid suspicion,' Ahmad replied. 'We can be sure the transhumanists have planted a spy or two in the centre to watch out for anyone who seems more interested in what's behind it than the centre itself. But we don't all have to engage at the same level. I used to work hard at keeping fit, but I've lapsed badly since I joined you. There just hasn't been time. So, I'm going to take it seriously, with an emphasis on physical fitness.'

'I feel exactly the same,' said George.

'We're ahead of ourselves,' Fred continued. 'Let's not forget that we're here to find out as much as we can about the transhumanists' base. We know there's a separate entrance, and we need to monitor comings and goings. I suggest we work out a roster that has one of us hidden by the side of the access road for at least four hours a day.'

'Makes sense,' said Julia, 'There's twelve days left, assuming the last day will be occupied with packing and making any final arrangements. If we all do two shifts, two of us will have to do three. I volunteer for one of the extras.'

'I'll do three as well,' said Fred. 'When we plan our programmes with Joan, we have to build in enough flexibility to accommodate our tours of duty. I suggest we roster morning and afternoon shifts on alternate days. Now, Sue and Julia, what sort of programme do you have in mind?'

'For me,' Julia replied, 'it'll be the least that's credible. I really need to rest. You all know how much I've been through. I've made myself keep going, but I'm hanging by a thread.'

'At NIDA,' said Sue, 'we were encouraged to keep fit, but like Ahmad and George, I've totally lapsed, so I want some emphasis on physical fitness. But I also want to learn about techniques that enhance mental strength and wellbeing. Techniques that I can take away with me.'

'I've never worried much about keeping fit,' said Fred, 'But I've got the beginnings of a paunch, which at my age is a bit gross. So I'll focus on physical fitness. Maybe a bit of mental stuff as well.'

At an early lunch the next day, the team compared programmes. Joan had been quite strict, insisting that an emphasis on physical fitness should include attention to mental wellbeing.

'The mind-body connection is paramount,' she preached. 'We ignore that connection at our peril.'

That meant the three men would do Qigong, Yoga and Tai Chi between vigorous gym sessions. Recovery from these would be aided by twenty minutes in the oxygen booth. Twice daily steam baths were necessary to eliminate toxins.

Sue's programme included some gym work, with twice daily steam baths, a daily mud bath, and a one-hour massage. As well as Qigong, Yoga and Tai-Chi, she would be taught additional meditation techniques and would spend time in the sound bath. There was no gym work in Julia's programme, which was otherwise similar to Sue's, though more flexible. At two, Julia left for her first tour of duty without arousing suspicion.

CHAPTER
TWENTY-EIGHT

Julia, wearing dark clothing, had found an observation point about half a kilometre away from the entrance to the transhumanists' base, which she observed through thermal binoculars. The entrance was guarded by massive steel doors, high and wide enough to admit the largest vehicles.

She was settled into a small depression screened by a robust rhododendron bush, a high-definition camera at hand. An hour or so into her stint, a white delivery van passed in the direction of the base. Another passed in the same direction an hour later. She snapped them, as she would all passing vehicles. About forty minutes before the end of her four hours, a third van passed in the opposite direction. There had been no more traffic by the time she'd left her hidey-hole and returned to the retreat. In Fred's tent, she screened the photos she'd taken. Ahmad downloaded the images of the delivery vans.

'Two different makes. One of those going out is a Renault Master Pro LWB, and the other is a Fiat Professional Ducato, also LWB, standing for 'long wheel base'. The one going down was a Renault. Both makes are very sturdy and reliable, with plenty of storage space. I assume they were delivering food and other supplies, and perhaps experimental subjects.'

The team had survived their programmes without mishap, except for Sue.

'My masseuse found that I was badly constipated. She urged me to have a colonic lavage, claiming expertise in the procedure. I yielded but wish I hadn't. She took me to an adjacent room, where I noticed an old-fashioned squat toilet set into the floor. She lay me face down on a mattress and stuck a tube up my bum. Then she poured in this herb-infused warm liquid. I had to lie there for a few moments while the herbs did their work. She helped me over to the squat toilet. There was an explosion, and I felt like my guts were falling out. The toilet overflowed. The smell was ghastly. After a shower, I confess I felt really good. But never again! From now on, lots of fibre will be on the menu.'

After the laughter subsided, the team planned for the next day.

'I'll excuse myself from the first half of my programme,' said Fred, 'and do the morning shift. I'll fire a tracker into a tyre of all the vehicles that pass. Later, we can follow one down.'

Fred's plan worked as he'd hoped. That evening, the team studied the tracking data.

Of the four vans that had left the transhumanists' base, three went to the same destination. Google maps showed it to be a warehouse in an industrial precinct about three kilometres from Bandung's city centre. The fourth van went to the city's outskirts, where the team viewed a large shed in a field at the edge of a small farm.

The next morning, Julia parked their 4WD off the sealed road and waited for a van to leave the transhumanists' base. She'd been chosen for this task because the flexible nature of her programme allowed her to be absent without suspicion. George had protested that it was far too dangerous, but Julia had firmly over-ruled him.

When one of the Fiat vans went by, Julia used the tracker on its tyre to follow it at a safe distance. When the van stopped at the steel door entrance to the warehouse in Bandung, she parked as closely as she could, training her thermal binoculars on the building. The steel door was raised and lowered so quickly that she only glimpsed the interior, which seemed unremarkable. She then walked around the warehouse, looking for windows and doors. There was one padlocked door in the back of the building, and several windows, all too high for access. There was evidence of a comprehensive security system, with several strategically placed closed-circuit TV cameras.

'I'd say it was impossible to get into the warehouse undetected,' Julia told the rest of the team that evening. Fred and Ahmad agreed after studying all the photos she'd taken.

'So, what next?' Julia asked.

'I think we should track one of their vans to that other destination,' said Ahmad. 'The shed in the field.'

The next morning, Fred and Ahmad claimed exhaustion as an excuse to avoid their programmes. They followed one of the Renault vans, which had two men inside, parking at a safe distance when the van reached the shed. There were enough trees and shrubs to hide their approach to the structure. The van had entered the shed, the door closing behind it. Ahmad and Fred heard a loud noise, which stopped suddenly. There were raised voices.

'It seems the machine, a crusher, has broken down again,' said Ahmad. 'They can't fix it themselves, and they can't wait for it to be repaired, because they're needed back at base.'

When the delivery van left, Fred and Ahmad studied the door to the shed. It was secured by a large padlock. Fred had come prepared. A device like a stethoscope magnified the sounds made by a skeleton key. The padlock was open in minutes. Inside the shed was a large commercial shredder, designed to make compost. The remains of a human body were stuck in the outlet.

They found two more bodies, both naked, partly hidden by a tarpaulin. Near them was a deep pit, clearly used to bury what was left of them. Ahmad retched when he pulled the tarpaulin back. Fred's face turned a shade of green. The men's bodies were covered in scars, ulcers, boils and pustules. Their eye sockets were empty. Wires protruded from grey matter exposed by large holes in their shaven skulls. More holes had been made in the bone just beneath their ears. The arms of both men had been amputated just above the elbow, and injuries to their upper vertebrae suggested that their spinal cords had been severed. After taking numerous photographs, Ahmad and Fred replaced the tarpaulin, locked the shed's door, and walked back to the 4WD.

That evening, the photos were shown to the rest of the team on Fred's screen. No-one actually vomited, but Sue retched repeatedly. It was some time before the team was ready to talk about the horrors they'd seen.

'Why dispose of the bodies there?' asked Julia. 'It's much riskier than doing it in the base.'

'Even transhumanists must have human sensibilities,' said George. 'From a psychological perspective, burying the bodies elsewhere may allow some of their unconscious guilt to be externalised.'

'Or', said Fred, 'they may use more experimental subjects than originally planned. Perhaps they just don't have room. But we don't need to speculate about this. We have to decide on a plan of action.'

'We could let the local police know about the shed. If they raid it while it's being used, they could interrogate whoever's there. Maybe get enough evidence to raid the base itself.'

'I'd strongly advise against that,' said Ahmad. 'The transhumanists will have connections to the police, and probably to the provincial government.

Exposing their activities is unlikely to yield any real action and may put us all in danger. These evil bastards must have almost unlimited funds. I haven't the slightest doubt that a big chunk of their profits is being used to bribe exactly the people who can stop any investigations.'

'We could get into their base by hijacking one of the delivery vans,' said Sue.

'What would that achieve?' Fred countered. 'They'd just grab us and probably use us as experimental subjects.'

Gloom descended, brought upon them by the realisation that they were powerless to prevent the almost unimaginable horrors that took place at the transhumanists' base. They all went to bed.

In Fred's tent the next morning, Julia said that she had something really important to tell them.

'You all know that George and I have been through a lot together, not only as part of the team, but well before that. We were lovers, and then just friends. But in the quiet moments that we have had in the tent, surrounded by the sounds of the forest, we reconnected. The strong sexual attraction that we once had has come back. We haven't yielded to it, of course, but the desire to do so gave me an idea.

We know that the transhumanists offer designer babies on their dark web site. I could contact them and say that my husband and I were desperate to have a designer baby. If they agree to take us on, we'll have to stay in their base. Once in, we might be able to do enough to bring them down. George is still thinking about all this.'

'I don't think Julia has thought it through enough,' George responded. 'During my time as a psychiatrist, I studied in vitro fertilisation. Let me explain what's involved, then we can have an informed discussion. First, Julia will take fertility drugs to stimulate her ovaries to produce mature eggs. These will be collected by inserting a needle into an ovary while she's under sedation. The healthiest eggs will be stored in a culture medium kept at body temperature.

While Julia is undergoing this, I will provide a sperm sample. The most active and healthy sperm will be added to a cytoprotectant so that it isn't damaged during storage in liquid nitrogen. Finally, the sperm will be unfrozen and inserted directly into the healthiest of Julia's eggs.

At the earliest stage of embryo development, while it's still a single cell, CRISPR-Cas9 will be used to modify its' genetic structure according to our wishes. When the embryo is sufficiently mature, it will be implanted into Julia's womb. She'll be prescribed hormones to support the lining of the womb and optimise the chances of the embryo's further growth. A pregnancy test after ten to twelve days will determine success or failure. If the test is positive, Julia will be allowed to leave the base.'

'When will Julia need to take the fertility drugs?' asked Sue.

'Early in the menstrual cycle. It takes up to twelve days for the ovarian follicles to reach the desired size. Then she'll be given what's called a trigger shot to make sure the eggs are fully mature before they're collected.'

'So, we're talking about a stay of at least a month,' said Sue.

'A bit longer if things don't go so smoothly. But the transhumanists may be able to arrange for Julia to take the fertility drugs before she enters the base, so she goes in only when a blood test confirms the follicles are sufficiently mature.'

'Actually George,' said Julia, 'I have thought things through. We're trying to destroy the transhumanists. That's what this is about. Once we're in their base, we'll have to start the in vitro procedure. But we can change our minds, stop the whole thing before the embryo's implanted. Insist on paying the full fee by way of compensation.'

'I stand corrected. But there's still one issue that we need to clarify. What if I want a child? A child with you.'

'I've always imagined myself childless,' Julia replied. 'Maternal instinct absent or suppressed, an exclusive focus on career. But things changed after my near-death experience. As you know, I've come to believe in a divine presence, an immortal being who looks after me, and by extension, all five of us. This being, which I hesitate to call God, spared my life. Saved me, I'm sure, for a purpose. I've struggled to understand what that purpose might be. Perhaps it is for me to have a child. For that, I'm now truly ready.'

'How strange,' said George. 'That it's taken a stay in a wellness retreat for Julia to realise all this. And for me to be certain that I want Julia's child.'

'Why do you think it's called a wellness retreat?' Sue quipped. 'What you call strange is the natural result of our efforts to blend in, to take part in the programmes.'

'We need to discuss all this as a team,' said Fred, 'but right now we must start our programmes. Do we need to continue monitoring the delivery vans' comings and goings?'

'I don't think so,' Ahmad replied. 'Let's focus on our programmes. We can't afford to raise the slightest suspicion of our true purpose here. And I need some time to digest all that I've heard this morning.'

That evening, the team gathered in Fred's tent.

'Here's how I see it,' he said. 'There's not a lot of danger in requesting a designer baby, or in the procedure itself. The danger lies in exploring the base. I'm sure the designer baby unit will be closed off from the experimental areas. We need to find out how these are accessed. If it's keypad entry, we need to discover the passwords. If cards are used, we must somehow copy one. I'll do one last shift tomorrow morning, get as close as I can to the base's entrance, and when it's opened for a vehicle, I'll take photos through the thermal binoculars. They might give us an answer.'

'Hold on a moment,' said Ahmad. 'We need the whole team to agree before going ahead. Sue?'

'I agree with Fred that the danger isn't in the designer baby programme, but in exploring the base. If it's too dangerous, George and Julia must not go ahead with it. On that basis, I support the project.'

'I support it on the same basis,' said Ahmad.

'That's all of us then,' said Fred. 'I'll screen the photos tomorrow evening.'

The photos showed that exits from the entry hall were controlled by keypads.

'I'm relieved,' said Fred. 'I was worried they might use retinal or iris scanners, although setting them up for a large number of people is very time-consuming. And retinal scanners, in particular, can be slow to work and are a bit unreliable. The transhumanists must be very confident about their overall security to rely on keypads.

After Julia and George have been accepted into the programme, I'll work on modifying our micro cameras so they can be used to capture the keypad entry codes. We have to assume that those in the designer baby programme will be allowed to keep their smart phones, although their messages will probably be monitored. But they won't be able to monitor the smart phones for anything else, including photography. If George and Julia are able to get into the research areas, they can photograph what they discover and safely save the images. With luck, they'll get enough material to reveal the full extent of what's being done. When they leave the base, I'll relay everything to my government contact. I assume he'll get

Interpol involved. We know the local police can't be trusted.'

'Let's establish a time frame,' said Ahmad.

'We can access the transhumanists' dark web site from here, but we'll route it through HQ, given that George and Julia are based in Sydney. When they apply to join the programme, there'll be a background check before they're accepted. We'll need to work on that. Everything should be ready within twenty-four hours or so.'

Early the day after next, the team assembled in Fred's tent. Ahmad told Julia and George that he and Fred had done everything they could to make sure their application was foolproof.

'If you're ready, we can send it now.'

'Let's do it,' said Julia. 'Put ourselves in the hands of God.'

CHAPTER TWENTY-NINE

Julia and George were accepted into the programme two days later.

'The fee,' George told the team, 'is four hundred thousand American dollars.'

'Less than a kidney transplant,' Sue quipped.

'Half the fee must be paid upfront, the rest only after a successful outcome. If a second attempt is agreed to, the balance of two hundred thousand covers it. They claim that so far, a third attempt has not been necessary.'

Julia spoke next.

'The fertility drugs have to be administered in the base itself, where progress can be monitored reliably. Because designer baby programmes are banned by the FDA and most other national health authorities, we've been told to observe the strictest secrecy. We can tell no one about the true purpose of our trip abroad. They've suggested that a stay in the adjacent wellness retreat be used as a cover, because the retreat and the transhumanist base share the same travel itinerary. This, they explain, adds authenticity to our deception.'

'More evidence of a clandestine link between the retreat and the base,' said Ahmad.

'A flight from Jakarta to Bandung has already been booked for us,' continued Julia. 'We'll be picked up from Bandung airport mid-morning the day after next. That'll give us time to fly back to Jakarta. We're supposed to be coming from Sydney don't forget.'

'You arrive just a day before our booking here expires,' said Fred. 'Sue, Ahmad and I will stay here for as long as you're in the base. I suggest we book for a further month. They still have plenty of vacancies, but let's insist on less demanding wellness programmes!'

'Knowing that you'll all be here is really important to us,' said George.

'How could it be otherwise?' said Ahmad. 'To quote D'Artagnan, 'all for one and one for all."

Julia and George were met at Bandung airport by a young man who introduced himself as Don

'I apologise for putting you in a van, but it has comfortable seats. We use vans for security reasons.'

Don took them to their quarters, a small room with an ensuite. It had a wardrobe, a double bed with side tables, a desk, a chair, and two small couches. It was of course windowless.

'It's small, I know, but I'm sure you'll understand that space is very limited in an underground structure like this. If it's any consolation, my room's not much bigger than a cupboard! You have full access to staff recreational facilities. When you've unpacked, I'll show you around.'

'Given the need for total secrecy, can we use our mobile phones?' Julia asked.

'Yes, we want you to use them to maintain the fiction that you're in a wellness retreat. We strongly prefer that you do not leave the base until pregnancy is established, so we'll provide you with photos of the retreat.'

'Are there any other couples in the designer baby unit?' asked George.

'Yes. Another five. That's the most we can safely handle at any one time.'

The staff recreational facilities were very generous. In one section was a small but well-equipped gym, a plunge pool, and a sauna. There was a small boutique cinema with a low stage. The main room had chairs and coffee tables with comfortable lounges against the walls. In the centre was a small pool table. A bookcase contained a variety of board games, CDs and jigsaw puzzles as well as books. Close inspection revealed that some were written in Indonesian.

'Ah, I see scrabble!' Julia exclaimed. 'Perhaps you'll be able to beat me for once, George!'

'All staff have to live in,' Don explained. 'We can exit the base only for work assignments, allocated leave, or medical treatment, so it's really important that we can relax and be entertained when we're off duty. I won't introduce you to anyone at this stage. You'll all be wearing name tags anyway. Partly for security. I'll show you the canteen now. You can have some lunch if you're hungry.'

George had brought with him an Indonesian phrase book and a dictionary.

'It'll keep my brain working,' he told Julia in their quarters after lunch. 'I don't want to just vegetate while you're being worked on.'

A little later, there was a knock on the door.

'I'm Nadia,' said a middle-aged woman with what sounded like a Russian accent. 'I'll be looking after you, Julia, during the programme. I trained in medicine at Moscow State University. Today I want to give you the fertility drugs that will stimulate your ovaries. These drugs, which we've developed ourselves, work at any stage of the menstrual cycle. They are totally safe and very effective. You'll need three intramuscular injections. You could be ready for harvesting in less than a week. We'll monitor progress using finger prick blood samples. Please come with me.'

'So, we'll just have to wait,' said Julia, when she returned to their quarters, 'but we can use the time to explore ways of getting into the research areas. Let's go to the recreation area, see if there's anywhere we can install the spy camera that Fred's developed. It has to be positioned to capture the keypad on the exit door.'

It soon became clear that it was impossible to safely install a camera. They were stuck.

The next morning, Julia and George rose early, unable to sleep. Armed with coffee, they went into the recreation area, planning to play yet another game of scrabble. At this early hour, it was almost empty. They'd just started their game when a young Indonesian woman came through the door in the far wall.

'Hello,' said Julia. 'Do you speak English?'

'A little. But not allowed talk. Must go.'

As she walked in the direction of the canteen, she gave a subtle sign for them to follow her. The young woman sat alone at a table, pointedly ignoring them. After collecting toast and scrambled eggs, they sat at a table some distance away. Quickly finishing a light breakfast, the young woman rose, subtly pointing to her empty plate. Casually, Julia and George walked to the table she'd vacated. A slip of paper edged out from under the plate. Julia carefully removed it under the pretext of studying the menu.

Back in their room, they read what was on it.

'Prisoner here. Always watched. Combination to door 81869002.'

'That's awful,' said George, 'but not entirely surprising. Involvement in conducting such hideous experiments can't always be voluntary. This young woman's been forced into it. How many others are in the same boat?'

'She's desperate,' said Julia, 'otherwise she wouldn't risk contacting us. If she's been observed, she'll be in even more danger. And so might we.'

'Let's assume she's avoided detection. She was pretty subtle in her movements. We'll know soon enough if her treason has been discovered. They'll come for us.'

'Let's wait a day or two before we try and get into the research area,' said George. 'We can spend more time in the recreation centre. Be sociable, get to know some of the other designer baby couples. And we should be able to chat with the staff who are allowed into the facility. There's a pool table. You're not as good at pool as you are at scrabble. Maybe I'll get my revenge!'

By early evening, they had chatted with four of the five couples in the designer baby programme. All were quite forthcoming about their motives. For three of the couples, the motive was primarily one or more genetic disorders. They needed to delete their embryo's harmful genes. Since they could afford it, they decided to add some beneficial ones. The fourth couple was different. The male partner was very short, almost a dwarf, though he radiated charisma. He owned a fleet of oil tankers and was fabulously wealthy. He and his wife admitted unashamedly that they wanted a tall child. None of the couples was concerned about the sex of the designer baby. They all knew that this could not be changed by genetic manipulation. It could only be achieved by abandoning an embryo of the unwanted sex and starting again. The second embryo might also be of the wrong sex. This genetic lottery was a most unattractive option.

The staff they chatted to were friendly enough, but not forthcoming about what they did in the research centre. George and Julia learned only that about thirty people were directly involved with research. There was a dozen or so more working outside the research facility. All, as they had already been told, were required to live in.

'We're a bit unusual, then,' said George when, after a meal in the dining area, they were back in their quarters. 'Neither of us is a dwarf or a carrier of a genetic disorder.' He then whispered in Julia's ear. 'Has that raised questions about out true motives? Are they bugging us?'

A careful search of the room and ensuite revealed no bugs, but they knew they might have missed them. Caution was needed.

'It's been a long day,' said Julia. 'I'm ready for bed.'

Three more days in the recreation area yielded no more information about the research facility. Julia's blood tests showed rapid maturation of the eggs in her ovaries.

'Nadia told me that they'll harvest my eggs tomorrow,' said Julia. 'I don't think we should try and enter the research area until that's done.'

'We should probably wait until the embryo is implanted,' George replied. 'They'll need me for the sperm sample, and they'll be monitoring you very closely.'

When Julia got up the following morning, she noticed that a slip of paper had been pushed under the door. She unfolded it and spread it on the desk.

'George,' she whispered, 'come and look at this. It's a floor plan. I think it's the research facility.'

'Whoever's given us this and the keypad code must have been waiting for a couple like us. A bit unusual. We know some of the research relies on forced labour. Perhaps there's an organised resistance. I've no idea about security in the research area. It may be lax, given that it's impossible for any workers to leave the base without authorisation.'

The floor plan showed the research facility to be divided into six areas, all labelled. The initial DB indicated where designer baby research was carried out. The other five labels were: Brain Implants, Drugs, Viruses, Cells, and Staff. The entry code was added to each area, except staff accommodation, which was by far the largest.

'We'll have ten days or so here after the embryo's implanted', said George. 'We need a plan of action.'

The implantation was achieved successfully, after a brief delay. Julia and George told Nadia that they'd changed their minds about modifying the embryo's genome. They wanted only a standard in vitro fertilisation. Nadia was taken aback.

'But you've paid all this money. Done everything needed. Why back out?'

'We're just a bit worried about something going wrong. Since we've been here, we've realised that the procedure is still experimental. We hadn't understood that when we signed up.'

'Yes, it's still in development, but it's very safe. We would never risk harm to the embryo.'

'We've made our decision,' said Julia firmly. Please go ahead as we've requested.'

After the embryo was implanted, Nadia insisted that Julia rest in bed for the remainder of the day. In ten days' time, a blood test would determine pregnancy – or otherwise.

CHAPTER
THIRTY

They could get into the research area. But how could they explore it, let alone take photos, without getting caught?

'We could go in at night,' George suggested, 'but it's likely that some areas are open around the clock. And there must be surveillance.'

'When staff members walked through the recreation area to the canteen,' said Julia, 'one or two were still in uniform. I noticed masks hanging around their necks. If we can get hold of a uniform, one of us could pose as staff.'

At three the next morning, Julia entered the code for the keypad on the door to the research area. It opened silently. They found themselves in a hallway with two exit doors. There were also shelves, and open closets in which hung uniforms.

'They're unisex,' said Julia, holding one up. 'This should fit me.'

George reached for another uniform, but Julia stopped him.

'I'm going in alone,' she said. 'They'll be less likely to query a woman than a man. Don't argue. My mind's made up.'

She saw blank name tags on a shelf and put two in her pocket.

Back in their quarters, George seethed with rage but remembered to speak in a whisper.

'How could you make this decision without discussing it? I won't let you do it. I'll be the one to go in.'

After George had calmed down, Julia painstakingly argued her case. In the end, George was forced to agree with her.

'I won't do it today. I'll be tired after being up half the night. I'll go in tomorrow morning.'

Wearing the stolen uniform, a mask, and a filled in nametag, Julia entered the research area. She was wearing a pair of spectacles. These added to her disguise, but they also functioned as a high-definition camera. This was controlled by a small device in one of her pockets. The device also stored still photos and videos. The uniform was tight enough to make it clear she was a woman.

She knew from the floor plan that the left-hand door in the hallway led to the designer baby unit. She chose the other door, relieved that it opened silently as soon as she entered the second keypad code they'd been given. For the rest of the morning, Julia managed to photograph all the research arears in the sector. The staff were so busy and task-focussed that no one paid her any attention. On the way out, she decided not to risk entering the designer baby unit. 'My extraordinary luck,' she thought, 'might run out.'

Back in their quarters, Julia immediately transferred copies of the photographs and videos to their smart phones. Then she asked Geroge to sit down.

'It's even worse than we thought. Have a look at these.'

Images of the area labelled Drugs showed two bodies lying on stretchers with fluid entering their arms through intravenous drips. The room was a well-equipped laboratory. Neither of the two uniformed staff appeared to notice her as they went about their tasks.

She paused at this point.

'I wondered why they took no notice of me. Then I thought about security. They must be used to someone checking that everyone's doing what they're supposed to. We know that some staff are working under coercion. It makes sense for them to be monitored. Especially at random.'

The area labelled Cell also contained two bodies, both strapped to stretchers. It was set up as a laboratory, but the equipment was very different from that of the previous area. There was only one staff member present, a woman wearing a mask. She was injecting fluid into the arm of one of the bodies, which caused it to emit a grunt of pain.

The Virus area contained only caged rats, although an empty stretcher suggested the use of human subjects when required. There was no one inside. The lab equipment differed from that of the previous areas.

The Brain Implant area was much bigger than the others. Inside was a body strapped to a stretcher. In its shaven skull were holes through which wires protruded. Twitching movements told that the victim was still alive. Another body lay on an operating table, in the middle of dissection. An anaesthetic mask on its' face showed that it also was still alive. The lab equipment was more varied and extensive than in any of the previous areas. In an alcove were a man and a woman, naked, bound and gagged.

Julia paused again. 'I knew they would die. The woman was young and pretty. I almost broke down, but by the grace of God, I kept it together.'

'The body on the stretcher,' said George, 'matches the description of those found in the shed by Ahmad and Fred. Except that it still has arms. Cutting off the limbs must come later. Perhaps they're using brain chips to control prosthetic limbs by thought alone. We know that Elon Musk has already had success with this technology.'

'It won't stop there,' said Julia. 'They'll be trying to develop more and more powerful brain chips. Chips that allow thought control from a distance. Imagine what that could do to complex electronic systems. Computers, hyperscale data centres, finance hubs, bitcoin mines, you name it. Mastery of this technology will yield enormous power.'

'We can't do any more,' said Julia when she'd shown George the last photo. 'We'll just have to wait for the result of my pregnancy test. Then we can get the hell out of here.'

The pregnancy test was positive. Nadia congratulated them.

'Now,' she said, 'we have to get ready for the next couple, so you have to move out at once. Please transfer the balance of two hundred thousand to the same overseas account.'

George did so at once.

Nadia accompanied them to the entrance hall, where Don was waiting for them in a van. He put their cases in the back. As they got in, Nadia put her hand in the sliding door.

'By the way, we did tweak your embryo's genes a bit. Just couldn't resist it.'

She slid the door shut and the van rolled forward.

George and Julia were speechless for a moment.

'How could they do that?' asked Julia.

Don overheard.

'It's an experimental centre. As Nadia said, they just couldn't resist it. They'll find a way to follow you up, check on the outcome of their experiment. But don't worry. It will be a positive one. They are transhumanists, don't forget.'

Their return flights from Badung to Jakarta had already been booked. The fiction that they'd flown in from Sydney had been successfully preserved. They cancelled the return flight as soon as Don had dropped them off. Ahmad picked them up in the 4WD soon after. Fred immediately sent the photographs and videos to his government contact, with a brief explanation of their context.

Almost at once, the Australian Government notified Interpol, who notified the highest levels of the Indonesian Government. With pressure from both Interpol and the Australian Government, the Indonesians were compelled to act. Early the next morning, a large force of soldiers and national police surrounded the transhumanists' base. Entry was forced through the door behind the wellness retreat. The soldiers made sure no one escaped through the main entrance. The operation took the entire day because the authorities had to be sure that all those in the base had been caught and placed in custody. Those able to prove their innocence would be looked after, perhaps even receive compensation.

The team knew that it would be weeks before the base was fully explored, documented, and closed down. Fred had asked his government contact to keep him informed of developments.

There was no need for the team to stay any longer in the wellness retreat. Citing a family emergency, they signed out and booked a flight from Bandung to Jakarta, where they planned to stay for two days. Ahmad hoped that his aunt Karina would be well enough to see them all. Fred had to leave his gun behind, slightly regretful that he hadn't used it.

CHAPTER
THIRTY-ONE

The first day of the stop-over in Jakarta was dominated by anxiety and rage about the transhumanists' clandestine genetic engineering of Julia's embryo.

'I know that Don was confident the outcome would be positive,' said Julia, 'but what does that mean? Higher IQ, stronger, taller, better immune system? Whatever they've done to my baby's genes, I didn't ask for it, and I don't want it.'

'Have you thought about termination?' asked Sue.

'We've decided against it. The child will be our own, although it won't have sprung entirely from George's loins.'

Julia's attempt at levity was a sign that her rage was beginning to soften. George had been just as angry as Julia, but less worried. In a biological sense, it was Julia's baby, hers alone. Understandably, she was more anxious than George.

On the second day of the stop-over, Julia was settled enough to join the team in a visit to Ahmad's aunt Karina, whose health was largely restored. They spent much of the day with her. She was very keen to know the outcome of a mission that she herself had instigated. When she learned that it had been a success, her relief was palpable.

On their return to HQ, all stayed the night. They assembled around the conference table after breakfast the next morning and agreed to rest for two days.

At the next team meeting, Fred outlined the three projects on offer.

'Why only three?' asked George.

'Paradoxically, it's because of our success with previous projects. The range of potential targets has got smaller. This leaves money laundering, once our main focus, and two of the three projects are in this area. The third is very different. It's about a dominatrix - a woman who specialises in humiliating men. Men who pay a lot of money for the services she provides. This assignment isn't from the Government, but a life insurance company. It's had to pay out large sums for two deaths that have raised serios questions.

Two bodies, both of men, were found by the side of a road in separate Sydney suburbs. They both had extensive bruises, recent and older, but the coroner determined that violence was not the cause of death. One died of a cerebral haemorrhage, the other of a heart attack. Both men were in their fifties and in good health, which makes their deaths extremely unusual. The coroner decided on an open verdict. She explained that although the causes of death were natural, the bruising suggested that they were provoked by some kind of external circumstance. She was unable to be more conclusive.

The insurance company wants us to explore matters further and has sent all its background information. It did employ a private eye. He illegally tapped the phones of both widows but overheard only one conversation of relevance. There was mention of a dominatrix called Morgana. This was enough for the detective to tell the insurance company that she was probably responsible for the deaths, but he had no proof. Without it the insurance company couldn't reclaim the money paid to the widows or seek reimbursement from their own insurers. The private eye didn't pursue matters any further, in spite of pressure from the insurance company. Perhaps he was warned off.'

'What more do we know about the two men?' asked Julia.

'Both men were very wealthy. One was insured for five million, the other for six. They were businessmen with their own successful companies. Work dominated their lives, at the expense of family. Perhaps the very costly life insurance policies were their way of compensating for this. There's nothing on record to suggest they were involved with a dominatrix, but that's hardly surprising. It's not something you'd want to advertise.'

'What payment are they offering?' asked Ahmad

'Three million for proof that both men died at the hands of a dominatrix. Fairly modest by recent standards, but the project is both interesting and challenging, and George has some knowledge of the area.'

'I do,' replied George. 'I did a lot of research during my involvement with the murdered cabinet minister who, as I've already explained, practised autoerotic asphyxia. This very dangerous perversion is undoubtedly sadomasochistic but, as its name suggests, is done alone. Would you like me to outline what I've learned?'

'Hold on,' said Sue. 'I'm worried about how dangerous this project might be. We suspect that the private eye was warned off, presumably by the dominatrix. She may well have powerful connections. The kind that could put us in real danger.'

'Dominatrixes can be very expensive,' continued George. 'For one with a stellar reputation, the fee would be at least two thousand dollars an hour. Fees for a whole day can be over ten thousand, and for weekend sessions, as much as fifty thousand dollars. So, only the very wealthy can afford the most celebrated dominatrixes. Amateurs, or professionals of less talent or experience, are much cheaper. So, it is certain that Morgana will have connections with powerful men. Men who will do anything to avoid exposure.'

After lengthy discussion, Sue agreed that they take the project on, but only if they withdrew at the first sign of any real danger.

'Now that we've decided to go ahead,' said George, 'I'll tell you what I've learned. The first thing to understand is that the professional literature is both sparse and confusing. This is because it's extremely rare for men to seek psychological help in stopping their masochistic activities. So those who do so are very unusual. Their psychopathology is probably very different from that of the great majority. There seems to be agreement on only two things. First, there is a genetic predisposition. Second, there has been childhood trauma regarding the expression of sexuality. When this is repeatedly punished by the mother, who is often unconsciously seductive, it creates a powerful link between sexuality and physical abuse by a female, a link that is carried through to adulthood.'

'I actually understand all that,' said Julia, 'and I'm not very psychologically minded.'

'It gets more complicated,' said George. 'Very common in men who employ a dominatrix is the desire to feminise, usually by cross-dressing or role play. To be convincing in her designated role, the dominatrix must be a very skilled actor, and intimately psychologically connected with her clients. These attributes are also essential for success in all her other activities. Only the most sophisticated dominatrixes possess these qualities, and that's why they are so pricey.'

'Why the desire to feminise?' asked Sue.

'Cross-dressing embraces the relatively vulnerable position of women, but it's also a way to escape from the male sex-role stereotype in which many of these men feel trapped. Some enjoy being forced to wear women's clothing as part of humiliation or control. Perhaps most important, these behaviours allow them to explore aspects of their gender identity, something they could never achieve otherwise. Any more questions?'

A negative response allowed George to continue. 'I'll talk in detail about the work of a high-class dominatrix. First the equipment. All dominatrixes have a range of restraints. They include metal or leather handcuffs, chains, shackles, silk ropes, collars and leashes. Spreader bars are strong metal bars that allow wrists and ankles to be attached at various distances apart. A St Andrews Cross is an X-shaped metal cross that permits a greater variety of limb positions.

Gags are a central form of restraint, and their variety is extraordinary. Ball gags involve putting a rubber or silicon ball in the mouth and strapping it in. Some balls are inflatable. A bit gag is like a horse's bit and allows some speech. Ring gags keep the mouth wide open. Muzzle gags cover the mouth completely and may be attached to other devices.

Tools for applying punishment are also standard equipment. They include canes of wood or metal, riding crops, and a variety of whips. A paddle is a flat rigid tool of leather, wood, rubber, silicon or metal. Some are double layered to facilitate loud, stinging hits. The choice of paddle depends on creating a balance between pain and humiliation. A favourite is the pizzle, made from a dried bull's penis.

A wide variety of other tools includes TENS units for graduated electric shock. More sophisticated is the Violet Wand, an electronic device that emits a purple glow and produces an electric arc when close to the skin. Intensity ranges from a tingle to sharp, painful shocks that may leave small burns. Permanent scarring can occur with repeated use.

A Wartenberg Wheel is a spikey metal cylinder with a handle. Depending on the size and sharpness of the spikes, and the pressure applied to the skin, it creates sensations ranging from tingling to acute pain. Clamps are used to create pressure on specific body parts, particularly the nipples and genitals.

Dominatrixes use a wide range of masks, mainly in role play, but also more generally to foster intimidation and control. Candles and ice cubes are used in temperature play.

By far the most dangerous equipment is that used in total body enclosure, or sexual mummification. This creates total immobility and a sense of utter powerlessness and subjugation, an ultimate escape from the male sex-role stereotype.

A straight jacket is relatively safe, as are specially designed bondage suits, made of rubber, spandex or lycra. They cover the whole body, including the face. Rubber suits require a tube for breathing, but spandex and lycra allow it naturally. Sleep sacks are more dangerous, especially those designed to create pressure change by pumping out air. Extreme pressure within such a sleep sack can be fatal, either through suffocation or causing strokes and heart attacks.

Most dangerous are vacuum beds, platforms covered by a clear plastic or vinyl sheet that's fully sealed around the body. A vacuum pump sucks the air out so that the sheet clings tightly. Breathing occurs through specially designed masks which are airtight and preserve the vacuum. The masks are closed off for some clients who enjoy what is called erotic asphyxia. The lack of oxygen greatly increases the duration and intensity of orgasms.

It seems, then, that our two men used either a sleep sack or a vacuum bed. If they were into erotic asphyxia, it would have been a vacuum bed.

Whatever the device, an error by the dominatrix, or equipment failure, caused their deaths.

'Do all high-class dominatrixes have vacuum beds?' asked Ahmad. 'They're probably very pricey and their use can be extremely risky.'

'I'm guessing here,' George replied, 'but given that mummification can be achieved more safely using other methods, probably only a minority have this technology. I won't go into detail about other extreme fetishes, partly because they are so disgusting and partly because they are so rare. Often, they involve faeces, urine, fisting, and other forms of anal assault. Frequently, there is specific attention to the penis. Very occasionally, minor surgery. Whatever you can imagine, it's almost certainly been done, or is being done right now.'

'If you're right about vacuum beds being relatively uncommon,' said Sue, 'this could help us track down Morgana. If our two men were into erotic asphyxia, they would have approached only those dominatrixes who had necessary equipment. This could narrow down our search. I think we've learned enough to start planning. So, let's share our thoughts after breakfast tomorrow.'

CHAPTER THIRTY-TWO

'I think there are two issues,' said Julia at next morning's team meeting. 'First, we have to find Morgana. Second, we have to prove our two men died at her hands.'

'Agreed,' said Fred, 'so any ideas about how to find her?'

'There's a way to both find her and incriminate her,' said George. 'I'll pose as a client with a particular interest in mummification and erotic asphyxiation. Because oxygen deprivation so powerfully increases the intensity and duration of orgasm, some couples use strangulation routinely during sex. It's called breath play. For masochistic men, strangulation by a woman during sex is doubly erotic. It both enhances their orgasm and meets their need to be dominated, degraded and controlled. So, it's not surprising that most dominatrixes offer erotic asphyxia as a key service. In itself it's not too risky, but becomes much more so when combined with mummification, especially at its extremes.

Some deeply masochistic men may even welcome this level of risk, at least unconsciously. Freud revealed the death wish as an intrinsic part of the human psyche. In masochists it is stronger than usual. It may be that dominatrixes who specialise in a combination of breath play and mummification are willing to accept the death of a client as an acceptable risk.'

'That's a very scary thought,' said Ahmad. 'It underlines the risk you'll be taking.'

'If Morgana accepts me as a client, I'll tell her that it will take time for me to trust her enough to submit myself to the very risky combination of erotic asphyxiation and mummification. I'll ask her how she manages the level of risk, and whether she's had any serious accidents. Of course she won't admit to killing anyone, but I was a psychiatrist long enough to be good at reading body language. I'll know if she's lying. As well, Morgana will have records of clients, their preferences, and what services she's provided to them. She may not have deleted all reference to our two men. I'll find a way to access her files.'

Julia exploded. 'You're being absolutely ridiculous George. I've heard enough. Why expose yourself to such risks for a project that isn't paying a fortune and isn't exactly going to save the world. Why do you care so much about the fate of our two men? If Morgana did kill them, she has surely learned her lesson. We have to assume the deaths were accidental, and not the result of some murderous impulse or intent, so more deaths are extremely unlikely. You won't be saving any lives, and far more important, you are soon to be a father. How could you even think of putting yourself in danger?'

'I promise you, Julia, that I will not put myself in any danger. I won't submit myself to either erotic asphyxiation or mummification, let alone in combination. I'll combine the discussions about safety with some harmless activities. I'm skilful and knowledgeable enough to prolong this almost indefinitely without arousing suspicion. Please trust me.

And we don't know if there have been other deaths, or even if Morgana will continue with very dangerous activities in spite of the two deaths that have been discovered. Morgana will know the sort of people to get rid of bodies without a trace. Our two men may have been dumped because she panicked or couldn't use her usual cleaners.'

'Surely,' said Sue, 'any deaths would leak out and destroy Morgana's reputation. Why would anyone use her services if they're so risky?'

'We just don't know enough about the world of the dominatrix. That's one of the reasons I want to do this. Now I have a confession to make. When I discovered the cabinet minister's addiction to autoerotic asphyxia, I started to research it. I even built my own apparatus. But what started as an experiment became an addiction. I stopped only because I came very close to death when the safety mechanism failed. I destroyed the apparatus and haven't used any other techniques, although I'm still tempted at times.

I have more to confess. I've always had self-destructive tendencies. That's one reason I got struck off the register. And I've been a compulsive risk-taker. This actually helped me survive the challenges around the cabinet minister's disc saga. And it explains my eagerness to get involved in our more dangerous missions.

I realise now that I unconsciously chose psychiatry as a way of dealing with these problems, but it obviously hasn't worked. I find this all incredibly painful to think about, let alone talk about. That's why I never had therapy myself. I've kept the whole thing secret, even from Julia. Becoming the client of a dominatrix will allow me to talk freely and might help me resolve some of these issues.'

'Well,' said Julia, 'you've been brilliant at hiding all this from me. I never suspected any of it, but I care for you even more now that you've come clean. We have a child. We still live apart. I hope that will change when our child is born. But sharing a home or not, we'll need to work closely together for the wellbeing of our child. We'll need to be intimate, honest, open. And George, you've just made a huge stride in that direction.

I'm looking forward to resuming our sexual relationship. I know you are. When that happens, we all know it'll make staying in the team difficult, perhaps impossible. But to be honest, I don't want to stay while I care for my baby. It's too risky. I'm raising this now because it seemed impossible not to. I know it's not timely. We're at a crucial point in a very challenging project. But we can at least think about what I've said. Meanwhile, George, I know you'll abide by your promise to keep yourself safe. So, I'll support you to the very best of my ability.'

Because George was approaching Morgana as a client, Fred and Ahmad were able to locate her website within hours. She replied after a short delay. Before agreeing to see George, she wanted to be sure he was genuine and not an undercover agent. It was easy to create a convincing background story because of the publicity around George's involvement with the cabinet minister. Then it was just a matter of proving that George was who he said he was.

Satisfied, Morgana asked George to outline his requirements. She then sent details of her location in the Sydney suburb of Homebush. Her initial fee was five thousand dollars, to be paid in advance.

Two days later, George arrived at the Homebush address in the early afternoon. It was a large, detached house set well back from the road. Entry to the driveway was barred by a metal gate. Geroge pressed the entry button, and the gate swung open. As he was parking, he saw a youngish woman emerge from the front door of the house.

'I'm Rosemary, Morgana's housekeeper. Please come through.'

A short flight of stairs led down to a metal door which opened after Rosemary completed a retinal scan. Revealed was a huge basement, out of which Morgana emerged. She was a slender, petite woman looking to be in her forties, with close cropped brown hair and an attractive angular face.

'Welcome George. Let me show you around. I'm sure you've done your research and know what to expect, but I'll run through what's here and answer any questions you might have.'

The basement was equipped with everything that George expected, including a vacuum bed.

'Very impressive,' he said. 'How much of this huge basement was here when you moved in?'

'About a quarter. I had the rest dug out in stages to avoid awkward questions. Now, let's get down to business. You've told me what services you are looking for, but I need more detail.'

George confirmed his desire for a combination of erotic asphyxiation and mummification.

'But I need to be sure I can trust you with what I know is a very risky procedure, so I want several preliminary sessions with more basic equipment. Is that acceptable?'

'Of course, but it will add to the expense. Have you got the funds? You already know that my fees are very high.'

'You're expensive because you're the best. I'm quite wealthy and will pay in advance if you want me to.'

'Today is just an introduction and to fine-tune your requirements. That's why it was only five grand. Let's book three more sessions before we move to the vacuum bed. Each session lasts four hours and will cost you eight thousand dollars. So, deposit twenty-four thousand in my account, and we're set. How often do you want to come?'

'Is twice a week okay? I want to move forward fairly quickly, to get to the vacuum bed as soon as I feel I can trust you.'

'Let me check my diary.'

Morgana moved to a computer screen in a small alcove. George watched carefully. This, he realised, was where he could download Morgana's files when the chance arrived.

'If you're happy with morning sessions, I can book you in on alternate days, from the day after tomorrow.'

Back at HQ, George updated the team.

'I know where she keeps her files, but to download them I'll need a diversion. Not during the first session, but the second one. Any ideas?'

'We need to get her out of the basement,' said Ahmad. This means creating an external diversion, but one that won't arouse suspicion. She'll have an alarm system. Fred and I should be able to hack into it before your second session. We'll aim to trigger it about half-way through.'

George's first session was in part a way for Morgana to assess his physical strength and ability to manage the demands of the vacuum bed combined with erotic asphyxiation. It also allowed George to question Morgana about her previous experience with this very risky procedure.

'How often have you done this? And have you ever had any accidents?'

'Clients who want this combination, and can afford it, are relatively uncommon. Which reminds me: the fee is fifteen thousand dollars, payable in advance after we've completed the first three sessions successfully.'

'In case I don't survive?' George quipped.

Morgana looked angry and then relaxed when she realised George was joking.

'I've done this combined procedure over a hundred times during the twelve or so years that I've been here. An average of eight or nine a year. Demand tends to come in clusters. Clients usually want two or three sessions over a week or so.'

'And never any accidents? Never any fatalities?'

Morgana looked George in the eye. 'You'll be completely safe. I've developed fool-proof safety mechanisms, so please stop worrying.'

George realised that Morgana had not answered the question, but decided not to pursue matters further.

The second session was a little more rigorous. It started with a Wartenberg Wheel, which Morgana removed when Gorge had reached the limits of his capacity to endure the pain. Then she used a variety of paddles to inflict more pain. Next, she employed a Violet Wand on the skin of his upper left arm. Just as the intensity of its application was becoming very painful, the alarm went off.

Morgana dropped the wand and rushed out. George attached a flash drive to Morgana's computer. He finished downloading just before Morgana returned.

'False alarm. Sorry about the interruption. Let's resume.'

Back at HQ the team studied the contents of the flash drive. As George had predicted, it listed the names of Morgana's clients, together with their preferences and activities. A search engine found the names of the two dead men, although all their details had been erased.

'Bullseye,' shouted Ahmad. 'She must have meant to erase all record of them but somehow missed their names. Probably because they're duplicated in her financial system. We can send all this to the insurance company. Case closed!'

'Hold on,' said George, 'We shouldn't send it until after my third session with Morgana. If we expose her before then, she may link it with the false alarm, and so with me. Given her extensive contacts, she may be able to plan revenge, even from prison.'

The rest of the team agreed to wait until after George's third session, at which Morgana arranged a date for the vacuum bed.

The insurance company acted as soon as it received the data on the flash drive. Federal Police, with a SWAT team, surrounded Morgana's house. There was no need for forced entry: Rosemary opened the front door at the first ring. With little persuasion she opened the basement door. Morgana was with a client. Both were arrested.

At the team's usual celebration, George expressed his concern about the possibility that Morgana had killed more men than the two of their concern.

'The police will look into that very closely,' Julia replied. 'Given our role in exposing Morgana, we'll surely be given access to any relevant data. You may have saved other men from the same fate, but even if you haven't, your still my hero. I'd like to drink to that, but my baby wouldn't be happy.'

CHAPTER
THIRTY-THREE

'Here's something completely different,' said Fred at the next team meeting. 'It's about an ex-member of a religious sect called The Church of Spiritual Enlightenment, which happens to be based in Sydney. Another ex-member had heard of us and suggested she make contact.

The woman's name is Rachel. We spoke at some length. She explained that the leadership of the church changed in mysterious circumstances about two years ago. Recently Rachel was made aware of criminal activities carried out under the new regime. When she realised their full extent, she left the church. This was an ordeal that she wasn't ready to talk about, but she'd memorised one of the key tenets of the church, and was able to repeat it:

"Sensitives, or mediums, communicate with those who have passed over, and who show their continuing love for us. From these messages, we know that they still exist, but in a different domain. We call this domain the Spirit World. We will enter it ourselves when we pass over, because only the physical body dies."

After a brief pause, Fred continued.

'Rachel went on to explain that seances were still at the core of the church's doctrine but had been corrupted, and were now used for criminal purposes. She herself had not been privy to these seances but had heard about them from the same ex-member who had told her about us. Although this woman had not attended a corrupt séance, she was given a full account of one by another ex-member, a wealthy woman who had been directed in a message from the spirit world to donate five thousand dollars to a specific charity. Under what she later came to believe was a form of post-hypnotic suggestion, she obeyed.

This information added to Rachel's reservations about the new leadership of the church. She discretely questioned a number of members. Some had, under the same circumstances, also donated to a charity, but the sums were relatively small, and the victims believed that they were doing good. They continued to be devout members.

Rachel suspects that the church advertises seances for those outside the church, although she doesn't know how this is done. She also suspects that the use of corrupt seances goes beyond financial extortion. There have been rumours about church members carrying out illegal activities, presumably, Rachel believes, under post-hypnotic suggestion.'

'Are you sure Rachel is a credible witness?' asked Julia.

'I've no reason to doubt that she believes everything she's related. For me, that's enough to justify some further investigation, but we need a consensus before going ahead.'

After a brief discussion, the rest of the team agreed to some preliminary enquiries.

'Let's start by accessing the church's website,' suggested Ahmad.

The site occupied only one page. It summarised the church's history and outlined its aims and activities, including seances. There was an address in the suburb of Crows Nest, about 5 kilometres north of Sydney's CBD. New members were welcome and were invited to take part in the church's activities without pressure to join it.

'Rachel,' said Sue, 'suspected that the church actively encouraged people to take part in seances, but there's nothing of that kind on the website. Perhaps she's mistaken, or perhaps there's another website offering seances as a way of contacting the departed. People are willing to spend big money to create a real sense of contact with a dead loved one. I've looked into this a bit. Organisations like Project December, HereAfter AI and Replika use similar technology. All digital traces of the dead person, including videos and photographs, are used to create a range of virtual presences. The most sophisticated and expensive technologies produce interactive holograms or immersive experiences using virtual reality.'

'Surely,' said George, 'those who pay for these seances know they're experiencing a digital representation, not an actual visit from the afterlife.'

'Presumably,' replied Sue, 'but the phenomenon shows an utter desperation for some kind of contact. This technology is very expensive. A séance may, for some people, seem an affordable way to meet that desperate need.'

'So,' said Ahmad, 'we must look for websites that offer hope to the bereaved. Hope the includes the possibility of direct contact with the departed. Fred, shall we get started?'

There were several such sites, but only one invited further attention. Although there was no mention of the Church of Spiritual Enlightenment, the address was the same, but with a different contact number. The site, Crossing Beyond, offered the certainty of contact with the departed. A phone call or a visit would explain exactly how this miracle would be achieved.

'Much more straightforward than what the Church offers,' said Ahmad. 'No religious palaver. Just a direct path to the afterlife. One of us will have to sign up. '

'That has to be me,' said Julia. 'All this connects perfectly with my near death experience. Now that I believe in an afterlife, I'll be totally convincing.'

'Assuming it's a scam,' said Fred, 'they'll check you out. Find out how much they can take you for. So we'll need to create a suitable background story. That'll take Ahmad and I quite a few hours. I think you'll be okay to contact them sometime tomorrow.'

'Before I do that, I want to do some research. I've never been to a séance, and I need to know what to expect. Give me a whole day. I'll outline what I've learned at our team meeting the day after tomorrow.'

'It's been absolutely fascinating,' said Julia at the scheduled gathering. 'I realised at once that a historical perspective was crucial. The modern spiritualist movement began in America in the 1840's and arrived in Britain about ten years later. There, the first well known medium was Georgina Houghton. Under the direction of her spirit guides, she drew the most amazing abstract paintings, described as "without parallel in this world." A selection of the hundreds that she created can be seen today in London's Courtauld Institute.

Other mediums followed a similar path, and their works were a major factor in popularising modern spiritualism, which spread throughout the world. As they became more popular, seances focussed on two-way communication with the spirit world. Many people attended in the hope of talking with departed loved ones, and this became the movement's central theme.

Spiritualism caught the attention of some of the great thinkers of the day, including Alfred Russel Wallace and Sir Arthur Conan Doyle. In between knocking off Sherlock Holmes' stories, he spent his later years promoting spiritualism.'

'It's interesting,' Sue interrupted, 'that none of Sherlock Holmes stories directly involved spiritualism. Presumably it didn't fit into the genre. But I read somewhere that Doyle used Sherlock as a challenge to his spiritual beliefs, as a kind of test of their truth.'

'Let's not stray too far from my own story,' said Julia. 'The movement is still active in Britain, where the Spiritualist Association has over eleven thousand subscribing members. There are some three hundred spiritualist churches across the nation.

In Australia, the numbers are smaller, of course, but the movement is still very active. The Victorian Spiritualist Union, founded in 1870, has about fifteen hundred members, with eight churches in the state. All the other states have their own spiritual unions, of which the largest is the Spiritualists National Union of Western Australia. In the latest Australian census, almost nine thousand people identified as Spiritualists, but there's no data on actual church attendance.'

'Is there a link to our First Nations' spirituality?' asked Ahmad.

'None at all as far as I know. The movement seems very Western focussed. I haven't looked at other spiritual religions. Buddhists make up over two percent of Australia's population. There may well be links between Buddhism and the spiritual beliefs of First Nation people. The Baha'i numbers are only about fifteen thousand. Then there are numerous cults, some very coercive. We could look at those another time.'

'There must have been efforts to expose the fraudulent nature of seances,' said George. 'Have you looked into this?'

'Yes. There's a whole industry devoted to it. Prominent is the work of Professor Richard Wiseman, a psychologist and magician. With a colleague, he used descriptions of Victorian seances to recreate them in a disused prison. One hundred and fifty-two volunteers took part in nine séances. With the use of fine wires and magnets, numerous objects were moved before their eyes, accompanied by mysterious sounds. Afterwards, one fifth of the participants believed that they had witnessed the spirit world.

Later the professor detailed some of the tricks and props used in seances. Central is a circular table with four to eight chairs. Participants hold hands, creating a sense of unity, and at the same time stopping any attempts at manual exploration. A suitable fragrance is combined with silence or soft music. The room is darkened, but initially not enough to stop 'Cold Reading' by the medium, aimed at picking up clues about the participants' hopes and expectations. Some mediums employ 'Hot Reading,' a detailed search of participants' backgrounds. Nearly always, an assistant is hidden behind a curtain or partition, and in full darkness comes out to facilitate complex illusions.

The medium starts by invoking the guardian spirits, each named personally. She may employ a cone-shaped spirit trumpet to amplify her messages from the spirit world. Some mediums are skilled ventriloquists. Table movements are achieved using magnets and steel plates. Other hidden devices, or the assistant, create knocks and raps. Fine wires allow the movement of objects, movements which can also be done by the assistant. Projections and reflections, sometimes combined with puppets, create the images necessary for total conviction. Cold breezes are sometimes used to reinforce the impact of key moments. I imagine that AI is used in the most sophisticated seances.

At the end, the medium releases the spirits, returning them to the spiritual domain. She may then collapse with exhaustion, feigned or real. Some mediums actually enter a trance-like state, and a surprising number believe in that spirit world as a reality. They use séances to convince others of this.'

'With all this evidence of fakery,' said Fred, 'how come so many people are sucked in?'

'Professor Wiseman deals with this at some length. He emphasises the power of suggestion, to which some people are particularly susceptible. The séance is crafted to maximise this. Darkness helps. Suggestion builds up as the séance unfolds, and even cynics can be duped.'

'So mediums have a range of motives,' said George. 'Some truly believe in the existence of the spirit world and use seances to promote their belief. Some use them to justify their special status within a particular church, or more widely. We know that many rely on seances as a source of income, but not in the same way as the one that Julia is about to engage with. The ruthless exploitation that occurs within it must be very rare, otherwise it would become known.'

'I think you're right,' Julia responded. 'I can't add anything more that might be helpful. Any final comments or questions?'

After a brief silence, Julia concluded her narrative.

'I'm ready to go ahead. I'll make contact tomorrow afternoon. First, I want to study the background story that Fred and Ahmad are creating about me.'

'It's nearly done,' said Ahmad. 'The first half is essentially true, although all reference to George and me is omitted. Because you joined us straight after the deep fake destroyed your career, your life since then has been totally private. This makes it relatively easy to create a fictional account of subsequent events.'

CHAPTER
THIRTY-FOUR

Ahmad and Fred began their fictional narrative by explaining that compensation after the deep fake had left Julia wealthy. She had lost a sister, Lucy, to whom she was very close. Lucy had been drowned in a boating accident about fifty kilometres off the coast of South Australia's Port Lincoln, an area notorious for freak waves.

Fred and Ahmad invented two brief media reports of the episode which they inserted into the on-line back issues of the Port Lincoln Times and the Adelaide Advertiser. The reports stated that Lucy had removed her life jacket to go for a swim, but had not replaced it when a rogue wave capsized the boat. Life jackets saved the other three on board. Lucy's body was never recovered.

The media reports both ended with: 'Sadly, what started as a fishing trip ended in tragedy.'

Julia committed the background story to memory. During her time as a barrister, she had memorised numerous documents, and her capacity for doing so had stayed with her. She knew she might be questioned about her background and could not risk errors.

'I'm ready to contact them,' Julia told the team at the next morning's meeting. 'Wish me luck.'

'There's one other thing,' said George. 'By my calculation, you're at least a month pregnant. I'm worried that any stress might cause a miscarriage.'

'It's actually twenty-nine days,' Julia replied. 'I'm booked into the ante-natal clinic next week. At this early stage, stress isn't an issue, but maybe later we'll need to think about it.'

Julia's phone call was answered after a short delay.

'Crossing Beyond here,' said a woman's voice. 'How can I help?'

'I've recently lost my sister. She was drowned, and her body was never recovered. We were very close. I'm desperate to find a way of contacting her. I believe in the afterlife. A friend suggested a séance. I found your website.'

'You're exactly the kind of person we can help. We've had consistent success, which in your own case we can virtually guarantee. When can you come in?'

'What about tomorrow morning? Say 10 o'clock.'

'We'll be expecting you.'

'For the séance itself,' said Fred, 'We'll fit you up with a hidden recording device. It's tiny and undetectable but doesn't have the capacity to transmit data to HQ. If these people are very concerned about security, they'll have installed technology that picks up transmissions of any kind. So we can't monitor what happens.'

The building that housed both Crossing Beyond and the Church of Spiritual Enlightenment was an old Anglican church. Declining attendance had made it redundant, and it had fallen into neglect until it was bought by the new church. The main building had been restored, and two new structures added. One was a large church hall, the other a two-story building with basement parking. Clearly, the Church of Spiritual Enlightenment was well funded. Julia found an above ground parking spot adjacent to the church itself.

The location of Crossing Beyond was indicated by a prominent sign on the front of the church hall. As Julia approached, the door was opened by a tall, youngish woman dressed in a grey smock.

'Welcome, Julia. I'm Ingrid. Please come inside. Let me show you around.'

The structure was divided into two. The front part had a small kitchen. Tables and chairs were stacked against the walls of the remaining area which was extensive enough to hold large gatherings. A door in the back wall led to a corridor in the centre of which was another door, wooden and ornate.

'You'll see another door at the end of the corridor,' said Ingrid. We usually access the séance room through that. Come in.'

The séance room was breathtaking. In the centre was a table surrounded by eight cushioned chairs. The ceiling and the walls were almost entirely covered in black velvet. Lighting came from a range of strategically placed lamps on pedestals. Each was a work of art designed to enhance an other-worldly atmosphere. There were two curtained-off alcoves on either side of the room, which was furnished additionally with four easy chairs and matching side-tables.

'It's perfect,' said Julia, 'I already sense the presence of the beyond. When's the next séance?'

'We don't want to rush things,' said Ingrid emphatically. 'It's really important that we prepare you beforehand. And we need to know everything about your loss, how you've coped with it, and what you hope to get from the séance. Our medium has an assistant who will take you through all this. He's very experienced and will understand how painful it will be to talk about your sister's death. He's not available today. He occasionally helps other mediums. But I can arrange an appointment for tomorrow. Let me check the diary. Our fees, by the way, just cover our expenses. You'll be up for only twelve hundred dollars per séance. If you're concerned about privacy, don't be. The séance room is completely soundproofed throughout. Not a sound can be heard from outside.'

Julia met the medium's assistant at three o'clock the next day.

'I'm Andrew. I've been doing this for nearly twenty years. You can trust me.'

Andrew was a man of medium height and build who looked to be in his early forties. His face was slightly lopsided, but not unattractive.

'First I'd like to understand you as a person, and especially how you're coping with your tragic loss. Then I'll explain what you should expect.'

'I was surprised that you were a man. I assumed a medium's assistant would be of the same sex. Please tell me about your role.'

'Virtually all medium's assistants are men. The spirits are more comfortable entering a space where the genders are balanced. As for my role, I don't take part in the séance itself. I'm in an alcove, behind a curtain or partition. Sometimes the medium gets into trouble. Contacts with hostile spirits, trances becoming too deep, complete loss of consciousness, collapse from exhaustion or overload. These problems are uncommon, but when they do happen, help from an experienced assistant can be lifesaving.'

The rest of the meeting was, as Andrew had explained, focussed on an exploration of Julia's personality and lifestyle, events around Lucy's death, and how Julia had coped.

'I need to share some of this with the medium,' Andrew concluded. 'Let's meet again tomorrow afternoon. Then I'll fill in any gaps and tell you what will happen in the séance, at least initially. Events after that can't be predicted with any accuracy.'

Back at HQ, Julia outlined what had taken place and dealt with the team's questions as best she could.

The next afternoon's meeting with Andrew was relatively brief. He asked a few more questions and then outlined what Julia should expect.

'There'll be three others at the table. You'll sit in a semi-circle so that you can hold hands. The medium will sit opposite, further into the room. Before she joins you, I'll ask you all to talk briefly about your departed loved ones and what you hope to hear from them. Then the room will be darkened. The medium will enter and summon the spirit guides by name. As I've already said, I can't tell you what will happen after that, but I'm sure it will be helpful and healing. The séance is scheduled for noon tomorrow. I'll see you there. Oh, I nearly forgot. No mobile phones. Their radiation disrupts communications from the spirit world.'

'They've really spun things out,' said Julia back at HQ. 'You'd think they'd get me into a séance as soon as possible, in case I changed my mind.'

'It's to give them time to check you out,' said Fred. 'They downloaded the background story we created. The conversations with you were designed to establish that your own account matched it exactly. I'm certain they've accepted our fake narrative, that they believe you are a very wealthy woman in a state of profound grief. Ripe for the picking.'

'Would you feel safer with some back-up?' asked George. 'One of us could park close to the church hall in case you need help.'

'I'm sure I won't be harmed. At least until they've finished trying to get my money. The amount of checking they've done suggests some insecurity. They'll be vigilant for anything suspicious. One of us in a parked car might give the game away. I'm happy to go in alone.'

CHAPTER THIRTY-FIVE

The séance room was fully lit when Andrew ushered Julia in. All four of the easy chairs had been arranged to face each other, and two were occupied. When he had seated Julia, Andrew went out, returning immediately with a fourth person whom he seated in the remaining chair.

'I'll leave you to introduce yourselves. The medium wants you to connect with each other emotionally as well as physically. If possible, share what has brought you here, and what you hope to achieve. You'll see a glass on each side table. The drinks contain herbs that will enhance your sensitivity to the spirit world, so please take them. They taste quite pleasant and are totally safe.'

'I'm Lenny,' said the one man present. 'I've just lost my wife Dora from ovarian cancer. She was only forty-two, three years younger than me. In a hospice towards the end, her pain was well managed, thank God. Even though I expected it, her death has devastated me. We had no children. It was always just the two of us. Dora believed in life after death, in a kind of spirit world rather than a Christian heaven. I'm not sure about all that, but if she's in that world, I know she'll try and contact me. That's why I'm here.'

A woman on Lenny's left spoke next.

'I'm Hilary. My husband Bill was driving our two sons to school when the car was hit by an out-of-control truck. All three died at the scene. Bill was forty-eight, the boys, Justin and David, were fourteen and fifteen. I'm forty-three. To be honest, I'm still in a state of shock. It hasn't fully sunk in. But I'm ready to try and contact them. I don't have a strong belief in an afterlife, but I'm open to the possibility, and I'm desperate enough to try anything that might ease what I know will soon become an unbearable pain.'

Julia spoke next. She felt acutely uncomfortable narrating her concocted story, but drew upon the skills she had honed as a barrister. Seeing tears in the eyes of both women, Julia knew that she'd been convincing.

The third woman introduced herself as Stella.

'I'm a passionate rock climber, or used to be. My favourite climbs are at Mt Arapiles, near the town of Natimuk in Victoria. It will help if I talk a bit about them. They range from easy to extremely hard. The three hardest are Somalia, Punks in the Gym and Light Weight Baby. My dearest friend Georgie shared my passion. We had climbed Somalia and Punks in the Gym together. Because we managed both climbs without too much difficulty, Georgie suggested that we climb the very hardest, Light Weight Baby. We trained hard for it.

We started early morning on a cloudless day, thinking the fine weather was a good omen. We use triple lock carabiners to link our ropes or secure them to cams. Cams are inserted into cracks in the rock face and expanded to allow weight bearing. Triple lock carabiners are strong, round pieces of metal and are the safest to use, but setting them requires both hands in three steps. Somehow, near the top of the climb, I got it wrong. My only excuse is exhaustion: the climb was much tougher than we'd expected.

The carabiner sprang open, and I fell, taking Georgie with me. A cam lower down halted my fall, but I was left dangling precariously. The cam started to come loose. Perhaps I hadn't set it in correctly. If it failed, both Georgie and I would fall to our deaths.

Georgie was dangling about four metres below me. She could see that the cam was close to failing. 'I can still pull you up,' I shouted. She shouted back. "No you can't. I love you." And she cut the rope.

I was able to get back down. Georgie's body had fallen all the way to the ground. Three other climbers were attending her. Her helmet had protected her head and face, but her body was just a mass of torn flesh and broken bones. I honestly can't remember much of what happened after that.

We had both made wills, knowing that we were not immune to accidents. Georgie had wanted a simple funeral, and for her ashes to be scattered at the foot of Punks in the Gym. It was only after I had scattered her ashes that I noticed how utterly sad and empty her death had left me. I thought seriously of suicide, perhaps in another fall. Then I remembered Georgie talking about seeing ghosts and hearing the voices of First

Nations people when we passed near their burial sites around Mt Arapiles. She described herself as fey, as otherworldly in the sense of being aware of the spirit world, which for her really existed. So instead of killing myself, I decided to come here in the hope of hearing from my dearest friend.'

Julia felt tears in her eyes and saw them in the eyes of the other three.

At this point Andrew reappeared. He had obviously been listening, either from an alcove, or through hidden microphones. Julia assumed that the medium had been listening also.

'We're ready to start. Please finish your drinks and take your seats at the table.

Lenny, please sit second from the left. The medium will arrive shortly.'

The room darkened and a woman dressed in white robes entered silently, seating herself at the opposite end of the table and facing towards the four bereaved. She wore a hood. This and the twilight made it impossible to make out her features. She gazed steadily at them, perhaps using cold reading to add something to what she already knew.

'Welcome. My name is Hestia. In a moment I will call upon my spirit guides. They are unpredictable, but their presence is vital. I promise that they will cause no harm to any of you. Please join your hands.'

The room darkened further. Hestia bowed her head in silence for a moment before speaking again.

'I call upon the spirits of Kathumi and Nada to enter this realm, to guide us and protect us while we cross into the spirit world.'

There was complete silence. Then a cool breeze, quite gentle, wafted across the table.

'They are here. We can begin. Julia, please be the first to speak.'

Julia was well prepared.

'Dearest Lucy, I'm praying that you can hear me. Please say something. Anything.'

There was a long silence. Them the medium's body twisted in a spasm, and she rocked back in her chair.

'I hear you, dear sister. I am well and happy in the spirit world. I miss you, but grief in this world is somehow a blessing, not a burden.'

The medium's voice was raspy and sometimes a little difficult to hear. Her delivery was unemotional, almost flat. Julia thought this might be to protect her voice from fatigue. After a pause, the voice continued.

'Please shed your tears Julia, but in the knowledge of my happiness and security. And then, I pray, get on with your life. You have so much to offer. I want you to know that I've made friends in this world. And two of them would like to speak to you. But at another time. My links with you are beginning to fade.'

The medium slumped forward, her head resting on the table. Some minutes passed before she raised her head.

'That was more draining than I expected. I need to rest before we continue. But not for long, I'm very resilient. You can remain seated.'

The room lightened to twilight and Hestia moved to one of the easy chairs. After about ten minutes, she resumed her seat at the table.

'Stella, will you please speak next.'

'My beloved Georgie. I miss you so much, and I feel unbearably guilty. If I'd closed the carabiner properly, you'd still be with me. I want your forgiveness, but most of all, I want to know that you are safe and happy in the world that you believed in.'

Hestia's body again went into spasm. Her voice, though still raspy and at times a little slurred, was subtly different from that in her first message.

'Of course I forgive you, my love. We should never have tried Light Weight Baby. It was beyond us. I'm as much to blame as you are. It was my idea, so stop feeling guilty. I'm happy and safe in the spirit world. I know you still have tears to shed, but when they dry, which they surely will, I beg you to resume life to the full. Maybe even start climbing again, or at least become a trainer, a mentor. We need many more of those. So, for now, my dearest friend, farewell.'

Hestia needed another break. Resuming her chair, she asked Lenny to speak next.

'Dora, my dearest love. I know your last days were full of pain, despite everything they did for you in the hospice. I pray that you are now in a place of tranquillity, free of all suffering.'

Hestia's body went through the now familiar spasms and contortions. She then spoke in a voice quite different from that of her first two encounters.

'Lenny, my dearest friend, know that I am free of all suffering in this new world. I am happy and safe. My only wish is for you to find again the love and joy that we shared. I've made a friend here and she wants to talk to you.'

After a pause, Hestia spoke again, but in a voice that was subtly different.

'My name is Denise. I was convicted of extortion and blackmail and sentenced to eleven years in prison, where I died. Dora has told me that you are very wealthy. She has given me permission to ask you to make redress. Please send as much as you can afford to a charity called Saving the Dispossessed. If you do, it will help me rest in peace, to forgive myself for causing so much pain to so many.'

Lenny promised to do so. The voice faded and was replaced by Dora's. 'It's really important to me, as well as to Denise, that you are as generous as possible. By doing so, you will add yet more to my happiness. Goodbye, my love.'

Hilary's introduction to Bill was along similar lines, followed by similar reassurances and hopes. The channel wasn't strong enough for the boys to speak, but Bill assured Hilary that, like him, they were happy and safe. There was no request for money.

By the time Hestia had recovered from communicating with Bill, it was just past four. The medium said firmly that Stella and Hilary should not risk another séance, in case the spirit guides played up and confused them. But Julia and Lenny would need to come again, Julia to receive more messages, and Lenny to confirm that he'd met the requests of his late wife and her spirit friend. A second séance was arranged for noon, two days later.

The team listened to Julia's recording as soon as she got back to HQ.

'It's all so convincing,' said Sue. 'If I'd been there, I'm sure I would have started to believe in the spirit world. What about you, Julia? And did the herbal mixture have any effect?'

'Although I believe in the afterlife,' Julia replied thought fully, 'I've never had a vision of it. It's always been something to be revealed only when I die. But now I have a vision: the one created in the séance. It's stuck in my head. I can't shake it, even though I know it was all fantasy. This could be the effect of the so-called herbal mixture. I suspect that in reality the drink contained a drug that increased our suggestibility. A hypnotic agent. Ensuring that what we experienced in the séance was somehow implanted in our psyche, and that we keep, at all costs, any promises we made to our dear departed. That's not only illegal, but potentially very dangerous. I'm due for my first antenatal check tomorrow. I'll ask about the risk of any drugs crossing the placenta to the embryo. Whatever they say, I'll use my pregnancy as an excuse to refuse the herbal mixture next time.'

'I'm pretty sure,' said George, 'that you were given a small dose of one of the barbiturates. Not enough to sedate you, but enough to increase your susceptibility, amplifying the overall effect of the séance. Barbiturates do cross the placenta, but a single lowish dose won't affect the embryo. But of course you must refuse to take the herbal mixture.'

'I'll check out the charity,' said Fred. 'Won't take long, so hang about.

Saving the Dispossessed is a registered charity,' explained Fred an hour or so later. 'It meets all the statutory requirements. Surprise, surprise. It's part of the Church of Spiritual Enlightenment, which itself has charitable status. Charities are protected from scrutiny unless there's evidence of wrongdoing. The church's charity has funds of just over eight and a half million dollars.'

'Have we recorded enough of the séance to take the data to the authorities?' Julia asked.

'I don't think so. We'll need a recording of the second séance. From what Hestia told you about it, that should be enough.'

Two days later, in the late afternoon, Julia gave the team a summary of events.

'It went as Hestia planned, apart from my refusal to take the herbal mixture, which she reluctantly accepted. Just Lenny and I were there. I now realise that involving two others in the first séance was to make it all as convincing as possible. They were stage props, but they undoubtedly benefitted from the experience. I was contacted by Lucy's spirit who immediately introduced her two friends, both women. One asked me to immediately give as much aa possible to Saving the Dispossessed, briefly explaining why this was absolutely vital. She prayed that other donations would follow. The second friend asked me to transfer one hundred thousand dollars to a bank account, making sure that the details had been transmitted correctly. Again, her reasons were totally convincing. Without the influence of the drug, I knew I'd be less susceptible to those demands, but still, to my surprise, I felt a strong obligation to meet them. I promised to do so.'

Lenny confirmed to Dora and her friend that he'd transferred funds to Saving the Dispossessed. Fifty thousand dollars initially, with the promise of more to follow. Hestia advised us both strongly against any further séance, with the same explanation she'd given to Stella and Hilary. She concluded by congratulating us on our courage and perseverance, and that she was delighted by the seances' positive and rewarding outcome.'

The team then listened to the recording, naturally much shorter than the first one.

'It shouldn't take me long to find out who owns the bank account for the hundred thousand dollar transfer,' said Ahmad. 'Even if it can't be connected to the church, I'm sure we've got enough data to send to the authorities.'

Although the account was connected to an intermediary, Ahmad traced it back to the church. The team then agreed to transmit all the recorded data to the relevant authority. By the following afternoon, Fred and Ahmad had done this, together with a comprehensive explanation of the context.

The head of the authority decided that the activities of the charity were not only in breach of its statutory code of conduct, but criminal. She contacted the Federal Police who, once they had digested the contents of the two recordings, decided to act.

Aware that investigating a registered charity was a delicate matter, the Feds delayed action until they had identified all those in the senior ranks of both the church and Saving the Dispossessed, which turned out to be the church's sole charity. Then, with the help of the local police, they arrested all of them in a single overnight raid.

'Let's hope they find a record of all the victims,' said Julia at the next team meeting. 'They should get most of their money back. The truth might be painful to them, but they deserve to know it. For me, it's been as tough gig. I couldn't have done it without your help and support. But it's been worth it. I'm really happy that we've stopped the ruthless exploitation of people who joined the church in a spirit of hope. And I'm especially happy that my vision of the afterlife has been restored to a mystery that will be revealed only when I pass across. Now, it's time for our usual celebration. Will someone please make me a lemon, lime and bitters?'

CHAPTER THIRTY-SIX

Julia didn't realise how stressful the seances had been until she woke the next morning and struggled to get out of bed. She was totally exhausted. After two days of complete rest, she joined the team at their next gathering.

'I'm fully recovered,' she announced. 'Ready for anything. What's new?'

'I've got a potential gig,' said Sue. 'But before I tell you about it, there's something I want to get off my chest. Please bear with me. I think we're too work focussed. I know we all feel exhausted after a tough gig and need a day or two to recover. This leaves little time for socialising together. For me, our post-gig celebrations have become a meaningless ritual. Except for Julia, we just get drunk. I want to know about how you're all coping with life, about your hopes and expectations. I'm asking you to put work aside. I want to know about your lives.'

There was a lengthy silence, broken by Fred.

'I've already shared a great deal with you all, more than I've ever shared with anyone. You know how, after my parents' murder, I struggled to make relationships, let alone intimate ones. I chose a life that was basically virtual, online. Of course, my hacking skills, together with Ahmad's, have been vital to our success. And I want to continue with all that. I feel close to all of you, but I struggle to express that, however much I want to.'

'I have an idea,' said Sue. 'Why don't we meet just to socialise? Outside of HQ. Finding a safe venue will be tricky, given our enemies out there. But it's do-able. And Fred, why don't you buy a house? Maybe living in HQ is part of the problem.'

'You're right, of course. If I had my own home, I could at least invite people round. It's time I started looking. I'd welcome some company during the search.'

'Count me in,' said Sue. 'Now, George. I know you've laid yourself bare to us, revealed your dalliance with autoerotic asphyxia, your self-destructive behaviour. You said that your time with Morgana might help. Has it?'

'Yes. The pain that she inflicted on me was beyond my capacity to bear. Somehow, it left me almost free of any impulse to injure myself. And the success of the gig boosted my self-esteem. I'm better able to control any residual impulses. Almost cured. Which is timely, given that I'm soon to become a father.'

'Ahmad, even though we've become close, I know less about you than I know about Julia, George and Fred. Not that you've been secretive in any way. It just hasn't come out.'

'I was always acutely conscious of being Anglo-Indonesian. That, together with acute shyness, probably a social phobia, took me into the IT world, a world empty of direct social contact. I was far too shy to date anyone. And that's where you found me. I lived alone, still do of course. You all, as a team rescued me. Since working with you, I've really come out of my shell.'

'We've noticed!' quipped Sue.

'But I still find it difficult to talk about myself, even to you Sue. Something I want to work on.'

'I've been rescued too,' said Julia. 'After the deep fake destroyed my life, George, Fred and Sue welcomed me into the team. Gave me my life back.

Meeting the challenges of our gigs has restored my self-confidence and my self-esteem. Most important, it's made me ready for motherhood. Falling back in love with George has been the icing on the cake.'

'There's yet another rescue!' exclaimed Sue. 'After NIDA, I couldn't get any gigs. The café assault was a blessing in disguise. It took me here, where the casino job plunged me into the deep end and let me use my acting skills at last! Working with you all has been scary, exciting, challenging and very rewarding. I'm so grateful I was given the chance, and for Ahmad's friendship. That friendship, that love, is my icing on the cake, together with the use we've made of my passion for art.

Well, that's about it. Thank you all for being so open and honest. Now I can tell you about the gig. But to explain how it came about, I need to tell you about the background. One of my favourite artists is Augustus John. His sister, Gwen John, was probably a better painter, but was much less prolific. Augustus was both an eccentric and a womaniser. So numerous were his liaisons that he once said in jest, 'If I pass I child in the street, I always pat it on the head, in case it's one of mine.'

There was a ripple of laughter.

'In spite of his many faults, I found him an engaging character, and I studied his life and work. Augustus had a passion for gypsies. He bought his own gypsy caravan and travelled with several gypsy communities. They welcomed him because he created many paintings of them, some of which he gave to the community depicted. Now, of course, those which have survived are worth a fortune. His 'Head of a Girl' sold for four hundred and eighty-eight thousand American dollars in 2021.

Infected by his passion, I joined a gypsy community for a couple of weeks, ostensibly to paint them. My painting skills were so inadequate that they saw through me. But I was still made to feel welcome, and I learned a great deal about their way of life.'

'How come you never told us about this?' asked Fred.

'It never seemed important. And I thought it would be seen as a foible, something rather silly. So, I kept quiet about it. And we've always focussed on my NIDA training and love for art. Anyway, I kept in touch with a gypsy woman, Kezia, who'd befriended me. Not regular contact, but frequent enough to keep the friendship alive.

Yesterday she phoned me for help. One of her community, a middle-aged man, had been shot dead. The police are hostile to gypsies and were unhelpful. The autopsy showed that the man had been killed with a rifle bullet, a 303. Almost certainly the work of a sniper. The community fears it will happen again.'

'Why would she turn to you for help?' asked Ahmad.

'Gypsies are frequently harassed, not just by the authorities, but by locals. Kezia has told me about some of the more serious incidents. I told her, without giving anything away, that I was part of a group that works for those who are marginalised, oppressed of persecuted. So that's why Kezia turned to me. I told her that I could help, but that I needed to brief my team and get their support before going ahead. Are you with me on this?'

It took only a few minutes for the team to come on board.

'I know we haven't got a plan,' said Fred. 'But we'll work something out. Meanwhile, why don't you tell Kezia that your whole team wants to help, and that we'll let her know when we're ready for action. You could add that it would take a day or two to come up with a plan, and that we wouldn't do anything without her approval.'

'Thank you all for your support. There's no question of charging a fee, of course. But we've done pro bono gigs before. We can well afford to do another one. Now, I need to tell you a bit about the gypsies. We can't come up with a viable plan unless we understand their history and culture. So again, please bear with me.

They originated in Northern India in the eleventh and twelfth centuries. As Hindus they were persecuted by the Muslims. They fled into central Asia, living peacefully in and around what is now Istanbul until the Turks forced them out in the fourteenth century. Subsequently, they were discouraged from settling in most of Europe because they were thought to be forerunners of a Turkish invasion.

Allowed into Romania, for the next five hundred years they were essentially slaves, forced to do work that the Romanians considered beneath them. Made redundant by the Industrial Revolution, an act of Parliament freed them in 1837. But with no training or education, they became beggars, fortune tellers and petty thieves.

In many other European countries, laws were passed to force the gypsies to leave, or to enslave them. Many of those who remained survived by acquiring skills such as basket-making and metal working, which made them an asset. But this positive element has been obscured by the prevailing misconception that all gypsies are thieves and scoundrels, to be constantly moved on, never to be trusted.'

'What should we call them?' asked Julia. 'Romanis, gypsies, travellers? And how did their name originate?'

'The gypsies call themselves Roma. The name gypsy arose because the early Roma described themselves as Egyptians.'

'When did they first arrive in Australia?' asked Ahmad.

'The first gypsies arrived in 1791, as convicts transported from England. By the time transportation ceased in 1852, some seventy of the convicts, including nine women, had Romani heritage. All except two had committed "victimless" crimes, against property rather than people. Their skills included knife-sharpening, horse-breaking, brick-making, pottery, basket-making, and most notably the construction of tents. This made those with this skill indispensable.

Once they had completed their sentences, the gypsies, like the other convicts, were given land grants. Most made good use of these, aided by their traditional skills in horse-breaking, animal husbandry, tinkering and craftwork. Because there were so few gypsy women, nearly all the men married non-gypsies, and began to assimilate. Practising their trades required a relatively dense population, something entirely absent in Australia at that time. This constraint was another reason for their assimilation: they had to take whatever work was available.

In spite of these problems, the gypsy population steadily increased. There was little immigration: gypsies were very wary of travel by sea, which had never been part of their culture. It was not until the era of steamships, judged relatively safe, that they arrived here in any number. Many gypsy men were drawn by work as riggers and performers in travelling fairs and circuses, entertainment made affordable by the wealth created in gold rushes. By the start of the twentieth century, encampments were not uncommon in areas where there was enough work for them, both men and women. Employment in travelling shows meshed with their traditional lifestyle of moving on as a soon as their services were no longer required.'

'How did they travel?' Julia asked.

'Those with regular work in the travelling shows generally went with them. Of the others, very few could afford caravans. Most travelled in carts, living in tents. Encampments, though usually quite small, sometimes attracted hostility, even occasional violence. Naturally this reinforced the Romanis' sense of difference, of isolation from society at large.

Industrialisation destroyed the market for their handicrafts and reduced the need for manual labour, especially on farms. Travelling shows and circuses fell out of fashion as other forms of entertainment emerged. By the 1970's, most Romani families were struggling to make a living. Then, the increased affordability of air travel spawned another wave of Romani immigration. In the late 1980's, the fall of Communist regimes allowed freedom of travel, which the gypsy populations took full advantage of. The increased Romani population led to the creation of the Romani Association of Australia, which launched its website in 2003. This connected Australian gypsies not only to each other, but to the rest of the world. It led to a cultural renaissance.

Today, there are some twenty thousand Romanis in Australis, comprising several subgroups. Although increasingly rare, gypsy encampments still exist, members travelling in cars, vans, trucks and modern caravans. My friend Kezia is from one of these encampments.'

'Where is her encampment at the moment?' asked George.

'In Western Australia, about ten kilometres inland from Albany. Fairly remote, but with enough of a local population for the group to ply some of its traditional trades. It's been there for over three months and will stay longer. These days, encampments don't rely on income from the services they provide. Members have learned to play the system. The dole helps fill gaps in their finances, which allows them to live above the poverty line, although not by much.'

'From everything Sue's explained,' said Ahmad, 'Some of us have to go out to the encampment. If Sue agrees, I'd love to go there with her. I feel a strong connection to the Romanis, perhaps because of my own sense of being marginalised as an Anglo-Indonesian. Sue, what do you say?'

'It's a no-brainer. I'll arrange things with Kezia. Then we'll fly to Perth, hire a car, and join the encampment.'

CHAPTER
THIRTY-SEVEN

Ahmad and Sue hired a 4WD at Perth International Airport. The journey to the Gypsie encampment, a distance of just over four hundred kilometres, took seven and a half hours. Kezia had given precise details of her location, so they found the encampment quite easily, even though darkness has fallen.

Kezia, told by text of their imminent arrival, waved at them as they drove in. Legally or otherwise, the site was connected to the electricity grid and was illuminated by the light from various vehicles and a few lamps on wooden poles. Kezia embraced Sue and after a moment's hesitation, gave Ahmad a quick hug. She led them into a mobile home.

'This is the only mobile home here, allocated to my husband and I because of our status. Ah, here he is.'

A short, swarthy man with a twirled moustache held out his hand with a smile.

'I'm Django. Welcome to our humble abode. It's late, and you must be tired after your long drive. We have two bedrooms, and you are welcome to one of them. Would you like something to eat before retiring?'

'We snacked on the way,' Sue replied, 'and you're right, we're both exhausted. So, we'll unpack and go straight to bed.'

During an early breakfast, Kezia talked a about the encampment.

'We have seventeen caravans, all fairly modern except a traditional one that we keep as a symbol of our culture. There are also three Winnebagos, which are meant for couples with young children but are not used for that right now. And of course, we have cars and vans for touring and local trips, together with a truck and trailer.'

'How many of you altogether?' asked Ahmad.

'The number varies a bit from time to time. At the moment, we have thirty-eight adults and forty-three children, including teenagers. The children are from only ten married couples. Our culture rejoices in children, and most Romani couples have at least four. Now, let me show you around.'

Kezia stopped a few paces away from the mobile home. 'The land you see before you belongs to a local farmer. We pay what is probably an exorbitant rent, and he needs the money enough to put up with the locals who don't want us here. He's let us run a couple of hoses from his water mains, so that we can keep tanked up. Charges us extra, of course!'

The site was almost square and occupied about two hectares. The vehicles were arranged around the perimeter. In the centre was a playground with a tall slide, a roundabout, climbing frames, swings, a seesaw and a small sandpit. There were no children. At just after eight, it was too early for them.

'If we needed any evidence of your love for children, there it is,' said Sue, pointing to the playground. 'I've not seen one better equipped.' She then pointed towards a marquee adjacent to a smaller tent. 'What are they for?'

'The marquee is for gatherings of the whole community. There's a stage inside which can be used for entertainment. We had a show for the locals, which went well, and helped those who came to accept us. But they are a minority. Most would like us out of here. I've arranged for you both to meet everyone in the marquee this evening. I hope that's okay. The smaller tent is for guests who can't be accommodated elsewhere in the encampment.'

'Before we meet the community, we need to have full details of the murder,' said Sue. 'I know it's painful for you to talk about, but we must know everything if we're going to be helpful.'

'Of course. As soon as we've finished the tour. Any more questions?'

'What about sewage? You must generate a fair bit!'

'Behind the smaller tent, there is a Biocell wastewater treatment plant. Biocell design these for specific locations. The one they've designed for us can be dismantled and transported in our truck. It's big enough to render all our sewage into harmless wastewater, which we use to water our herbs. And it meets all the requirements of the local council.'

Back in the mobile home, they were joined by Django. Kezia began the conversation. 'For reasons that will become clear, this murder has frightening ramifications. Bear with me while I explain why. Django will, I'm sure, add any-thing important that I forget. Our finances are at the core of all this. No-one wants our traditional services like knife-grinding, basket-making, horse-breaking, metalwork. We have a stall in Albany selling clothing and handicrafts. Our embroidery, crocheting and lacework are exquisite, but the stall doesn't earn much. Several men and women work in and around Albany. Manual labour mostly. And we make full use of the dole. But we only just break even. Shortage of cash has turned some of us to drug production and trafficking.'

'What?' exclaimed Sue and Ahmad simultaneously. 'You can't be serious,' Sue added.

'I'm afraid we are,' replied Django. 'Our truck and trailer house the production and storage facilities. Making crystal meth is incredibly smelly. It yields odours described as cat urine. So, we put the truck and trailer as far away as possible. But many of us know about it.'

'Two families are involved,' said Kezia. 'Both include several men and women seriously addicted to crystal meth. That's why it's been impossible to stop them making the stuff. We've tried, but they make threats. Serious ones. Those who know about it have learned to keep quiet. The man who was shot was a key dealer. He'd managed to create a distribution network in and around Albany, with some contacts as far away as Perth. You wouldn't believe the demand for crystal meth, although fentanyl is becoming steadily more popular. If demand for fentanyl overtakes that for crystal meth, they'll learn how to make it.'

'How can we help?' asked Ahmad.

'At tonight's community meeting in the marquee, Django will introduce you as researchers, planning to write a book about Romanis. He'll stress your positive attitude towards us and invite people to be generous and honest in answering your questions. We hope this fiction will obscure the true reason for your interest, which is, of course, to permanently eliminate all drug production and trafficking within our community.'

The meeting in the marquee went as planned. Afterwards, several men and women approached Ahmad and Sue, expressing their wish to help as much as possible.

'That's a good start,' said Ahmad, back in the mobile home. 'Now we just need a plan. Any ideas?'

'I've given this some thought,' Sue replied. 'You could pose as a buyer. Explain that you and your friends are recreational users but can't get the drug in Sydney without paying more than you can afford. Say that Kezia told me all about the situation here. When I told you, you realised it created the chance of getting plenty of the drug at a much cheaper price. That's why you decided to join me.'

'Posing as a recreational user is much more plausible and safer than posing as an addict,' said Ahmad. 'I think it'll work. But we'll need Kezia and Django to back the story up.'

'That's no problem,' said Django. 'It might make Kezia look a little loose-mouthed, but that's a small price to pay for stopping this evil trade. Am I right Kezia?'

'Absolutely. Looking a bit of a flap jaw might tarnish my impeccable reputation, but if we win this fight, we'll all be heroes!'

'Before I contact the drug dealer, I need to learn all about crystal meth. Give me the rest of the evening.'

After breakfast the next day, Ahmad outlined what he'd learned.

'Most users heat the crystals in a container until it vaporises and then inhale it. The effect is almost instant, and the dose can be titrated. Some snort it, with a slightly delayed effect. If it's mixed into food or drink, the effect is delayed for at least half an hour but can last for up to twelve hours. A few hard-core addicts inject it intravenously, which allows an instant big hit. I'll tell the supplier that my strong preference is to inhale.'

'They'll expect you to try a sample,' said Django. 'How will you manage that?'

'I'll inhale the vapor. But instead of holding it in, I'll sneakily exhale it. If they watch me too closely for that, I'll get high, but let's hope it won't limit my capacity to be rational and coherent. I'll need all my wits about me to plant the two microphones that will transmit their conversations to my receiver. I'll relay the data to Fred back at HQ. We can't analyse it here.'

'I'll come with you,' said Kezia. 'I'll introduce you to the key players and back up your story. They'll want to be sure you're the real thing.'

Kezia knocked on the door of one of the Winnebagos. It was opened by a young woman with bleached blonde hair.

'Hello Kezia. What can we do for you?'

'I want to introduce Ahmad to your family. He's interested in buying some of your product.'

'You're in luck. The boss is in. Come on through.'

The boss, a stout middle-aged man with a shiny bald head, shook Kezia's hand.

'Duke, meet Ahmad. He wants to buy some of your product. I can vouch for him.'

'Given your hostility to our operation,' said Duke, 'I'm astonished by the introduction. You'll have to convince me Ahmad's the real thing. Since my brother-in-law was shot, we're being extra careful about security.'

'I've brought Ahmad here under duress. He threatened harm if I didn't cooperate. Bear with me while I explain how he came to be here.'

'You've convinced me Kezia,' said Duke when Kezia finished talking. 'Please leave while we get down to business. Ahmad, how much do you want to buy?'

'That's depends on the price. My fellow users and I have clubbed together, so I'm well-funded.'

'I can do it for seventy dollars a gram. You won't get it cheaper anywhere else.'

'A gram's about five hits. So that's fourteen dollars a hit. Can you bring it down a bit?'

'Only if you buy a lot. A minimum of half a kilo. I can do that for sixty dollars a gram. That's thirty grand. Are you up for that? Or maybe even a kilo?'

'I'll need to discuss it with the others. It's a good offer. They'd be crazy not to agree to half a kilo. Might stretch to a kilo. Bur before we go any further, I'd like to try a sample.'

Duke put a quarter gram in a glass container with a handle and heated its base with a Bunsen burner. They watched the crystals melt and then vaporise. Ahmad took the container and placed its opening under his nose, inhaling cautiously. Pretending to hold his breath, he surreptitiously exhaled.

'You're not holding it in,' said Duke. 'I promise you it's pure. Absolutely safe. So, take it like you're used to.'

Ahmad didn't have to feign intoxication. He rose to his feet, wobbled, and fell back into his chair.

'It's much stronger than anything we can get in Sydney. I'm feeling sick. Where's the loo?'

Ahmad made loud retching noises in the toilet before flushing it. 'Give me a few minutes,' he called out. 'I might be sick again.'

After a few more retches, he flushed the toilet and cautiously opened the door. The adjacent room was empty. He planted one of the tiny microphones. Feigning disorientation, he entered the kitchen-dining area and planted the second microphone. Then he rejoined Duke.

'Sorry about that. But at least I know your product is of the highest quality. That will help persuade my friends. For now, I'll buy just five grams. And a glass pipe. I didn't bring mine just in case I was searched at the airport. It'll take a while to connect with my fellow users, but I can't buy the half-kilo without their say-so. I'll get back to you as soon as I can.'

Back at the mobile home, Sue was waiting for Ahmad. Still a bit woozy, he related events as best he could. 'We need to spin this out as long as we can,' said Sue. 'Record as much as possible. Can you buy us a couple of days?'

'I think so. Duke wouldn't give me his phone number, on security grounds. But I'll go over, invent reasons for a delay. Duke will understand that getting the agreement of a bunch of dope-heads might take some time. Now, I have an idea. Why don't we try a bit of crystal meth ourselves? I've got the doings. We just need a source of heat. There must be a hikers' stove around somewhere.'

'You'll remember that my older sister was a drug addict, and that she died of a heroin overdose. Since her death, I've avoided all drugs. Except booze of course. But I've got some of her genes, and I have strong impulses to get high, escape, during bad times. I've always resisted them, but I'm still at risk. If I do this with you, it'll be kill or cure. I'm willing to give it a try. But only because I'm doing it with you. Should we tell Kezia and Django?'

'I think so. We'll need a hikers' stove to heat crystals, and if they haven't got one, I'll ask them to borrow one. I'll tell them that Duke wants some feedback about the product. That I need to experiment a bit to be plausible. Let's aim to get things organised for tomorrow morning.'

In their little bedroom, Ahmad and Sue watched the crystals melt and vaporise. They both inhaled deeply, holding the vapor in. They became a bit giggly and disinhibited.

'Ahmad my dearest. I know you want to make love to me, and I really want it too. We've never done it because we thought it would create problems in the team. But that's not the only reason, is it?'

'I'm a virgin,' Ahmad replied after a brief pause. 'You know how shy I was, especially with women. I've been scared that I'd disappoint you, maybe put you off.'

'I'll be gentle. Patient. Let's give it a try.'

'You're a fast learner,' said Sue, nearly two hours later. 'That was fantastic. Multiple orgasms! How about you?'

'Not to take away from your skilful and loving tuition, but I think the meth was a big help. It took away my anxiety, boosted my confidence. It was all amazing. Wonderful. I came three times!

I can hardly believe it. We'll have to do it again sometime.'

Sue laughed. 'But not right now. I'm orgasmed out!'

Ahmad laughed in return, and then closed his eyes, feeling better than at any time he could remember. Sue cuddled up to him and let herself fall asleep.

It was mid-afternoon before they woke up.

'Well,' asked Ahmad. 'Do you feel like another hit? Is it kill or cure?'

'I think the hit's worn off completely. But I don't have the slightest desire for another one. Early days, I know, but I'm pretty sure it's cure, not kill.'

'Then I'll flush what's left down the toilet. You okay with that?

'Absolutely. Then let's go and chat with Kezia and Django. They'll want to know about our trip. And we need some advice about how to be convincing in our role as researchers.'

'Good thinking, Sue. Tomorrow I'll need to talk to Duke again, create more delays before finalising the drug deal. By then we might have heard form Fred about the recordings.'

Fred had not yet contacted them when Ahmad knocked on the door of Duke's Winnebago just after ten the next morning.

The same young woman opened it.

'Is Duke in?'

'Yes, I'll see if he's free.'

She quickly returned to usher Ahmad into the room where Duke was waiting. He shook Ahmad's hand and indicated an easy chair.

'What progress, Ahmad?'

'Not much I'm afraid. My so-called friends are arguing about how much to order. Some of them want to buy two kilos and on-sell it in Sydney for more than twice the price. Others want to order just enough for personal use. And they're wondering whether to transport it back to Sydney by car or on the Indian Pacific, or if you have a courier service.'

'Almost none of our product goes to Sydney. Too much competition. So I'm not worried about your friends entering the market there. But others will be, and it'll come back to me. Things could get very nasty. So on-selling our product is out of the question. And of course I don't have a courier service to Sydney.'

'That's settled then,' said Ahmad. 'I should know how much they want to order by some time tomorrow. But if there's still no agreement, I'll make the decision myself.'

'I've heard from Fred,' said Sue when Ahmad had got back to the mobile home. 'He's excited.

There's already enough to send to the Feds, but he'd like another day or so to clinch it. The data even included a phone number, spelt out for accuracy.'

'Perfect timing. Tomorrow afternoon I'll see Duke and order half a kilo. That's thirty grand, but we have to buy it, or he'll suspect that we were the ones who tipped off the Feds. That could put us in real danger. Meanwhile, let's do some of the research that's expected of us.'

They spent the rest of the day talking to caravan residents. All were welcoming and willing to answer questions that were not too sensitive. In the early evening, they gave Kezia and Django a summary of what they had gleaned.

'We asked them all,' said Ahmad, 'why they chose to live here rather than in regular housing. A majority explained that they couldn't afford to rent or buy near other Romanis, most of whom had got into the housing market early on, when it was much more affordable. Being part of a Romani community is very important to them, and this encampment was both welcoming and affordable.'

Sue continued the narrative.

'Others said they could afford to rent an apartment near other Romanis but could not bear the confines of such a dwelling. Encampment life was far more desirable. The others emphasised the importance of Romani culture, and especially the Romani language. We learned that this is more complex than might be thought, as there are several dialects. Traditionally, we were told, all Romanis learned the language of their host country. This allowed them to talk to each other if their Romani dialects were too different. In Australia, apparently, most speak the Kalderash dialect, and this is what the children here are taught. But we couldn't find out how many children actually speak it when they grow up.'

'Fewer and fewer,' Kezia replied. 'We have to send the older children to a local school, and that creates competing demands. More generally, many choose to leave their encampment as soon as they are old enough, but most of them stay connected to it one way or another. Our culture simply won't survive without ceaseless efforts to keep it alive. Even little things are important: playing our traditional musical instruments, eating our traditional foods like the goulash we call Yogray, having Romani weddings, cooking in pits. Django and I work really hard at keeping all this alive. But it's increasingly hard work, increasingly unrewarding.'

Sue and Ahmad spent the next morning visiting more caravans. In one of them, a woman called Esmeralda insisted on telling their fortunes, explaining that this was a central aspect of her culture. 'It's my trade, but these days there's little demand for my services. I won't charge a fee. You'll help me keep in practice!'

Esmerelda had a crystal ball in a small, darkened room. Sue entered first.

'I see an approaching watershed,' said Esmeralda to Sue, gazing into the clouding crystal ball. 'Soon you'll have to make a decision that will change everything in your life. I cannot divine what choices will confront you, or what you will decide, but I can see that making the choice will be very difficult. And that it cannot be undone. You must live with its consequences, good or bad. I can see no more.'

When Sue told Ahmad what had transpired, he decided to pass. Esmerelda was disappointed but said that she understood.

After lunch, Sue returned to their bedroom. Ahmad knocked on the door of Duke's Winnebago, to be ushered immediately into his presence.

'I've made an executive decision,' said Ahmad. 'I want to buy half a kilo at sixty dollars a gram.

I'll transfer thirty thousand dollars to your account as soon as I get the product. I don't need to test it.'

Back in their bedroom, Sue tossed the package in her hands. 'Thirty grand's worth. What'll we do with it?'

'I'll bury it in a precise location, so that it can be used as evidence if necessary. Otherwise, it will just stay there. I'll do it as soon as it's dark.'

When he got back from the burial, Fred had contacted Sue.

'He's got enough data to get the Feds into action. He'll keep us up to date as best he can.'

Because of the sensitivity about the arrest of gypsies, the Federal and local police spent two days preparing for action. Those identified in the recordings and their contacts were watched. Overnight, all suspects were taken into custody. At the same time, Duke's Winnebago, together with that of the second family involved, were silently surrounded.

The arrests were carried out as quietly as possible. In the morning, Kezia convened a meeting in the marquee to give a carefully edited account of what had taken place. She omitted all mention of the part that Ahmad and Sue had played, maintaining the fiction of their research. She confirmed what many had suspected: that the man who was shot had been killed because he'd stolen from a drug syndicate.

'We've been here nine days,' said Ahmad to Kezia, once they were back in the mobile home. 'There are still a couple of caravans we planned to visit, but with all this turmoil, that's out of the question. So we'll rest today, maybe go for a drive. Tomorrow we'll head back to Perth. I'll book the flight back to Sydney.'

'We're so grateful for what you've done,' said Kezia as she and Django sat down with them for a late breakfast. 'We'd like to give you something as a token of our gratitude. What you did was risky, dangerous.'

Django opened a large box. Inside was a replica of a traditional gypsy caravan.

'It's exquisite,' said Sue. 'What craftsmanship.'

'Yes,' Kezia replied. 'Done by a legendary craftsman, now long dead. I have a feeling that you two will end up living together. It will be perfect on your mantelpiece.'

Back at HQ, Sue and Ahmad were greeted by the news that Fred, with Julia's help, had found a house in Redfern, not far from the dwelling that had been blown up. He'd already paid the deposit. During the ten days that Sue and Ahmad had been away, the rest of the team had done all the things they'd been unable to do while on assignment. Fred had some new projects but wouldn't discuss them.

'Let's celebrate tonight. I'll tell you about them tomorrow.'

CHAPTER
THIRTY-EIGHT

'Ahmad and I have a confession to make,' Sue announced at the start of their next team meeting. 'We've become an item.'

Fred's face went red. 'You mean you've had sex?' he asked bluntly.

'I'm afraid so,' Ahmad replied. We need to work out what this means for the team.'

'George and I also have a confession,' said Julia. 'The past ten days have been quiet. No gigs. We found ourselves spending a lot of time together. We've started having sex again.'

'I was waiting for this,' said Fred. 'I'm surprised it's taken so long. So now I'll have to join you. Once I'm settled into my new home, I'll get on a dating site or two. Scary, but I'm ready to give it a go. So, what does this mean for the way we work together? Can the team survive?'

'There's only one way to find out,' said George. 'Take on another project. Fred, what's on the list?'

'Two of the usual money laundering gigs, and two more in areas we've covered already: deep fakes and industrial espionage. The fifth is from a woman called Daphne. She heard about us through Rachel, the ex-member of the Church of Spiritual Enlightenment. Rachel gave her our contact details, which, you'll recall she had our permission to divulge in matters she judged important enough. And from what Daphne told me, this may well be one of those.'

'Before we hear more,' said Julia, 'there's something I want to discuss. We've done several pro bono gigs, including the last one. I'm glad we did, of course, but I'm a bit concerned about our finances. I'm thinking of Ahmad and Sue, who aren't wealthy like the rest of us.'

'You needn't worry. We have a total of just over nineteen million dollars in interest-bearing accounts and various bonds. And HQ must have gone up a lot in value since we bought it.'

'Ahmad and I aren't exactly poor,' said Sue. 'We've done very well from our paid projects. Living here at HQ has worked well for me, but like Fred, I want my own home. I can easily afford to buy what I want in the city or a good suburb. Both Ahmad and I will then have our own homes. No pressure to cohabit!'

'I'm reassured,' said Julia, 'about both financial and cohabitation matters. So, let's hear more about what Daphne had to say.'

'She didn't know me and was initially cautious about telling me her story. But it all came out. Her only daughter, Veronica, joined a religious cult called Heaven's Stairway about fifteen months ago. Daphne hated what was happening but kept in touch with Veronica as best she could. Only the high-ups were allowed mobile phones, so they were restricted to a land line. The two women assumed their calls were monitored, but they were able to use a code that they'd invented when Veronica was a child. This code had protected them, to some extent, from physical and mental abuse by Daphne's husband, of the First Nations people.

'Using this code,' continued Fred, 'Daphne learned that the cult was located in what Veronica judged to be an old logging site in tropical woodland that was now protected. The adjacent river, once used to transport the logs, was still flowing, but less than when it carried logs. Heaven's Stairway had upgraded the old logging tracks.

This made the site, remote and isolated as it was, fairly accessible. It was surrounded by a tall barbed-wire fence that could be electrified. The area was slightly elevated and was hot and humid in summer.'

'That might be enough info for us to locate it,' said Ahmad. 'There can't be that many old logging sites that are slightly elevated, adjacent to a river, and in tropical woodland that is now protected. I'll make a start on finding it right now.'

'I'd like you to hear the rest of Daphne's story before you do,' said Fred. 'She'd been able to learn very little about life in the cult. Even with their code, getting the truth was almost impossible. At any hint of it, the land line was cut off. The cult wanted her mother to believe that Veronica was happy, so that Daphne wouldn't try to get her out. If Veronica didn't stick to their script, she was punished. Daphne soon learned that the cult's regime was harsh, punitive and oppressive, brutal at times. And that escape was impossible.

Three days ago, Veronica phoned her mother in great distress but was cut off before she could explain what was happening. Daphne called the landline repeatedly, with no response. She believes that her daughter is in serious danger.'

'Has Daphne called the police?' asked George.

'Yes. Straight after telling me about Veronica's call. We have to decide whether to leave it to the police or to get involved ourselves. I suggest that we leave it to the police and tell Daphne that we'll monitor their missing person's website. We'll act if the police don't get anywhere.'

. Late morning the day after next, Fred learned from the police website that Veronica's body had been found in a motel room in Cairns. The coroner had not yet ruled on the case, but an autopsy suggested that Veronica had died of a drug overdose. A verdict of suicide was almost inevitable. The police had delayed contacting Daphne until they were certain of Veronica's identity. She'd learned of her death before Fred, but she'd been too distressed to tell him until he already knew.

'I did my best to comfort her,' Fred explained at a quickly convened team meeting, 'promising that we'd try to find out what really happened. Daphne was certain it wasn't suicide, and I agreed with her. Heaven's Stairway have created this false scenario to obscure any links between them and Veronica's death. She couldn't have escaped from the cult, let alone gone to a motel in Cairns, without it being orchestrated by Heaven's Stairway. The police will learn no more about the cult than the little Daphne can tell them.'

'I hate to say this,' said Julia, 'but Veronica being Aboriginal will affect the investigation. I've learned this only too well during my time as a lawyer. The matter will be given low priority. The police will accept the coroner's inevitable verdict of suicide and will close the case. I believe Veronica's death must be investigated. We have to expose her killers and deal with them as they deserve.'

'I see we all agree with Julia,' Fred stated. 'I'll call Daphne and say we're determined to help her find justice. That we'll locate the cult, identify Veronica's killers and make sure they'll never harm anyone again. That we'll totally destroy Heaven's Stairway.'

Fred sipped at his diet coke before continuing.

'Someone will need to do background research into religious cults. Let's meet the morning after next. Once we've worked out some sort of plan, I'll invite Daphne to comment on it. We'll need her input, and her permission to go ahead.'

George and Julia had done the background research into Australian religious cults, but before outlining it at the scheduled gathering, they and

Sue wanted to hear what Fred and Ahmad had learned about the location of Heaven's Stairway.

'There's only one site that ticks all the boxes,' said Ahmed. 'It's an abandoned logging camp about seventy kilometres inland from Gladstone, a coastal city in Queensland about five hundred kilometres north of Brisbane. Gladstone has a population of nearly fifty thousand, so it's big enough to supply most of the cult's needs.

Google maps showed several buildings within the central fenced-off area, which occupied about three hectares. The forest has reclaimed some of the original logged area, leaving a total of eight or nine hectares. A few trees and shrubs have sprouted among the stumps, and there are several cleared areas bearing crops. The relative lack of cover will make it difficult to get close to the central buildings without being spotted. We can't get enough definition on google maps to be certain, but there's evidence of closed-circuit cameras at regular intervals. Security is obviously very tight. Heaven's Stairway seems as well guarded as a Nazi prison-of-war camp. And just as difficult to escape from.'

'Do they have a website?' asked Sue.

'Yes, two actually. One on Google, the other on the dark web. We haven't tried to access the dark web site for fear of arousing suspicion. If we can't get into it safely, we'll have to visit the cult's physical location to find out anything more. Now let's hear from George and Julia'

'What we've found,' said George, 'is quite disturbing. There are currently fifty-six documented religious cults in Australia. This includes those with significant secular elements, such as the Church of Scientology. Most have websites. We started by searching for those cults that seem similar to Heaven's Stairway, in so far as we understand it. There were six. Then we searched their websites for links with Heaven's Stairway, either online or through shared locations and activities. We found only two. The first said simply that the cult had been disbanded. The second site was that of a cult called 'Lost and Found.' It offers free food, shelter and friendship to entice the vulnerable to the cult's headquarters.'

'The site,' said Julia, 'has links with those dealing with homelessness. Presumably, this is a form of advertising. The cult must hope that service providers will link some of their homeless with Lost and Found, either directly or through its website.'

'How much have you discovered about Lost and Found?' asked Sue.

'Their website' continued Julia,' has a section about the cult itself. It outlines its history, structure and current aims and expectations. But it's too perfect, too contrived, and is undoubtedly false. Then we found that Lost and Found have created several almost identical websites, designed to make it seem larger than it really is. These multiple websites create vulnerability, and we accessed them enough to learn at least some of the truth about Lost and Found.'

'And what we learned was pretty bad,' said George. 'The cult is based in the Brisbane suburb of Newstead, about three kilometres north of the city centre. It's become fashionable, with new up-market housing, but there are still quite a few old industrial sites. The cult's HQ is on one of these. It's a single-story building about three hundred metres square. Behind it are two large sheds. Several of the old industrial sites have some of their original buildings, and two of these have become gathering places for the homeless. Many of them previously roamed the streets in and around the CBD but increasing police harassment has pushed them further out. Lost and Found is in reality no longer a cult, but a facility for the homeless.'

'What's so bad about that?' asked Sue.

'Lost and Found' said Julia, 'offers some of the homeless employment and secure accommodation in outlying suburbs. But they choose only women, selecting the most attractive. According to rumours among the homeless, those women who take up the offer are never seen again. We need to check this out. Which means going to Brisbane.'

The team decided that the situation was serious enough for all of them to go. Fred got the go-ahead from Daphne. Two days later they'd settled into a three-bedroom apartment about two kilometres form Lost and Found's HQ. Early on the first morning they parked their hired 4WD close to the site, walking casually past it. There was already some activity: a few homeless men and women were waiting for the building to open its doors.

'I can see two white vans parked in front of the shed on the right,' said Ahmad. 'If they are transporting homeless women elsewhere, they'll use one of those. Both look like Fiat Master Pros, the same as those used by the transhumanists to transport people and bodies. There may be more vans inside the sheds. I'll come back dressed as a homeless man and wander about. I'll put a tracker on a tyre of all the vans I discover.'

'You already dress like a homeless man,' Sue quipped. 'Just dress down a bit more.'

'Four vans altogether,' Ahmad reported on returning from his mission. 'All Fiat Master Pros with a long wheelbase. Now we can track them. I think one of us should watch the building to let Fred know when a van leaves and get a sense of other comings and goings. Not all day. Just morning or afternoon.'

George took the first shift, hidden behind a low wall. Between periods of inactivity, homeless men and women entered the building. George tried to work out if the same numbers left, but the maths escaped him. There was some activity around one of the vans. George saw a woman get inside. As soon as the van left, he notified Fred. A second van left shortly before the end of George's four-hour shift.

'The first van is heading north,' said Fred, studying the equipment he'd set up in the kitchen-dining area of the apartment. 'It's more than halfway along the five hundred or so kilometres to Gladstone. It must be heading for the Heaven's Stairway HQ. The other van has stayed local, stopping now and again, presumably for supplies.'

'Why on earth would Lost and Found send women to Heaven's Stairway HQ?' asked Julia.

'That's exactly what we need to find out,' Ahmad replied. 'We need to come up with a plan. Let's start with another look at the cult's online connections and activities. Try and get into their dark web site. Fred, want to give it a go?'

'The site is strongly protected,' Fred reported some hours later. 'We couldn't risk being traced back, so we weren't aggressive. But we did enough to trace their connections to other sites on the dark web. One really shocked us. It claims expertise in making snuff movies and wants anyone interested to contact them.'

'I've heard of snuff movies,' said Julia, 'but I've never looked into them. George, I'm guessing you might know a bit more than I do.'

'Not really. But give me an hour or so. I'll do a bit of research.'

'First,' said George, 'some background. If we look at how humanity evolved, central aspects were inter-group competition and competition for status within a particular group. The hominids most likely to survive were those most willing and able to kill competitors. We still have their genes, but the drive to kill other human beings is supressed deeply in our subconscious. Except in times of war, when it is legitimised, even glorified.

Gory and violent movies are a way of satisfying the drive to kill by proxy. Their popularity tells us that this drive is still very much with us. And my work as a psychiatrist told me that most people have fantasies in which they commit violent acts, including murder. But they know they would never carry them out in real life. There are some people who have escaped this prohibition, or who never had it. For them, killing another person, or seeing others do it, is what they crave. And there are more of them than you might think.

Snuff movies are designed to meet this craving. Nearly all involve actors who try to convincingly create the illusion of murder. These movies can be addictive. Eventually, some addicts can be satisfied only by seeing the real thing or even taking part in it. I suspect that Heaven's Stairway provides this evil service. It explains why their HQ is so heavily guarded: far more than is needed to stop cult members escaping.'

'How can we expose them? Sue asked. 'We can't get into their HQ. Might it be possible to place a micro-camera inside, or some other recording device?'

'That's worth thinking about,' said George. 'Let's spend the rest of the day discussing how we might do it. Think about other approaches. Then sleep on it. Try and come up with a plan at tomorrow's team meeting.'

'I've put something together,' said Fred, after breakfast the next day. 'It's the product of all your suggestions with a twist or two of my own. If we go ahead with it, we'll have to do a great deal of planning and preparation.

George and I will pose as two policemen from Gladstone. Go to their HQ with a fake search warrant. Once inside, create a diversion so that one of us can plant a micro-camera and two or three bugs. Julia, from a legal perspective, how realistic is this?'

'It's a great idea. I think only one of you should wear a uniform. The other can pose as a plain clothes detective. An Inspector, to add gravitas. We can try and get a uniform in Gladstone, but otherwise we'll need to take photos and get one made up in Brisbane. Too risky to get it made in Gladstone. I'm sure Fred and Ahmad can come up with fake badges. The warrant isn't a problem. We just need to find out the format and whose signature to fake.'

'They'll try and delay our entry as long as possible,' said George, 'and will almost certainly contact police HQ to verify our credentials. We've got the equipment to divert that call to one of us. I suggest

Sue manages this because of her acting skills. It means Sue coming to Gladstone with us. Are you okay with that?'

'Of course,' Sue replied, 'but I'm wondering how you'll know where to plant the camera and bug. The buildings are extensive. And they'll hide any evidence of snuff movie production.'

'We'll use a drone,' said Ahmad. 'I'll go to Gladstone ahead of you. I'll study the buildings, analyse the movements of people around them. This might help us pinpoint the movie studio. Even if it doesn't, having a map of the structure will be useful. The latest surveillance drones are almost impossible to detect, because they can operate effectively from a height of at least a kilometre.'

'I'll come up to Gladstone as well,' said Julia. 'I don't want to be left alone in Brisbane, and I could be useful if there are problems with the warrant. So, we'll need a three bedroom apartment. Why don't we book one now? Ahmad can go up as soon as he's got the drone, and it'll be a base for all our comings and goings.'

CHAPTER THIRTY-NINE

The best surveillance drone that Ahmad could obtain immediately had a flight time of 45 minutes, about average for such machines. To make optimal use of the flight time, he had to launch it from a position as close as possible to Heaven's Stairway's HQ. This would also allow him to position the drone visually, ensuring it hovered precisely above the building. Recharging the drone's battery took forty minutes, even with a fast charger, so Ahmad couldn't maintain uninterrupted observation.

He found a suitable site about seven hundred metres form the cult's HQ. His car was almost completely hidden, but Ahmad could see the building. He launched the drone, which was almost silent, and settled down to make the most use of it before nightfall.

Back in the apartment he sent the data to Fred in Brisbane.

Before resuming surveillance the next day, Ahmad made discrete enquiries about acquiring, a police uniform. It was impossible to get one, so he took photos of uniformed policemen, making sure he captured their badges. He then relayed them to Brisbane where the team had decided that Fred would wear the uniform. George would be the Detective Inspector.

While waiting for a uniform to be tailored to Fred's measurements, he and Julia created a fake search warrant. This took longer than expected because of difficulties in getting the identity of the official who would sign it. They used the time to fashion the necessary police badges using a 3D printer.

Two days after Ahmad had left for Gladstone, the rest of the team joined him. The data from the drone had been helpful. It confirmed that the cult HQ was enclosed by a tall, barbed wire fence. The main building was a single-story rectangular structure of about a thousand square metres. It was linked to a smaller structure by a short passageway. Careful analysis of the footage showed that a small group of men and women entered this annex once or twice a day. The team couldn't be certain, but the data suggested that during the two day observation period, one person failed to leave. There was no evidence of the disposal of a body, but this could have occurred while the drone's battery was being recharged.

'It makes sense to have a separate building,' said Sue. 'It's probably sound-proofed. Exactly what happens inside it can be hidden from the broader community, although some members must be involved in movie making. I'm beginning to suspect that the cult and its members are just a front for Heaven's Stairway's real business: making movies.'

'If that's true,' said George, 'those movies will be made available for purchase. Let's try to buy one. See if it's what we think it is. Fred and Ahmad should be able to manage the deal.'

The two genius hackers quickly found a site on the dark web linked to Heaven's Stairway. Its main page offered 'Porn for Special Tastes', but buying the films required preliminary registration.

'I'm guessing,' said Fred, 'that you'd have to be part of a network to get registered. We haven't time for that. The site offers samples. We should be able to access them without being traced back.'

The samples showed a range of perverse sexual activity, some involving small groups. Violence to women was a central theme. There were no snuff movies.

Julia made herself watch the screen. 'I'm utterly disgusted,' she exclaimed. 'I actually feel sick. They're even worse than the deep fake that destroyed my life. But obviously they meet a demand. The trade must be very lucrative. These abhorrent films can't be cheap.'

'We didn't see any prices,' said Ahmad. 'Presumable these are revealed at the point of purchase. I'm wondering why there's no mention of snuff movies. Not a hint of them. Perhaps we're wrong about this. But what we've just seen must be against the law. Showing recordings of it to the police will surely be enough to trigger intervention.'

'I'm afraid not,' said Julia. 'Heaven's Stairway will argue that it is all consensual and provide witnesses to confirm it. The police won't act. Arresting porn movie producers isn't at the top of their to-do list.'

'Then we have to go ahead without them,' said George. I suggest that Fred and I knock on the cult's front door tomorrow morning. Are you ready Fred?'

'I'm ready. But we have to get this right. Let's do some role play. I'll put my uniform on, and George can dress in his suit and tie. We'll go out and knock on the apartment door. The rest of you can play it by ear. '

The role play descended into chaos and hilarity. They roared with laughter. It turned out to be the perfect remedy for the tension that had arisen without the team fully realising it.

At nine o'clock the next morning, Fred and George stopped the black 4WD in front of a gate in the barbed-wire fence. They'd placed what looked like a police siren on the roof. It was linked to Fred's phone. When set off, the noise would be ear-splitting. Fred would trigger it if they needed a diversion.

George pressed the car's horn button. The gate opened slowly. A man came out of the building and waved them towards him, pointing to a parking spot. As they got out of the 4WD, he held up his hands.

'I'm Jeff, in charge of security. Before you come any closer, please tell me why you're here.'

'I have a search warrant,' said George. 'It gives us right of entry and authority to search.'

'Please let me see it.' Jeff examined it carefully. 'We run a tight ship here. There's been a previous attempt at entry that was fraudulent. I need to contact your HQ to confirm your identity and the validity of the warrant. Please wait here.'

Sue was ready for the call.

'Gladstone police station. How can I help?'

'I'm head of security at Heaven's Stairway. Please put me through to Inspector Douglas.'

'I'm afraid he's not in yet. Perhaps I can be of assistance.'

'I want to confirm that your station sent a Detective Inspector and a Constable up here with a search warrant.'

After a brief delay, Sue confirmed that all was in order.

It was about ten minutes before Jeff came out again. Fred and George assumed that he'd given instructions to prepare for a search.

'I've got the all-clear. Come on through. Before we start, can I ask why the warrant was issued?'

'Fair enough,' replied George. 'Several parents of cult members called us because they believe their children are being kept here against their will. Their level of concern justified a warrant. '

'You're free to talk to anyone. I'm sure that when you do, you'll find that the parents' concerns are totally unjustified.'

There were small dormitories, all with adjacent bathroom and toilet. Benched areas for study or work were clean and well lit, as were the two kitchens. There was an auditorium for formal instruction and gatherings of the whole community, and two large dining rooms. A recreation area had shelves of books and games, easy chairs and a pool table. Two small rooms had to be unlocked for inspection.

'Those are used for retreats when a member needs to be alone,' said Jeff. 'They can be locked to ensure the occupant isn't disturbed.'

All those members to whom Fred and George were allowed to speak were adamant that they were free to leave the cult at any time. Fred had no trouble placing several bugs in the most frequented parts of the building. After they'd completed their search of the main buildings, they entered the annex.

'This is amazing,' said George. He saw a stage at one end of a well-equipped film studio. There was specialised lighting, three movie cameras, and strategically placed microphones.

'What kind of movies do you make here?'

'They're mostly for education. We make documentaries and short films, most about the work of Heaven's Stairway, some of more general interest. We use them to educate our existing members and to attract new ones.'

George moved to inspect a movie camera adjacent to a wall.

'This looks really high tech, he exclaimed while attaching a movement-activated micro-camera to the wall behind, where it was obscured form view. 'Must cost a fortune.'

'We're lucky enough to be well-funded,' Jeff replied. 'It's all top of the range stuff. Now, have you seen enough? If so, I'll escort you back to your car.'

'We didn't need to trigger the siren,' said Fred, back at the apartment. 'We had no trouble placing the bugs and the camera. Now we just have to be patient.'

The next few days tested the team's endurance. They watched the shooting of two porn movies and were so disgusted they almost gave up watching. At the shooting of the third film, their disgust turned to abject horror. A snuff movie unfolded. Towards the end of it, a murder was committed. The team had not the slightest doubt that the victim, a young woman, had been killed. Close-ups of the murder showed every detail of a brutal final assault.

'I'll get onto my government contact,' said Fred when he'd recovered enough to speak. 'Give him the background and send him all the bug and camera recordings. He'll liaise with the Federal police. I've asked him to let me know exactly what happens. We don't need to stay here any longer. Let's get back to HQ.'

True to his word, Fred's government contact gave him a full account of subsequent events, including footage of police activity. As soon as he received it, Fred convened a team meeting. He showed the footage and then relayed the government agent's account.

'The victims in the snuff movies were the women sent to the cult's HQ by Lost and Found. Most of the cult members believed that the studio was used only to make the kind of educational material that they were shown. A few members were coerced or bribed into the shooting of porn movies, but only the cult's hierarchy were involved in the snuff movies. They alone profited from the money these earned.'

'Did the police learn anything about Veronica's murder?' asked Julia.

'The cult's hierarchy denied any involvement. But it's very likely that Veronica found out about the snuff movies and tried to tell her mother about them. So, she had to be silenced. She'd already told Daphne that life in the cult was harsh, and this was confirmed by police investigations.

Members had to work in the outlying cultivated areas, which yielded fresh vegetables, mainly for the elders. They also had to keep HQ clean and tidy, do all the laundry, carry out routine maintenance, and prepare the meals. Some were coerced or bribed into providing personal services to the elders. These services included sexual ones.

As we suspected, the cult's main business was making and selling porn movies. Occasional snuff films, highly lucrative, were an additional source of revenue. The eight men who created Heaven's Stairway borrowed enough money to build their HQ, with the connivance of local authorities. It's almost certain that bribery was involved, but there's not enough evidence of this to justify any prosecutions. These eight men became the cult's elders.

The cult's HQ was completed only about five years ago. The elders planned to close it, and the cult itself, when they'd accumulated enough wealth. Threats and bribes would ensure the silence of any ex-members who knew the truth. HQ would be sold. End of story.

'Have you spoken to Daphne?' asked George.

'Not yet. I thought I'd wait until I know the whole story. I'd like to invite her round. Tell her everything as gently as possible. Perhaps over a meal. Is that okay?'

Daphne came round the following after-noon. Over tea and cake, Fred began to tell her the full story. When she wept, the team comforted her. The narrative continued into the early evening, when Fred paused it while they had a light supper. Once the story was complete, Daphne thanked them all for what they had done. As she left, promises were made to keep in touch. The team had a quiet cele-bration before going to bed.

CHAPTER FORTY

The mood was sombre the following morning when the team assembled for breakfast. They knew they had to make decisions that would change their lives. They put this off as long as possible by indulging in reminiscence.

'Before we talk about what comes next,' said Fred, 'why don't we talk about the gigs that most affected us. It won't change the decisions we've made, but it might help to explain why we've made them.'

'For me,' said Julia, 'it was the organ harvesting gig. When they put me on the operating table to gut me, I was certain that I was about to die. Then there were two miracles. The first was my rescue, through your combined heroism. The second was the near-death experience that changed my life. It left me with an unshakeable belief in a divine presence, and the conviction that this entity had spared my life for a purpose, a purpose that I've struggled to find.

Soon I shall give birth to a child, who we now know will be a boy. George and I were devasted when Nadia told us that the transcendentalists had tweaked the embryo's genes. We hope this will yield a positive outcome, but whatever qualities my son has, I'm going to devote myself to his care. That is the purpose that at last has been revealed to me. Before I say anymore, I'd like to hear from George.'

'No particular gig stands out for me,' George replied. 'I'm profoundly thankful that I survived many dangerous situations. Julia is sure that I owe my survival to the grace of God, and I won't argue with that. The more time I spend with Julia, the more I'm beginning to share her beliefs. But I'm not quite there yet.

I want to share the upbringing of our son equally with Julia. Irrespective of our son's attributes, it will be a challenging task for both of us, especially Julia. She'll need me there. So, I'm not going to put myself in danger again. That's why I've decided to resign from the team.'

'I don't want to do anything that risks my pregnancy,' said Julia. 'And I want to be here for our boy. That's why I'm handing in my resignation.'

'I expected this, of course,' said Fred. 'Now I'd like us to hear from Sue and Ahmad.'

'First,' Ahmad replied, 'I'd like to thank you all again for inviting me to join you. I was a socially phobic recluse. Now, thanks to what we've done together, I'm in danger of becoming an extrovert.'

Ahmad continued after the laughter subsided.

'Helping my aunt Karina is a real stand out. Especially the transcendentalist gig. Not only did we help her, but we destroyed a lethal organisation. The gypsy gig's another stand out, mainly because of what happened with my relationship with Sue. You all knew that we'd become close but held off having sex to preserve the integrity of the team. Sharing the caravan and trying the meth made sex happen. I love Sue very much. I want to share her life in safety. To do that, I have to resign from the team. If this seems ungrateful, I'm sure you'll understand. And forgive me.'

'Of course,' said Sue, 'the gypsy gig was a highlight for me. But my absolute stand outs are the ones to do with art: art forgery and the theft of Berthe Morisot's portrait. My doubts about being a fully-fledged member of the team vanished completely after we pulled them off.'

'What you say surprises me,' said Fred. 'You were truly heroic in the casino money laundering gig. And you'd only just joined us. Surely you felt you'd earned your spurs after that?'

'I thought I was just lucky. And it wasn't very dangerous. Anyway, I know I'm truly a part of the team. Which makes it incredibly difficult to resign. But I must. Ahmad has said he wants to share my life in safety. I feel exactly the same way.'

'And apart from developing our relationship,' said Ahmad, 'we're going to be quite busy. You know that Sue's decided to buy a house. The option of living in separate homes is important to us. Finding the right place may take some time. I want to help.'

'Well,' said Fred, 'that leaves me. For all of my adult life, I've lived and breathed in the world of IT. I've especially valued being part of the hackers' network. My hacking skills match Ahmad's, and we're two of the very best. I don't know if I want to go on in the same way, or if I can. George and I set up our HQ with the money he got from the Iran saga. He's the one to decide what happens to it.'

'Fred, that's totally up to you. I'm as wealthy now as when we bought HQ. You can stay here as long as you like, do whatever you want. I'm sure the team will be happy for you to use the funds we've accumulated.'

'Thanks George. I'll need some time to think about all this. Sue and Ahmad, what are your long term plans?

'In a way,' Ahmad replied, 'I'm the same as you, Fred. IT and hacking have been my life. But I want to get away from hacking. Maybe set up a network or school to help people manage the internet. With the advent of AI, it's going to dominate our lives even more. There'll be increasing dangers to our wellbeing. I'd like to help people manage them. Exactly how I do this depends on Sue. I don't want it to get in the way of our relationship. Money isn't an issue, of course. Thanks to our work in the team, we're both very wealthy.'

'I know exactly what I want to do,' said Sue. 'I want to set up an art gallery. Use it to sell the work of young artists who show promise. If I need help in choosing them, I won't hesitate to ask for it. It won't be a money-making endeavour. My mark-up will be just enough for me to break even. Where to set it up depends on the location of my new home. I'd like to be able to walk to work.'

'Julia and I,' said George, 'have given a lot of thought about how our lives might unfold when our son no longer needs close care. Julia still believes that the deep fake porn video has destroyed any chance of her resuming her career as a barrister. I want her to reconsider this, because it's still her calling. People have short memories about what they see in the media.'

'George may be right,' said Julia, 'but I doubt it. If I can get back, I'll combine it with more university study. If not, I'll study full time, aim to do a PhD on transhumanism. Publish it as a book. People need to know how dangerous it could become. George, I've taken over from you. Share your plans.'

'I really don't have any. You all know I'll never go back to psychiatry. And anything after the work we've done together will be an anti-climax. But I'm thinking about doing a Julia. Going back to university. Perhaps do a PhD on anti-psychiatry!'

'He's joking of course,' laughed Julia. 'It wasn't psychiatry that destroyed his career, it was me.'

'It was a blessing in disguise. I was becoming a bit jaded, a bit bored. Anyway, that's all in the past. We have to look to the future.'

'There's one last thing,' said Fred. 'We've worked as a team all this time but never given ourselves a name I suggest *Dark Web Spiders.*'

After the chorus of agreement, Fred continued. 'I suggest that tonight we have a wake. An
Irish one that somehow celebrates as much as it
mourns. It'll be our final meeting as Dark Web
Spiders, but I'm sure it won't be our last gathering. I know we'll want to go on sharing our lives,
however they may unfold.'